The Creature's Curse

Paul Braus

Lauren —
Happy
horror !

Special thanks to my editor, Charles Maurer. Also, thanks to: Ed, Lily, Dave, Luke, Brandon, Billy and (of course) Mom and Dad.

Interior Book Design and Layout by
www.integrativeink.com

ISBN: 978-0-615-36517-6

CHAPTER ONE

The stirrings from nearby put him on edge. There are voices. The creature's muscles strain beneath charred and petrified flesh. He digs reflexively at the dirt in which he resides – like a cat – with his long, sharpened talons.

He senses the invasion of his territory. This is his home...at least as much as the creature can comprehend that he ever has a place he can call 'home.' The voices he hears create confusion within him and there is a pulsing onslaught of pain coursing through him. And with the pain, the anger rises. There is a snowballing of emotions within him and when he experiences this he must find the release to try to eradicate these feelings.

They weren't accustomed to the night. The real country night. They had been living in the city where it never got truly dark.

"What makes you think this is the place, Jeremy?"

"Dude I'm telling you, this is it. This is Buck Tree Road. This is the house. The cupola at the top on the – let's see, which direction is that – west side of the house. There it is, man." He pointed upwards in the direction of a conical structure at the top front corner of the house.

"OK. Well, what do you want to do now?"

"Let's go inside."

"Fuck that, man. We got a lotta ground to cover. I told Melanie we'd be at Bennington by midnight."

1

"C'mon Alex, let's go see what's in there."

A night breeze blew briskly, and then died down. The cloudless Western Massachusetts sky was a showcase of a million stars, and a thin, crescent moon. The two friends stood out in the chill, fall air in front of the house that Jeremy so wanted to enter. Nearby there was only an old barn and, beyond the barn, a neighboring house with no car out front and no lights on. Jeremy had insisted they take this slight detour off of Route 7, down the dark road that headed east. They had parked the car up the road 100 yards in an unpaved patch near a marked trailhead. The two of them – 19-year-olds on a long weekend road trip up north – stood twenty feet away from the front door, as scattered leaves blew by them in the front yard.

Their voices were now like shards of glass piercing his mutated flesh. He let out a muted, anguished growl...

"Yo, J, did you hear that?" Alex asked, as he stoked a flame to a fat joint he had pulled from the pocket of his flannel shirt.

"Hear what, dude?"

"I just heard something," he said, as he inhaled on the joint. He now spoke in the strained tones of someone who's lungs were full of fresh pot smoke. "Like an animal sound." He exhaled.

"It was probably the wind in the trees. Or just these leaves on the ground rustling around," Jeremy said, kicking up a clump of crisp, fall leaves, then taking a long stoke off of the joint.

"I guess," Alex concurred, without enthusiasm. He took a deep hit off of the joint. "This is good shit, huh?"

"Yeah, it's sweet...d'ja get it from Jo-Jo?"

"No, man. I found out about some new dude uptown."

"Cool," Jeremy said, taking another hit. He passed it over and exhaled. "Look at that sparkling sky, Alex. We can't see shit for stars in the city."

"I know," Alex said, joining his friend craning his neck skyward. "It's incredible."

"Stash this for later," Jeremy instructed his friend. Alex took out a black plastic film container, and removed the grey lid. He tossed the roach in and clicked the top back on.

"C'mon J, let's hit the road, man."

"No, we're going in, Alex. Let's check this place out."

"You suck, dude."

"What? Are you scared, Alex?" he said, taunting his friend, putting it out there, a challenge in the air that he knew would make Alex bite.

"You're such a dick, Jeremy. I'm not scared," he said. "I just want to get laid tonight."

"Don't worry, man. You'll get some," Jeremy said. "Poor Melanie, pining away for her man."

"She'll be pissed if we're really late, dude."

"Shut up. Let's head inside."

They walked side by side up the front path of slate stones. As they were poised to head up the three-step entry stoop, Jeremy felt a sting and then a stab in his ankle.

"FUCK...WHAT THE FUCK!?!"

The yell unnerved the creature even more. He slashed out at the man who was the source of the loud yell and grabbed again...

Alex looked over and Jeremy was on the ground.

"Yo, J, stop dicking around. What are you doing?"

"Ahhhhh, my ankle is...AAAAAAAAHHHHH!"

Suddenly, there was a roar and a rush and Alex saw a huge, dark form, with a misshapen pinkish face, and mottled hair, slashing at his friend. Jeremy tried to fight off the form, but it was futile. Alex – his mouth forming an "o" of shock – was at a loss. His friend's anguished cries filled the air and he could see a huge hand cut through the air – and then the left side of Jeremy's face was filled with ribbons of bloodied flesh.

Jeremy was being mangled, and Alex tried to punch the beast in the back of the head. A reach-around swipe sent Alex sprawling onto his back on the leaves and dirt on the ground. He looked up and couldn't believe what he saw next. The starry sky was blotted out of his vision by the massive creature – he must have been close to 7 feet tall.

He took Jeremy's head in his hands and lifted him like a rag doll. He shook him. A crack rang out into the night, as Jeremy's neck snapped. The lifeless form hit the ground with a dull thud. The creature took another swipe at the prone form, and then turned to see Alex, who was just now getting up from the ground.

"No!" Alex said, his eyes wide open with fear. "Please...no!"

Alex got up, dizzy from the fall, turning to run. The creature reached out and swiped. His long talons dug into Alex's right shoulder.

"Aaaaahhh!" Alex screamed. His left hand went to his right shoulder, the knifing pain surging through him.

The creature had him now. And pounded Alex, negating his feeble efforts at fighting back. The creature wanted the silence that had been here before these two arrived. Holding Alex's head in his left hand and pushing – and grabbing his right arm and pulling and twisting – the force was overwhelming. The man's right arm was pulled from the shoulder socket. The excessive loss of blood put him into shock – he was dead within seconds. Muscle, bone and tendon hung from the shoulder socket. The body fell. The creature threw the arm aside and swiped at the dead form of the man – punching and swiping in frustration and anguish.

One dead history major lay near the front stoop of the house, blood from gashes on his face gleaming in the moonlight. The Russian Studies major lay face down in the front yard: one-armed, clothing torn – pulpy lifeless flesh. The wind stirred up again and leaves rustled against the bodies. Then the wind stilled, and it was quiet again in the cool Western Massachusetts night.

NOVEMBER 9TH, 1990: NEW YORK CITY

"Oh, yeah, it was right here, in this shop," Eldon told her. "Well, actually right over there." He pointed to a spot a few tables over. The waitress walked over to their window-side table at the Cup of Joe coffee shop and clunked down mugs in front of them, cappuccino for Eldon and Cinnamon spice tea for Abigail.

Eldon thanked the waitress, who seemed overly put out by the whole transaction and essentially ignored his 'thank you.' The pretty waitress' only response was to let out a big, exasperated breath, and brush aside a blonde curl that had fallen across her forehead. It was raining steadily on the other side of the glass on the gloomy November afternoon. The Cup of Joe was situated in Manhattan's East Village on Avenue A. Abigail and Eldon were new to the responsibilities of true adulthood, both 22 years old and fresh out of college.

"T.D.," he said, making a sarcastic face at Abigail.

"What's that," she asked. "T.D.?"

"Tip deduction," Eldon said, with a chuckle. "That waitress is a total bitch."

Abby nodded her head with a neutral look. She had been a waitress in school in Northampton, and always had empathy for others who had the gig.

"I guess that's typical Manhattan for you," Eldon continued. "All these wannabe actresses who think they're too important to do the job they're paid for."

Abby didn't want to dig any further into this topic. She liked Eldon. She didn't want to get soured on him because of a silly conversation about a downtown waitress. The girl did have a pretty lousy attitude, Abby had to admit. Still, she didn't like Eldon's stereotyping of women. She had heard him do it a few times before.

"So get back to the story, Eldon," she said. "How did it happen?"

"Right," he said, lifting his mug up for a sip of the frothy drink then placing it back down. "Like I said, I was sitting at a table closer to the counter, along the middle aisle, just reading the paper, and this tall, skinny wretch in a black ski mask runs in from the front door to the counter, and pulls a little gun – I don't know, I guess what they'd call a Saturday Night Special."

"Did you know what was happening right away?"

"I saw the whole thing. There were just maybe five other people in the place. He holds the gun up – trains it right on the girl behind the counter – and tells her to empty the register."

"What did the girl do?"

"She looked petrified, you know? She didn't say a word. Just hit the button on the register and forked over the cash. The guy with the mask – he just seemed jumpy, like he was just a stinkin' crackhead or something, totally desperate. After he gets the money from the register, he reaches into the tip jar on the counter and grabs the $1 bills."

She sipped her tea, trying to visualize the guy pulling the day-time robbery.

"Then it was all a blur," he said. "Maybe I just flashed back to when I played on the high school football team. I don't know. But the guy turned tail to get out of here. He was right by my table and I just dove and took out his legs."

"What? No, you didn't Eldon."

"Yeah I did, I even have the newspaper clipping to prove it," and he started to dig it out of his pocket to show her the short piece that ran in the *Daily News*:

COFFEE SHOP HERO TRIPS UP GUN-TOTING ZERO

The story detailed the events in a couple of paragraphs. It even mentioned Eldon by name. Now Abigail was even more smitten.

"So," Eldon says, "the guy goes sprawling on the floor – the gun goes flying. Then me and two other guys held him down while the girl behind the counter called the cops."

"And then?"

"Oh, the cops came and arrested the guy. He's probably already back on the street. Some legal services guy probably helped to spring him. You know – it's not *his* fault he's a crack head loser."

"Wasn't the owner here grateful?"

"Well, one of the managers, Joey, yeah. Whenever he sees me now he picks up my tab. He's not here today."

They sat there sipping their drinks, and then Eldon decided to prompt Abigail to talk about herself

"So, tell me more about your college days."

Abigail smiled and began launching into a story about one of her favorite creative writing professors at Smith. Eldon sipped cappuccino and seemed interested, as far as she could tell. Eldon Bailey had dirty blond, straight hair, neatly combed in a part. He was six feet tall, solidly built and ruggedly handsome – high cheek bones, narrow nose and a strong chin. Abby had known him for two months now. This was their fifth date. Abby was statuesque, tall and thin, with a long mane of curly blonde hair. Her facial features had a sharpness, giving her almost a bird-like visage. Men generally found her to be quite striking, with her long, shapely form and cute – if not beautiful – face.

One of the "episodes" she so dreaded was coming again, though, she knew it. She had finished telling him her anecdote, and he was talking, and smiling at her. It was a lascivious look. God, she'd seen it so many times before, from so many guys. Just then, as she could feel the discomfort of the message-from-the-past tingling through her, he reached under the table, and rubbed her knee with his right hand.

She pulled back abruptly, and the silverware on the table jingled, and tea and cappuccino spilled over the sides of the mugs. A couple at the next table glanced over. The rain intensified at that moment, and there were a few "oohs" and "aahs" in the coffee shop as the wind-swept rain pelted the shop's picture windows.

"I'm sorry, Abby," he said. "Did I do something wrong?"

"No, not at all Eldon," she said shaking her head. "You just surprised me, that's all." She tried to reassure him, and reached above the table to take his left hand in her right.

The rain backed off to just a steady downpour. It was coming, she knew. There was no way to stop it. She let go of his hand, and her hands were curled into fists, tightly closed, set uncomfortably on the table. The conversation continued and she tried to hold up her end, even though she was now distracted by the voices in her head. She looked down and noticed her balled up fists and loosened them and placed her hands in her lap. Then, just as she had to struggle to fight off the urge to yell out, she noticed that he had that look in his eye again. He was undressing her with that leer, she could tell.

Then she heard it.

[he just wants to fuck you. that's all they ever want. he's nasty and lustful. he's selfish. he wants to go between your thighs. they all want that…]

"So come on Abby, what d'ya say?" he asked, with a smile and an arched eyebrow. "Why don't you come away with me to my parents' country house this weekend? It's beautiful up there, and no one's gonna be around this weekend."

"What, Eldon? I'm sorry, I'm just lost in my thoughts."

[then he can have his way. he'll get you drunk, and then he'll try to fuck you. just to use you.]

"Forget it Abigail," he said crossly. "I don't know who I'm talking to sometimes when I'm with you. Or, let me re-state that: I feel like I'm talking to myself."

"I'm sorry, Eldon," she said. "I'm just stressed out about this job interview I had yesterday, and…oh God…I'm such lousy company sometimes."

['sympathy, dear,' the female voice said. 'now he tries to gain your sympathy. don't fall for it. they just pull that trick when they're horny. he wants one thing from you…]

"You're great, Abby. I think you're fantastic. It's probably my fault, it's umm…"

"Let's just enjoy this afternoon, together, OK Eldon?" she said. "We don't need to be so stressed out about…us."

[slimy, selfish, lustful, pig-shit, user. you've got something they want, dear. they always pretend there's more to it. then, when you've fallen for the lies, and they have you…that's when they chase after the girl down the street.]

"Yeah," Eldon agreed. "Maybe we can just catch a movie together Saturday, if you'd like?"

"That sounds good, Eldon," Abby said. "A movie seems like a nice idea."

[dirty, horny, fuck-anything-with-two-legs, schemer, liar...]

Eldon smiled at Abby warmly and raised his hand to signal the put-upon actress/waitress for the check. The rain continued its *rat-a-tat-tat* against the window, falling nearly sideways now.

"I hope you have a decent umbrella, Abby," he said. "One of those cheap-o models will get blown to pieces today."

She turned towards the window. He saw her bird-like profile. Abby watched a yellow cab pull over and splash dirty, city water up onto the sidewalk from a street puddle. A calm came over her, and she closed her eyes. The voices in her head – the messages – were gone for now. She blissfully heard nothing but the clinking of cups and silverware, and the chatter of others in the Cup of Joe. She turned to face Eldon. He was smiling at her. She reached across the table and took his hand into hers. He placed his other hand on top of hers, so her right hand was held by both of his, and he rubbed her hand affectionately.

"You're so hard to figure out, Abby," he said, "but I think things are going just fine between us."

She nodded her head slowly, and smiled warmly at him. "I like being with you, Eldon," she said, "I really do."

[fuck, fuck, fuck....that's what he wants...that's all they ever want...]

Abigail returned home to her small, studio, walk-up apartment on East 97th Street just before 9:00 pm. In the upstairs corridor, she gave her umbrella one more shake to remove remaining rain drops before she entered the apartment. She turned on the overhead track lights, placed down her handbag on her dresser, and removed her black overcoat and hung it in the closet next to the front door.

She shook off the flats she wore for the rainy weather, and removed the ankle-length dark green flowered skirt she had been wearing. She unbuttoned the canary, silk blouse and could feel exhaustion sweeping over her as the blouse slipped over her shoulders and she let it fall to the floor. She knelt down to pick it up and placed it on a hardwood chair next to her dresser.

The rain had lightened to a drizzle and she got a dreamy feeling looking out at the light spray of rain sweeping across the street lamp just below her 3rd floor window. She turned and caught a glimpse of herself in her vanity mirror, slim and fit, standing there in her black bra and panties. Oh, how could she forget to close the drapes first? Certainly, there was a desperate man or two peeking out of the windows from the apartment building across 97th Street. She faced the window, and saw her reflection. She lifted her hands above her head, and her palms met. She gave a slithery snake move, a full-body gyration back and forth – just for a few seconds.

It actually kind of turned her on to tease the slimy perverts across the street like that. Maybe she would just "forget" to pull the drapes closed for a few more minutes while she sat in front of the vanity to wipe off her make-up and eye-shadow. That would provide a sideways glance to onlookers from across the street. Surely, any observers would appreciate her bra-clad breast from a side view. Yes. She clicked on the desk lamp next to her vanity so that any curiosity-seekers on the north side of the street would clearly see her chest, her shapely midriff and her firm left thigh also.

When she tired of that game for the evening – and had finished removing her make-up with cotton balls – she walked to the window and gave a brief, knowing grin to her public. Yes, she was standing full body right at the window now, her curly, blonde hair flowing across her shoulders. She started feeling excited. For a few seconds she stood there, just for the thrill of it all.

That's enough, she told herself. She flung the dark blue curtains closed with a metallic "swoop" from the curtain rings and laughed a hearty, crazy-sounding cackle.

"Men are so predictable," she said. "Mother was right. Mother was always right."

She took her red, silk full-length robe out of the closet and slid it on. She was actually turned on by the idea that a simple night-dance in her apartment could get a rise out of nearby strangers. She felt a slight gleeful tingling in her upper thighs and brought her head back, eyes closed, to prolong the moment. All of a sudden she needed to lie down on the hand-stitched navy blue coverlet with a thin crescent moon and stars that stretched atop her single bed. It had been a gift from her mother. Her dear, departed mother.

Abigail liked dark hues, like deep navy blue. The white walls provided the only contrast to the preponderance of dark colors in her room.

She took a deep breath in and a full exhale. She caught her breath again and ran her hands down across her pert, mid-sized breasts. She immediately slid her right hand down the front of her silk panties, and her left hand flopped down to the side of the bed.

"Hmmm," she moaned, as she touched herself gently... just gently and slowly. The way those college boys can't do it, because they're so worked up from their own rising excitement. It's zero to sixty in ten seconds with those slobbering morons. She quickly put them out of her mind. Zack. Tommy. Albert. They were nothing to her now. She thought of Eldon, and started to stroke herself more rapidly.

"Ahhhh," she cried out, and then began to give out quick, short breaths as she worked herself to a peak.

Release...full release. Her left hand gripped the side of the bed as pleasure surged through her from head to toe. Her heart was beating rapidly and she closed her eyes, just drinking in the moment. Never had sex with a man brought her such pleasure. Not once.

It wasn't only the inexpert handling of the college boys she had been with. She knew it was her own baggage that made the experience with members of the other sex so...anti-climactic, for wont of a better term.

And with Eldon at the coffee shop, it was all there again. Even though she hadn't yet had sex with him, the signs were there. The voices. The internal struggle she went through just to conduct a conversation with him, for God's sake.

Scurrying around in her apartment the next morning, having just poured a cup of chamomile tea and letting it steep, Abby was headed towards the bathroom when the phone rang.

"Hello"

"I'd like to speak to Abigail Merriweather."

"Speaking"

"Oh, Ms. Merriweather, this is Sherri Garfinkel at Ingelhard and Meyer Publishing."

"Oh, hello."

"I'm looking at your resume. We'd like you to come in for an interview for the editorial assistant position."

"That's great," Abigail said, trying not to sound too excited – even though she was thrilled.

Sherri from human resources gave Abigail a choice of dates and times and they settled on an 11:00 interview the following Tuesday – five days away.

After hanging up the phone, Abigail felt much better. She wanted to call someone to share the good news. She no longer had her mother since she passed away last year – her father had been dead for many years. No siblings. She didn't have the kind of relationship with Eldon yet that she could just pick up the phone and tell him the good news. She didn't have any close friends in New York at this point.

She'd call Becky, her college roommate who was now in Boston. Now, if she could only remember where she had written down Becky's work number...

She stared out the window at the activity on 97th Street and smiled.

Chapter Two

When the bodies were discovered the next day, a slew of officers from the local police department and the county sheriff's department descended upon the house on Buck Tree Road where the slaying of the two young men took place.

Rumors were swirling in and around Stockbridge and Housatonic. Could this have been the work of a bear that the two "flatlanders" had enraged? After six hours of crime scene investigation, the yard in front of the house was cordoned off with yellow crime scene tape. Soon night fell, and again it was cool and clear in the Berkshires.

Burt "Oak" Alderson drove his blue Ford four-door down Buck Tree Road, and pulled over along the road near the crime scene. A mountain of a man with a scruffy full beard, he emerged from the unmarked police cruiser. He checked his holster to make sure his .38 was loaded and that the safety was off. Hell if he was getting caught off guard by whatever may be lurking out here.

He was nicknamed "Oak" because of both his stature -- he was as solid as a thick-stumped tree -- and his time chopping down lumber. Alderson was 6'4" and weighed nearly 275 pounds. All through his teen years he had worked with his father in the Berkshire mountain towns of Washington and Becket, clearing sites for residential construction. If Alderson wasn't big and strong enough to start with, he made himself even more solid through the work of clearing trees. He had managed lumber and moved the cut, treated wood throughout his high school years and during the summers when he came home from college.

Alderson, now a special agent in the sheriff's department based in Pittsfield, was instructed by his boss to make a nighttime stop at the crime scene, without the bee hive of activity that had been going on all day. Like everyone else in Berkshire County, he had heard the rumors about the house on Buck Tree Road. He knew the history. Certainly after this slaying the talk would get much worse and perhaps would never die down.

Alderson didn't buy it. He didn't believe in ghosts and other unexplained forces that made things go 'bump' in the night. He surmised that it probably *was* a bear that had attacked these two flatlanders. Well, if it was, and if the bear was still in the vicinity, three or four shots from Alderson's .38 would be plenty sufficient to dispose of him.

He stepped onto the property, walking up the gravel driveway. His vibram-soled boots stepping on the pebbles produced a crunching sound that reverberated in the night air. Oak lifted the yellow tape, stretched across wooden posts in the front yard, and stepped into the crime scene. With his large steel flashlight shining the way, he looked around the lawn, eyeing the silhouettes of white crime scene tape.

Alderson didn't know how his boss Earl Cummins had gotten the information; he was just following orders. Cummins had called him and told him there was a charm or an amulet necklace that he had to get his hands on. Was he playing by the book? No. Trying to lift something from a crime scene. Not good. But Earl, the county sheriff, had instructed him to do exactly that. If there were any repercussions, Cummins would take the bullet. Nobody locally wanted rumor-mongers and conspiracy theorists to get their hands on that amulet.

If there was a problem in Berkshire County, let it stay in Berkshire County. Nobody likes a whistle blower, and nobody in the county wanted rumors to start circulating beyond county lines. Many locals had already been interviewed by reporters from New York City – hopefully they were keeping their wits about them and just saying it was most likely a bear attack. The word was spreading around the county – don't give these big city types any reason to poke around here. Hopefully, this thing will die down – it *was* a bear attack and that's that.

Earl Cummins told Oak that people might come looking for this charm – or whatever it was – and if the papers and TV stations got wind of it, nothing good could come out of it.

Seemingly unafraid of what might be inside, Alderson moved up the three steps on the front landing and used a key that the sheriff's department had to open the front door. Since the house had previously been a crime scene, the sheriff had obtained a copy of the front door key in the prior investigation. Periodically, the lock was broken on the front door since curiosity seekers invaded the house to poke around. This lock had remained secure for three months now. Following his flashlight beam, he turned a corner around the half-wall to his left that separated the entrance way from the rest of the house. He eyed the high-backed, red upholstered chairs and low-lying coffee table in the living room and the Shaker dining room set in the adjoining dining area. He shined his flashlight up the stairwell that separated the entrance way and living room from the dining area and kitchen, and made his way up the stairwell.

The only sounds were those of Alderson's footfalls as he moved up the staircase. He kept the flashlight trained straight ahead and took a right at the top of the staircase. What he was looking for was said to be in the turreted room on the west end of the upper floor. He saw the window at the end of the hall was opened a crack, and he proceeded along the upstairs corridor and was stopped in his tracks when he heard the first of a series of distant howls from out behind the house:

"Damn coyotes," Alderson told himself, still unconcerned.

He listened to another howl and then a high yelping sound – high pitched squeals of desperation followed. The pack of coyotes had pounced on their prey, perhaps a squirrel or a groundhog. He reached the door of the turreted room. The sheriff's department had placed a padlock on this door, and that had never been pierced. Oak located the proper key on his chain, turned the lock, and opened the door, which responded with a *'creek.'* He shined the flashlight beam into the round room. There was a rectangular black carpet and navy blue curtains pulled closed covering the windows.

To his right, a low-lying book case with three levels had a top shelf containing brass and bronze candle holders with partially spent candles of various dark hues; dried wax dripped over the sides. On the next shelf were horizontally stacked, wire-bound notebooks. At the far end of the second shelf, stacked vertically next to the spiral bound notebooks, he eyed the faded titles on a couple of book spines:

Incantations in Darkness
Potions and Poxes

On the lowest shelf were a collection of small, clear glass and brown glass vials, with black caps. Some were marked with paper labels, some unmarked. When he moved the flashlight beam left there was a waist-high table, curved on both sides, that fit along the rounded wall. There was a yellow legal pad on the table with hand-written notes next to an ancient-looking, leather-bound book, with hard-to-read lettering on the cover. The letters, in gold-inlay on the cover, were printed, in a gothic, curved style. Beneath the title was a gold-inlay illustration of a bird; it appeared to be a raven. The book was titled:

In The Company of Familiar Spirits

"Shit," Alderson said. "Cuervo, Yukon Jack, Johnny Walker. Those are the spirits I'm familiar with."

Next to the book was the rectangular, brass jewelry box his boss had told him about. There was a swirling design of intertwining circles on the lid of the box. The sides were worn and curved over from wear.

"Bingo." Oak opened up the jewelry box, and pushed aside rings and bracelets. Beneath the other jewelry, he saw a round, pewter amulet, about the size of a quarter, attached to a thread-thin silver chain.

He looked at it and immediately realized it was the piece he had been sent to get. There were two design elements shaped into the pewter: a half dozen stands of wheat, stooped over like old men, as if swaying in a breeze. The amulet had a thin line down the middle of it, and on the other half were three raised five-pointed stars. Oak closed his big hand around the charm and the chain and put it in the pocket of his jeans. He shut the lid of the jewelry box and headed straight out of the turreted room. As he hit the top stair headed down, he flipped open his cell phone and hit auto dial to call home.

"Hey," he said, "It's me."

"When are you gonna be here?" his wife, Claudia asked, a bit impatiently. "Your dinner's waiting for you."

"I'll be there in five minutes," he said. "Guess where I am?"

"C'mon Burt, stop it. I don't have time for games – Tommy, stop hitting your sister! –" she called out at peak volume. "Just come on home, Burt."

"I'm on Buck Tree Road."

"No! You're not at that awful house, are you?" she asked, the fed up tone in her voice mixed with a hint of fear. "You've got no sense at all Burt."

"I'm not only at the house, I'm inside of it."

The creature heard the voice, and immediately was stricken by a surge of pain. His lone, working eye was flashing in his underground lair in front of the house's front stoop.

"Burt, please, don't do this. Just get out of there."

"Claudia," he said in a louder voice, as he hit the bottom of the staircase, "there's nothing here but a bunch of old furniture and some crazy books and potions upstairs in that room they always talk about."

It was the voice, the human contact, that started the process within the creature. It was immediate. Emotions were stirred up within the creature when he heard voices. And the emotional response for the creature was to feel discomfort – and that created pain.

"Well, what happened to those two boys last night, Oak, huh?" she asked. "Get out of that house, now."

He turned left at the bottom of the staircase, the flashlight in his right hand, the cell phone propped against his ear, and headed to the jutting out half-wall that separated the living room from the houses entrance corridor.

"Baby, sure as shit what happened last night was the work of one angry brown bear, and I've got my .38 locked and loaded," he said, calmly, as he reached for the front door knob.

"Bull shit, Oak!" she snapped at him. "You know about that house!" her voice was getting louder.

"OK, OK, sweetie, I'll be home soon." He locked the door with the marked key on his key chain, and headed down the landing. "Keep that beef stew nice and hot for me."

He took a second step on the front lawn and pushed the button to disconnect the call. She was still yelling at him. He dropped the phone into the pocket of his overcoat. He laughed, and took another step. The sole of his boot pressed down the leaves atop the grass and soil, and virtually directly below where Alderson was walking, a hand with charred, pinkened flesh, and long, razor-sharp talons, emerged from the ground, and reached out in the direction of that laugh. The creature knew this person was laughing at him, mocking him.

The hand swiped, Oak lifted his right foot to take another step, and the creature barely missed its mark, slashing through air.

Alderson kept walking, nearing his car. He heard a muted, guttural sound behind him, and pulled his gun with his left hand, the flashlight still in his right. Oak nodded his head, in an open challenge to whatever was out here on Buck Tree Road. He sprayed the area with light once more, like a lighthouse flashing the sea, and kept the gun in his left hand while he continued walking backwards towards the car. The creature didn't hear the voice any more, and he settled back down in his lair. After starting up the Ford, Oak checked his pocket, to make sure the amulet was still there. He took another look at the odd design – wheat stalks and three stars.

NEW YORK POST
October 24, 2008

College Kids Victims in Grizzly Country Killings

STOCKBRIDGE, MA – The bodies of two Columbia University students were found horribly disfigured near a deserted house on a country back road last week, the victims of a violent slaying. Local police are stumped as to who – or what – may have committed the brutal murders. The most popular theory says the two may be victims of a bear attack.

Alex Corrigan, 19, was found in the front yard of a vacant house on Buck Tree Road in Stockbridge. Officials said Corrigan had his right arm literally torn off and he was viciously slashed, with deep cuts on his face, neck and torso.

Jeremy Stiles, 19, suffered a broken neck and was also found with numerous cuts and slashes on his upper body and face.

Corrigan of Manhattan, and Stiles of Bradenton, Florida, were on their way to visit friends at Bennington College in Vermont, a friend of Corrigan's at Columbia said. "This is awful," said Judy Ericsson, who attended classes with Corrigan. "Alex was a sweetheart. I knew Jeremy, also. He was such a nice guy. People here are just devastated."

The two were reported missing by family members early last week. Stiles' car was found at the crime scene and local police contacted officials in New York. Family members of the victims could not be reached for comment.

Officials have not ruled out the possibility of an animal attack. Reports of bears in the area have become increasingly common in recent years.

"I have trouble believing that a brown bear could do this, but it certainly is possible," said Rick Hancock, regional administrator of the federal government's New England Wildlife Management and Control department. "If these two encountered a bear and somehow the creature became upset or confused...who knows? Bears are extremely strong. It's not often you see an attack that is this brutal, however."

Sources say that the slash marks on the victims may be consistent with cuts that could be caused by swipes from a bear.

According to an NYPD police source, there are scant details coming from Massachusetts police. "These guys are not being particularly helpful," an anonymous source told the Post. "We're trying to investigate on our part, and we don't know why they're not more forthcoming with information."

"We are in the midst of a criminal investigation, and it would be irresponsible to comment on any details at this time," said Stockbridge Police Chief Tom Eisler. "This is a tragic crime, and our hearts go out to the family members."

The families of the two victims are offering a $10,000 reward for anyone with details leading to the apprehension of those responsible for the murders.

DECEMBER 2ND, 1990: NEW YORK CITY

This is the night, this is the night, she told herself.

A week earlier, Abigail had finally agreed to go away for a weekend with Eldon. The weekend had exceeded her expectations. She felt his warmth and how caring he was. And she especially appreciated his sense of humor. It seemed like they were laughing the entire weekend. Also, he was completely respectful of her desire to "take it slow." It was different with Eldon. In college, all of the guys she had been with just wanted to get her clothes off as quickly as possible. Now she was feeling a close bond with Eldon and felt that if he was ready to make love to her...she was ready to let it happen.

An hour later they were together at Gino's, a tiny Italian restaurant on Second Avenue at 88th Street. It featured simple décor with little gilded-frame prints of Venice and Florence and Verona on the walls. Their jackets hung on the backs of their chairs. Outside, passersby were huddled up tight, in overcoats and hats and gloves as the winter chill bore down on the city.

Eldon sipped the pinot grigio from his glass and placed it down.

"Still settling in at work?" he asked.

"Yeah, it's fine so far," she said. "A lot of clerical stuff and typing up memos for my boss."

"It's what you've wanted, Abby," he said, holding his glass up. "Here's to new beginnings."

She picked up her glass and reached across to toast with Eldon.

"Yes," she agreed. "To new beginnings." She took a sip of the wine, and placed her glass down. " I hope it works out. You know, my boss –"

"Diane..."

"Right, Diane. She's such a typical type A, super demanding. I think she likes me, but it's sort of hard to tell."

"She hired you, right?"

"Yeah, everything seems cool. She's just...a 'yeller' sometimes. Maybe I just need to develop a thick skin. She'll be really crazy one minute and then all nice and supportive the next."

There was a pause in the conversation, and Eldon veered the talk away from her job.

"You know, I had a great time with you last weekend, Abby. I hope you enjoyed it."

"It was so nice, Eldon. You're so easy to be with."

Their eyes met and he smiled at her, his warm, gracious smile that she found irresistible. He reached across the table and brushed her cheek. She smiled demurely and his hand stroked her neck

"That feels nice," she said.

"*You* feel nice, sweetie," he said. Eldon brought his hand back over to his side of the table. He eyed her again, her collar bones visible in her v-neck top. "Abby, what's the story behind that necklace? It's cute."

She reached to grab the pewter charm attached to the thin, silver chain. She held it momentarily, and let it fall against her chest again.

"It's a...family heirloom," she said. "My grandmother gave it to me. I loved her so much. She gave me a beautiful old jewelry box, and let me open it up, and there were earrings, and a locket and a lovely bracelet, and this necklace. She told me that this was the piece that I should always wear. And I always do." She reached up to touch the pewter amulet again. "It came down through the generations. You know, I don't actually know how old it is. It was probably made hundreds of years ago."

"I can see the stars there," he squinted, trying to look closely at the piece, "but what's that on the other half?"

"Those are supposed to be wheat stalks."

He nodded.

She continued: "The earth and the sky, you know?"

"It's totally unique," he said. "Is there any significance? Were there farmers in your family?"

"I've told you, Eldon, my family goes way back – old time Massachusetts. DAR and all that stuff. I suppose, living in the 1700s, maybe even earlier, *someone* in my family was a farmer."

He shook his hand, truly amazed. "I want to learn more about your family's genealogy sometime. It must be some story."

All of a sudden, she had a slight scowl on her face; she seemed a little spaced out and shaken by his remark.

He lifted his glass, and tried to lighten the mood. "C'mon," he told her, "let's finish this wine and get out of here."

She smiled, a bit wanly, and lifted her glass to take a sip.

※ ※ ※

As they left the restaurant, a stiff breeze whistled up Second Avenue and the overhanging awnings on the buildings across the street rustled.

"It's so cold, Eldon," Abby said, as she gripped his hand in hers. "Hold me."

He draped his right arm around her, and then pulled her in with both arms. They kissed, and she closed her eyes and held him tight. They walked up the avenue and wordlessly headed to her apartment. Taxis were rushing by downtown and people traveled the sidewalks in small groups, some silent, some laughing aloud, spilling out of bars and restaurants. They arrived at her building on 97th Street. He stood silently with anticipation as she reached inside her handbag for her keys.

They walked up the stairs to her place and after removing their overcoats, were both seated on the knit bed spread of the stars and sliver moon. She caressed his cheek and stood up to close the window shades. Next she lit two candles on her dresser with the vanity mirror atop. She clicked off the lamp by her bed, so that the flickering lights of the candles created a soft, romantic glow in the room. They kissed and held each other, and their hands explored one another's bodies.

When Eldon started to unbutton her navy blue, silk blouse, he didn't know what exactly her response would be. He was pleasantly surprised when there was no physical or verbal objection. He unfastened the two bottom buttons and cupped his hand over her breast, caressing her, feeling her hardened nipple through the sheer bra she wore. He slipped the blouse over her shoulders and took it off of her and then reached to her back to undo the clasp and gently remove the bra. In the glow of the candles, her breasts were beautiful and firm. His mouth fell to her chest and he enjoyed the light utters of pleasure she emitted as he ran his tongue over and around her nipples.

He paused long enough to pull his sweater and shirt over his head. The scattered clothing was on the floor by her bed.

Her hands ran over his firm muscles, his shoulders and chest, and she kissed his chest and ran her tongue along the slim line of hair that made its way down from his chest to his fit stomach. Eldon was feeling extremely excited. The natural momentum left him momentarily breathless and seeking ultimate pleasure, which, he felt was not particularly likely tonight.

"Abby," he whispered. "Whatever you want to do is cool. Don't feel any pressure."

Her response was wordless. She started to unbutton his pants, and then slid the zipper down. She felt him below. He was fully excited and now was moaning lightly as she stroked him. He looked to reciprocate and undid the side zippers on her skirt. They paused again to remove more clothing. His pants and her skirt were tossed onto an easy chair in the corner of the apartment. She removed her stockings and they fell to the floor. Eldon wore only checked boxers, and she was in her white lace panties.

He guided her to face the bed board, looking away from him. He caressed her breasts and pressed himself against her from the rear. She reached around to feel his hardness, and his hand was around her belly, fingering her below. He stroked her and felt her excitement.

"Ohhhhh," she moaned. "Yes, that's good."

He sucked in breath, and let out an "aahhh" as she caressed him.

"Abby, I think I should take out a condom."

Her only response was to take her hand off of him, slowly turn around to lie on her back and lift her legs in the air to methodically remove her panties. The candlelight flickered in the room, and she tossed her panties to the floor. He stood up to reach into his jacket pocket for a condom and then took off his boxers.

"I want to be on top," she said to him, rising to sit at the bedside. He laid down on the bed. She straddled Eldon and pressed her hands against his chest. He found her and inserted himself.

"Slowww," she said. "Ahhh, that's it."

He braced himself and held her hips and they rocked gradually up and down. Her breasts were hanging before him.

[slut...you fucking idiot]

They began to rock faster as her excitement and her lubrication created a natural sexual path that begged for speed.

"Ohhh, that's so nice, Abby," he cried out.

[he's a fucker...a user...how can you be such a stupid little bitch...]

Her breathing was stilted as she moaned repeatedly, "oh... ohhhh...ohhhh...," trying desperately to ignore the voice in her head.

[you are such a fucking idiot...you never listened]

"I did," she cried out. "Oh...ohhhh...I did listen to you..."

"Ahhhh," Eldon moaned. "What Abby? What are you talking about?"

[he's a user...they're all users...he's a pigshit, selfish, lowdown...]

"SHUT UP!" she yelled. "Just shut up!"

He was so confused now, but tried to stay in the moment. There were tears streaming down her cheeks. He didn't say anything and gripped her hips even more firmly as he felt himself rising to climax.

[see, slut...he doesn't care. He only wants one thing...]

She was so conflicted that her rise towards orgasm had been completely disrupted.

"Ohhhhhh," he moaned and exhaled, as she felt the moment when he finished inside her.

She rose and pushed herself off of him. She stood in the room, her beautiful body there before him – tears in her eyes.

"I'm sorry, Abby," he said, as he removed the condom, utterly confused. "What did I do? Did I hurt you?"

[such a typical shit licker, asshole]

"No," she cried out, "I *don't* want to say that." It seemed to Eldon that she was not talking to him.

[tell him. don't be a dumb bitch]

"Abby, what is it?"

Through her tears, her shoulders shuddering, she told him: "Please, Eldon. I think you better go, now."

[user, fucker]

"What the hell, Abby?" He had never had a sexual experience like this before. Highs and lows and the whole fucking thing tossed together in a big god-damned mess.

[let him have it, girl]

"PLEASE ELDON!" she cried out. "If you care about me, get your clothes on and leave."

She turned and went into the bathroom with a rush, still naked, and slammed the door shut. He could hear her crying.

[you are such a fucking idiot. I tried so hard. everything in my life was for you. to convince you to see the light. he wants your pussy...now. of course. they all want it *now*...]

She was sitting on the toilet seat, her head in her hands, crying uncontrollably.

"Shut up," she said, in a barely audible voice. "Why won't you leave me alone?"

Eldon was lacing up his black boots, truly in a state of shock. Should he say goodbye to her? Should he just walk out of the apartment? He walked to the bathroom door, and still heard her weeping and muttering.

"God...why...why?"

Completely perplexed, he said quietly, "Bye Abby." He pulled open her front door, put on his navy blue pea coat, and made his way down the steps. Eldon had no idea whether she had any interest in seeing him again or not. He still felt a pull towards her, a strong pull. He opened the front door to the building and felt the brace of the bitter cold, snapping him out of the bizarre spell that had taken hold of him in Abby's apartment. He walked along the street, and took a right turn on Second Avenue. He heard a loud rush of laughter from a group of three guys passing by. For a second he thought of grabbing a stiff drink in one of the bars, but he felt that a shot of JD wouldn't be quite the sufficient elixir to clear his head of the indescribably freaked-out experience he just had.

His hands in his pockets of the pea coat, Eldon kept his head low and steady and walked to catch the subway downtown. The revelry of everyone else's Friday night continued to unfold around him.

CHAPTER THREE

Stories had trickled into Oak Alderson since he had retrieved the medallion from the house on Buck Tree Road. More accurately, he had poked around out of curiosity and information had come back to him from various sources. Reporters from the city had finally stopped snooping around a week after the murders. There were no solid clues leading to any likely suspects, and the prevailing sentiment kept the notion alive that a bear in a shitty mood was responsible for killing the two college kids.

The day after obtaining the strange looking pewter medallion with the stalks of wheat and the three stars, his boss Earl Cummins told him he didn't even want it stored in the evidence room in the basement of the Pittsfield headquarters. He asked Oak to get a safe deposit box at a local bank – Earl didn't even want to know which bank – and store it there. Earl figured, in case anyone tried to question him about it, let's say over a few cocktails, it was best that even *he* not know where the medallion was stored. Oak had dutifully brought the medallion to the Lee Savings Bank, placed it in the box the sheriff's office rented, and that is where it remained. Let the taxpayers pay for its safekeeping.

Curiosity, however, did slowly gnaw away at Oak. Eventually, he conducted a Google search and tracked down an article in *Modern Demon Spirit*, a self-proclaimed on-line 'zine of the occult. There was a professor from Umass at Amherst quoted extensively in the article who seemed to know all about the pewter medallion. He had put in calls and left messages on the voice mail of the prof – Dr. Peter Earnhardt – but hadn't heard back yet.

DECEMBER 3RD, 1990: NEW YORK CITY

"C'mon, dude, get the fuck outta here."

"No, I'm dead serious. That's what happened."

Miles Adamson, Eldon's best friend in New York, was sitting on his low-slung bachelor pad couch, on West 71st Street, working the TV clicker, mindlessly flipping through bad TV options on a Saturday morning, with the phone propped against his ear. Telephone pole skinny with a shock of red hair, Miles possessed a devil-may-care attitude that Eldon leaned on to offset his own insecurities.

"OK, you guys were getting busy," Miles prodded him.

"Don't be so fucking crass," Eldon said, sipping a cup of coffee he had brewed in his small studio in the East Village. He glanced out the window at two black-clad, short-haired girls walking along 4th Street right past the bum curled up on the sidewalk under a box and a bunch of papers and rags. "We were making love, man."

"OK," he said, "you two were 'making love,' and then…you finished, right?"

"Yeah, I mean, it started to get weird right in the middle."

"What did you do to her, Eldon? Why did she freak out?"

"I don't know, man," Eldon took a sip of coffee. "I can't remember exactly what she said, but I swear, it was like she was talking to somebody else. Believe me, there was nobody else in the room."

"Look," Miles said. "You scored with this hot chick you've been telling me about for two months, now, right? It's all good. Whatever else happens is gravy."

"Why can't you figure it out, Miles?" Eldon said. "It's not always about scoring, and just scarfing whatever 'pussy' you can."

"It's not?" Miles asked – he knew that would get a rise out of Eldon, so he had to deliver the called-for response.

"Don't be such a callous asshole," Eldon said. "I have serious feelings for Abby. I mean, I think she might be the one."

"Oh, that's good," Miles said. "This chick bugs out and tosses your sorry ass out onto 97th Street 30 seconds after your little bear has been hibernating in her den – and she's the one? You know, I don't think I'm the person who's confused in this conversation."

"You're right," Eldon said, in an exasperated tone. "You're not the one who's confused. I know I'm the one who's confused. Remember, I called you this morning looking for advice, pindick?"

"Oh, yeah," he said, humbly. "Well, have you talked to her since?"

"No. I think I should call her, but..."

"Eldon, what was she saying after you guys...*made love*?"

"You know, it was like, she was yelling at someone 'no, I don't want to do that, I don't want to say that.' It was weird. Then I tried to ask her what was going on, and if I had done something to hurt her. Next thing I know she's crying, and telling me I had to leave."

"Better you than me."

"Thanks again for your endlessly supportive sentiments."

"Sorry," Miles said. "I couldn't resist. OK. Look, call her, alright? Just see how she's doing."

"Maybe she doesn't even want to talk to me," Eldon said.

"Give me a break, Eldon," Miles said. "You've been telling me how great things have been. Hey, think about the fact that she helped you get over you know who." Miles tried not to mention the name of Eldon's ex-girlfriend, Cindy, because he was well aware how devastated Eldon was for at least a year after that one. Eldon really finally got over the Cindy heartbreak by meeting Abigail.

"Yeah," Eldon said, grudgingly acknowledging the dynamics of that situation. "Hey, that's why I want to make this one work.

I'm not a free spirit like you, Miles. I mean, you can just bounce from one to the other."

"Whatever. That scene's not that great. I'm looking for the right girl, too, E. I mean, I want to settle down," he said, with partial sincerity. Being 22, and in New York, he didn't really want to leave the single life. But he knew that's what his friend Eldon needed to hear.

"Well, that's my point," Eldon said. "You know what I mean."

Miles rolled his eyes and stayed silent.

Eldon continued: "I don't like the dating scene. I want this to work out with Abby. I think she's right for me."

"Even though she freaked out when you had sex."

"Look, I think it's probably something she has to work through."

"I guess so, brother. You've always had that soft spot in your heart for stray puppies and kittens, too. Maybe you just want to help the damsel in distress."

"It's not just that," Eldon said. "She's a great girl, Miles. I want you to meet her. You'll see. I think she just has...some intimacy issues."

"I'll be glad to meet her," Miles said. "Maybe she's got some freaky friends."

※　　　※　　　※

They worked through it, Eldon and Abigail. They both so wanted to make it succeed.

For Abigail, it was the first time she had experienced a truly deep emotional bond. Previously, it had been situations in which guys saw her as a sex object – or there were guys like Tommy. It was his striking good looks that were the lure. Tall, muscular, with curly brown locks. After a month together, she recognized his amazing shallowness, and that more than anything his love was reserved for his own image in the mirror. He was like a beautifully wrapped gift box -- thick, colorful paper and lovely tied bow -- that was mistakenly left empty at the department store. It took her a few weeks to remove that gorgeous wrapping paper to discover the vacancy within.

Eldon was so iron-willed and firm – and a cute guy, to boot. Tall and strong, with his dirty blonde hair. What really got her was his sincere interest in her side of the conversation. He was endlessly curious, and wanted to know how *she* felt. Soon she realized it wasn't an act. She was falling for him – mostly because it was just easy and natural to be with him. Now, if she could only fight off the demons that made her intimate life hell – just when it seemed that this relationship was coming together.

※   ※   ※

Eldon had been through a rough period at Syracuse after Cindy left him. He had been so much younger then – just two years before. But he realized that his collection of insecurities at the time had ultimately pushed her away. And there had been something else: an incident that he dreaded thinking about, but couldn't eradicate from his memory.

Cindy – raven-haired, athletic, beautiful, short and shapely. She played soccer in high school in New Jersey. A Management Information Systems major...this girl was *all* business. She must of tired of Eldon's artistic sensibilities. He could remember her digs at his interest in teaching.

"Those who can't do...," she'd say, leaving off the rest of the cliche.

God, what a bitch she could be. Yet it all became a web that was woven in his mind and his body. Yeah, she infuriated him, but she was bewitchingly attractive, with her always perfectly shiny, flowing black hair, and her athletically toned frame. Her seductive beauty and her athleticism in the bedroom – that's what had really made him crazy for her. Sexually, she had taken him where he had never gone before. She had this mojo like a chick out of a porn film:

"Give it to me baby...yeah...yeah...oh yes, baby..." It took him a long time to simply get over not having *that*. Something about her "yes, baby" – it just stayed planted in his memory banks, taunting him. However, the core of the story – and what really went down during the break-up – took him far longer to get past.

There they were, standing in the university's busy main quadrangle, people walking by them on both sides.

"You're just getting to be a complete drag to be around, Eldon," she said, in her sharp cutting voice. This wasn't the sexual tigress Cindy; this was the cold, analytical, CEO-of-the-future Cindy. "God, I just don't want to be with you – when I think of you whining and throwing a hissy fit because I was *having a conversation* with John at that party Saturday."

'John' played on the football team – middle linebacker. The way she was smiling at him, fawning over him. How was Eldon *not* supposed to feel jealous?

"Cindy, I said I was sorry," he said. "My god, I'm not perfect, I know that. I just…I'm crazy about you. You know how…"

"Crazy," she cut him off. "*Crazy*, period, Eldon. Maybe that's what you are. You don't give me any room to breathe. I'm starting to feel like you're looking over my shoulder every minute. I almost believe that if I'm chatting to the guy sitting next to me in class, I'll look over, and you'll be peering in the classroom window or something."

"No, it's not that. God damnit," he said, sounding flustered. "I was drunk when I got angry about you talking with John at that party. It was the booze talking. It wasn't me."

"Eldon, Maureen saw you two weekends ago, in your car, in our parking lot, in the middle of the night. What the hell were you doing there?"

Shit, he thought. Maureen was her roommate in the dorm. It was McMurney house: a small, grey-stone dorm building, with just five stories. There was a parking lot out back where he could see Cindy and Maureen's window. He had become obsessed. On a Friday night, when Cindy said she had other plans, Eldon couldn't help thinking she was with somebody else. She was cheating on him; he feared it, horribly. He had no good reason to suspect it. He was just…irrational at this point. The situation was truly spiraling out of control.

He drove his Ford Escort to the parking lot after midnight. He stared up at her window. Should he call? Should he ring the buzzer in the lobby? No, he couldn't do that. So he just sat in his car…for hours. Wanting to know where she was. Was she upstairs? Was she alone? Maureen must have come home late and seen his car; must have seen him. Damnit. That bitch.

Eldon looked up at the sky in anguish, trying to come up with the right answer to give Cindy. There was no serviceable lie that would work at this point. His car broke down? He was studying for a test, and that was the only place he could get peace and quiet? Her eyes bored into him – she was staring at him, a scowl on her face.

"Cindy, I…" he stammered.

"Goodbye, Eldon," she said, matter of factly, seemingly without emotion. "I need to get to class, pronto." She turned on her heels, and headed away. No kiss goodbye. No nothing.

"I'll call you later," he lamely called out to her.

She didn't even reply.

The next two days and nights were pure hell. He tried to call her; left messages, spoke with her roommate (that bitch, he thought again). Finally he tracked her down on campus, cutting a class to find her. He got a decidedly cool reception, and when he tried to kiss her, she turned, and his lips found her cheek. She agreed to have dinner with him. He couldn't figure out where he stood. In his mind, Cindy was still his girlfriend. He hadn't been told otherwise.

He had vague recollections of the dinner conversation, probably because after starting out with a screwdriver – "make it a double" – he kept ordering beers throughout the meal. Cindy remained stone cold sober. This, in itself, was a bad sign. She would usually at least have a couple of glasses of wine. They were leaving the restaurant when she finally helped him see the light.

"Eldon, we're so different," she said. "I just thought you were fun at first. You made me laugh. Recently, things have taken a turn in the wrong direction. It's not fun at all. You're dragging me down."

"Dragging you down?" he asked in a disbelieving tone. "Where? What the hell does that mean?"

"A relationship is about two people caring for one another, OK Eldon? It is not about one person living her life and feeling trapped by the other person's jealousy and paranoia."

"Paranoia?" he repeated incredulously, his words a bit slurred. "Why are you being like this. I-I-I love you. What are you saying to me?"

They were in the parking lot now, standing behind his Ford Escort.

"I'm just telling you the truth, Eldon. What I'm saying should come as no surprise to you," she said. "You're a smart guy. Now, wake up and figure it out. We had a good run, Eldon. It's just not...*good* anymore. Are you OK to drive?"

"I'm *fine*," he said, expressing annoyance.

"Then let's get in the car, OK Eldon?"

"Yes," he said softly, as she walked away from him to the passenger side.

Uncomfortable silence filled the car. His apartment was five minutes from Antonio's, the Erie Boulevard restaurant. It was closer than her on-campus dorm. He drove them to his place. His roommate was out for the night.

"C'mon in Cindy, please?" he asked. "For a cup of coffee."

"Eldon, I'm trying to be nice about this. I don't think we can date anymore."

"Cindy, just hear me out. Give me ten minutes. Please come up?"

Her face expressed utter frustration mixed with boredom. How long would this break-up take, she thought to herself?

Inside, after he fixed two cups of coffee, they were sitting in the messy living room. She was on an old brown leather recliner, seated upright; he was on the ratty couch, sinking in, the way everybody did on the old junker piece of furniture. He didn't even touch his coffee, while she was sipping hers. He was actually still quite drunk.

"Cindy, can't we give it one more chance? Don't you see? Talking it out has been good for us."

She raised her eyebrows while taking a sip of coffee.

"Yes," he insisted. "We've worked through a troubled patch in our relationship. We-we-we've communicated. That's good. You've let me know that I'm acting too jealous, and stuff like that, and now I'll change, OK honey?"

"I'm not your *honey*, Eldon," she said coolly. "Not anymore. And it's not OK. None of it. You are who you are. You're not about to change." She tried to soften her tone. "But, you're a great guy Eldon. Please, understand, this is simply not working out. I can't see you anymore. I think I should get going."

"No...no...no," his eyes were becoming wet with tears. He held his hands to his temples, looked down towards the dirty socks on the floor. "A year and a half together. I've told I love you. We can work through this."

She was standing, and now moving towards the door. She stopped, turned towards him, and put her hands on her waist. He walked over to her, his hands in a pleading position, palms raised, elbows at his side. He was nearly a foot taller than her, yet he felt so small. She leaned her head to the right and gave him an icy cold look.

"Eldon, you know what? You're not even *man enough* to realize you've been *dumped*," she said conclusively and derisively.

He was drunk; he was devastated. His world was falling apart right in front of his eyes. It was surreal and it was incredibly fucked up. Now he felt pure rage on top of everything else:

"You fucking...," and instead of saying "bitch," he drew his right hand back and punched her in the face. It was delivered at a downward trajectory, and it landed high on her cheek, close to her ear. It wasn't full force, but it was a good belt. Eldon was genuinely stunned and looked down wide-eyed at his own closed fist. What the hell did he just do? He genuinely didn't recall throwing the punch.

Cindy was thrown three steps to her right, yet remained on her feet. She was a little dazed, but she was one tough co-ed. She started yelling.

"You piece of shit!" She felt her cheek, and rubbed it. "You mother-fucking piece of dog shit!"

She walked up and slapped him in the face, and it stunned him for a second. He was taken aback, but he was already so regretful, he wasn't about to hit her again. He just stood there, paralyzed, while she had fire in her eyes. Now he tried to take it back – to show contrition...to apologize.

"Please Cindy," his hands were back on his temples, "I don't know what came over me. I-I-I'm so sorry." He reached out his left hand towards her, and she pushed his arm away.

"Don't even touch me. As a matter of fact, if you do, I'm calling the cops."

"Cindy, it was a mistake. You just," he was blubbering now, "you hurt me so much with what you said, and the thought of losing you, and..."

"What do you mean 'losing'? It's not present tense, you idiot. It's past tense. I am lost to you. It's over." She was headed towards the door. "I can't believe you *punched* me, you abusive fucking asshole!" She expressed her rage by slamming the door extra hard as she left.

Eldon stood there – bewildered, broken, and still drunk. He had lost Cindy. That was worse than awful. But the punch. Where the hell did that come from? Never in his life had he raised his hand to a girl or a woman. What was inside of him? The details of this episode would haunt him for even longer than the actual loss of Cindy.

His right hand was shaking. He laid down on the couch, and buried his face in a grimy throw pillow – and bawled like a baby.

When Eldon now examined it objectively – isn't that an oxymoron? – he realized that Abigail was the antithesis of Cindy. Tall, lithe, blonde, curly hair. Certainly no pure beauty like Cindy. But very sexy, nonetheless. Also, where Cindy had endless confidence and grit, Abigail was mysterious and questioning. Cindy was granite; Abigail was quick-sand, pulling him in. The more he came to know her, the more he was attracted to her quirks and vulnerabilities.

On top of his growing affection for Abigail, what made him stick it out past that first bizarre night of lovemaking was the survival instinct: he didn't know if he had it in him to make it through another break-up. Underneath the bravado, Eldon was a tightly wound ball of insecurities. He sought out a support structure to fight those off – he needed someone to be with.

※   ※   ※

While they forged past the uncomfortable incident of their first lovemaking, similar episodes did occur. Oddly enough, none of it was enough to push Eldon away. He just got pulled in deeper, ever more curious about what was behind the emotional Rubik's cube of Abigail Merriweather.

Once they were at her apartment on a Sunday morning. They had made love. She was crying, telling him to leave. He refused to do it.

"Abby," he said, knocking on the bathroom door. "Let me in there, or you come out. Come on now, we've got to talk about this."

He heard a garbled response, through choked tears.

"What? I can't understand you, Abigail."

Nothing. Just fits and starts of whimpering from behind the door. He sat down on her bed, on the coverlet of stars and the sliver moon. After another ten minutes, she figured he had slipped out of the door – and she emerged. Her eyes were red, and she looked exhausted, even though they had both gone to sleep early and had just been through a vigorous wake-up, love-making session, which should typically be invigorating.

"Oh," she said, quietly. "You're here." She turned away from him – making a sharp right into the built-in kitchenette. She grabbed the kettle off of the stove-top, and the only sound in the apartment was the rush of the water filling the kettle.

"Do you want some tea, Eldon?"

"You know I'm a coffee guy, sweetie."

"Suit yourself."

He stepped across the apartment to where she stood and gently placed his hands on her shoulders. She flinched, like she had been spooked by a ghost. She exhaled with full cheeks, looking upwards, and reached back to take his hand in hers.

"I'm sorry, Eldon. I'm so sorry I do this to you."

He held her by the shoulders, and guided her around to face him.

"You're not doing anything to me. I don't believe that. I think it's something you're doing to yourself."

"Why do you stay, Eldon?" she asked, looking him in the eyes. Her blue eyes, even after a crying jag, were beautiful.

Eldon thought for another few seconds before he said: "Because I love you, Abby."

Her tears welled again and she held him close, resting her cheek against his muscular shoulder.

[lies, lies, lies]

"Thank you. Eldon. Thank you so much for being so understanding."

He waited for her to reciprocate. He had never said this to her before. He had only told one other girlfriend that he was in love. And he would end up feeling like a fool for saying it to Cindy.

[it's what they do. it's how they fuck with you. say sweet nothings…and that's what they are: nothings. don't be a stupid bitch.]

"I can't handle this, Eldon," she said, now breaking down. "I love you, too, Eldon. But please, go…just go."

He stroked her hair and now she was pulling away.

"No. There's something else we need to work out here…today."

"Please Eldon. You just don't understand."

"I know that, Abby. I know that very well. But I think that you don't understand, either. It's time for both of us to know more about what's going on with you. I want you to see this doctor. He comes highly recommended."

He pulled a business card out of his wallet, and she looked at it.

"Dr. Orlow. What kind of…?"

"He's a psychiatrist, O.K.? I insist that you see him. Whatever is going on – whatever is getting in the way of our happiness, we've got to figure it out."

"But I've never been to a shrink before. I'm not crazy. I'm not that weak. I'm not…"

"Honey," he looked into her eyes, at her tear-stained face. "That's so irrelevant. I would never say those words about you. You're the person I care about more than anyone else in this crazy world. That's what's crazy. The whole damn world. That's why I want you to find answers. I want you to be with me, so we can make it through this together. Whatever it is that is…," he struggled for the right phrase, "tearing us apart. Let's figure it out and beat it."

CHAPTER FOUR

"I'm calling for Agent Alderson please."

"Speaking."

"This is Peter Earnhardt from Amherst. You called me a few times."

"Ah," Oak said, in happy recognition. He was at his desk, in the open, bullpen style sheriff's headquarters – he didn't have his own office. "Thanks for getting back to me, doctor."

"Call me Peter, please."

"And you can call me Burt. What I called you about was a certain object I have obtained here at the sheriff's office." Oak would draw the line right there at revealing anything else about how he got the medallion. He felt quite uncomfortable about violating a crime scene to obtain the medallion. No one else (aside from his boss Earl) would ever hear that he had done such a thing.

"And how did that point you in my direction, Burt?" Earnhardt asked, in a friendly tone. Sitting in his cluttered office at the university, surrounded by stacks of books on his desk, and more books on all the conceivable shelf space in the small, square room, Earnhardt had long grey and brown hair, and a scruffy beard. He had a growing bald spot at the top of his pate, and his tall, gangly frame stretched out – his legs extended next to and behind his desk – the area beneath the desk didn't allow him to sit facing forward comfortably with his chair close to the desk.

"I think you know about it. It's a pewter medallion – it was worn as a necklace. It has a distinctive design. There are curved-over stalks of wheat, and then a line down the middle…

"…and three five-pointed stars," Peter Earnhardt interrupted, finishing for Oak.

Oak chuckled. "You do know about it, then."

"It sounds like the Sibber medallion," he said. "You have it in your possession?"

"Yes I do. I have it stored away safely."

"For one thing, it could be a copy," Earnhardt said. "The actual medallion seems to have strayed. It was passed down from one family member to another, but at some point in the last 30 years, someone got it – maybe a family member – and no one knows where it is."

"Maybe it's here in the Berkshires."

Earnhardt let out a ponderous sigh. "It certainly is possible." He wasn't convinced that what Alderson had was the real thing. In fact, Earnhardt felt that he was dealing with a lawman who was well-intentioned, but probably misguided. Earnhardt had received phone calls like this in the past. When all was said and done, he had devoted lots of time and energy to examine reproductions of the medallion.

"Burt, let me explain why people are so interested in the Sibber medallion."

"Great. I'm all ears."

"I'm a history professor here. My specialty is early American history, focusing on the New England colonies. A sub-specialty of mine is the witch trials in Salem – and some of the repercussions of those events."

"Repercussions? I don't know much. I can remember they told us in high school that there were apologies and regrets way after the fact," Oak said, reaching back in the memory banks to his days at Pittsfield High School

"That's one way to put it."

"The Commonwealth finally acknowledged that many people were wrongfully executed. Reparations were made," Oak said, completing his thought, restating what he recalled.

"Nickels and dimes, Burt. The Commonwealth sent out form notes of apology fifty years after mass executions. A descendent might get a check for a nominal sum with a note of apology: 'we are very sorry we killed your maternal grandmother in 1694.' Pretty callous stuff."

"It's hard to believe that happened."

"Yes and no," Earnhardt said. "Fear and ignorance can wreak amazing destruction. Look at Iraq right now."

"I think that's a bit different."

"Do you think more innocent people were executed in Salem and Beverly and Marblehead in the 17th Century – or in Iraq in the past year?"

"Fair point," Oak responded.

"Anyway, Burt," Earnhardt said, "Try to imagine what Salem was like: neighbors turning on neighbors over petty squabbles. People had land disputes – and saw the solution in accusing their neighbors of witchcraft. It was wealth-building. Some made their fortunes as a result of alleged witch executions."

"Unreal."

"What they say is if you give a blind man a gun in the woods, eventually he'll hit *something*."

"Your point?"

"There were instances in which some of the people executed people in the 17th Century may have been genuine witches. You know – from the old country: women whose descendents practiced witchcraft in Europe and maintained the belief systems when they came to the Colonies. To put it simply, Ann Sibber was said to be a genuine practitioner of witchcraft."

"She was put to death?"

"Drowned, from what I've heard, in 1694. She was wearing a medallion around her neck. Her daughter removed the piece. As I told you, one of my fields of study is the repercussions of the events that took place in Massachusetts at that time. It's not commonly discussed, but I am convinced that something akin to 'karma' emanated from some of those places..."

"I guess it's not good karma," Oak said.

"No," Earnhardt answered, exhaling in a sigh. "Essentially, there are those who believe that the evil of those executions – the will of the people who were wrongfully put to death – those forces exist in the very heart of the Sibber medallion."

"Now, come on Doc," Oak said, his skeptical nature showing through. "This sounds a bit far-fetched."

"I suppose it's all about belief, Burt," he said. "I'm not here to try to convince you, or alter your thinking. I've spent years researching this topic. For those that *do* believe...well, there have been chilling stories. People in Marblehead and Salem may not like to discuss it much – there's a reason for that – but there are few in those towns who would dare say a cross word to a Sibber, particularly one who wears the Sibber medallion."

"Why?" Oak asked, still skeptical. "Where's the evidence that this thing is...evil?"

"The Sibber medallion has been passed down the line, generation to generation. A female descendant in the family always ends up in possession of the piece." A shadow crossed his desk from the window at the rear of his office – he could have sworn it was a clear blue-skied winter day earlier – and he felt a strange chill. "Look, I don't really feel comfortable discussing this anymore right now, Burt."

"What do you mean?"

"I'm sorry," Earnhardt said, his voice sounding a bit strained. "Give me your fax number there. I have a book I'm working on. Is it alright if I see the piece, and photograph it, and get some details about the crime scene?"

"Of course, Doc, no problem."

"Good, thank you. I'll fax you an account that will clarify some of this for you. Look, virtually any of the stories that I know of can be debunked with the proper degree of cynicism and, I guess, close-mindedness. I've heard plenty; I've read too much to think that all of the stories I know of have no connection – that they're coincidental. I'll fax you a piece that exemplifies what I'm telling you. There's something in that medallion – if it's not pure evil, I don't know what it is."

An hour later, Oak had received a fax and he was reading it over, sipping coffee from a Styrofoam cup:

It was a document informally prepared by Dr. Earnhardt – it was not in published form.

Subject: Patricia Sibber born: 1813 Marblehead, MA died: 1880 Salem, MA

Sibber was six generations removed from Ann Sibber; a direct descendent. From available documentation she is said to have possessed and worn the Sibber medallion.

Her husband, Stephen, a farmer, died in 1857 of a debilitating illness brought on by unknown circumstances. Reports state that within two years time he shriveled from a hearty, strapping, tall figure to that of a gaunt, sallow-cheeked, hacking sickly man. It was suspected by some neighbors that she poisoned him – perhaps gradually, through an elixir that she served him on a regular basis.

The most significant event that she was connected with occurred after the death of her husband. Reportedly, she was in an ongoing dispute with her next door neighbor in Salem, Elias Dartmond (1829-1872).

One element of this story that should be made clear: There was an overwhelming collective sense of guilt in the region – stemming from the events of the late 17th Century. When it was well established that most of the executions that occurred as a part of the witch trials were wrongful deaths – neighbors accusing neighbors and having them executed – few in the region ever wanted to delve into the area of "witch accusations" ever again.

The point being that the people of the areas near Salem were extremely reluctant to make and/or support such accusations. The results had been so catastrophic and disastrous and remained a glaring black mark in local history.

As far as the history of Patricia Sibber and Elias Dartmund:

A few years after the war between the states – in April, 1868 – Dartmund hired an attorney and attempted to bring legal action against Patricia Sibber.

County court papers indicate that Dartmund directly accused Sibber of "placing a curse" on he and his family. No court in the jurisdiction would honor the accusations by actually bringing a jury trial.

Aside from the obvious problems in gathering evidence, there was the collective sentiment in the region referred to earlier in this document – a reluctance to make accusations of such occult doings in general; and a reluctance to accuse any local residents of anything resembling witchcraft.

Oak's cheeks puffed up and he exhaled deeply, and he gave his head a little shake. As much as he didn't believe in things that went bump in the night, he was getting intrigued by this crazy story. He took a sip of coffee and resumed his reading.

All we really have to go on at this stage of the story are the facts of Elias Dartmund's life:

In 1869, one year after Dartmund's lawyer submitted legal papers, Dartmund's youngest son Edward, eight years old, was said to have been attacked and killed – his body torn apart – by a pack of marauding wolves or perhaps coyotes. Such a seemingly unprovoked attack – one that took place during the daytime hours in a wooded area – was unprecedented at the time and remains a highly unusual occurrence.

In 1870, Dartmund's fourteen year old daughter, Annabel, was run down in the middle of Salem town by a stage coach – and dragged beneath the wheels to her death -- driven by a drunken man. The man was only described as a "dark stranger" without any form of identification, a person unknown in the area. He was punished by execution for his crime. An editorial in a local newspaper reported that even the hardened scribes and law men in the area were given a "strange feeling" by the distinct lack of remorse shown by the killer of the young girl.

Later the same year, Dartmund's wife Emily plunged onto a rocky bank at the Massachusetts seaside. An apparent suicide, it was reported that she leaped off of a high cliff and crashed into the rocks below, her crumpled, broken body never reaching the sea.

The following year, Dartmund – said by locals to be something akin to a raving lunatic at this time – repeatedly went to the police harboring accusations of murder against Patricia Sibber.

There were no witnesses that placed Patricia Sibber in any of the locations where the deaths took place. No evidence of any sort was ever found that could connect her in any way to either a pack of animals killing a boy; a mad stranger killing a girl; or the tragic, apparent suicide of an understandably grief-stricken woman.

In 1871, Dartmund was removed from his home – said to be a danger to his neighbors and to himself – and promptly delivered to the State Hospital for Mental Dysfunctions in Northhampton, MA.

He would die there the following year.

Oak put his coffee cup down and scratched his bearded chin thoughtfully. A note was scribbled at the bottom of the page from Dr. Earnhardt:

Burt:

This is one of several stories revolving around descendants of Ann Sibber. I have established to a degree of near certainty that Patricia Sibber was in possession of – and indeed wore around her neck – the Sibber medallion that you now possess.

It's a fascinating story to be sure, Burt, but it's a bad business. To put it bluntly, there is an overriding record of evil and tragedy associated with that family. All of it seems to emanate from the horrible events that occurred in and around Salem in the 17th Century – and a sustained dark energy that may indeed exist in the heart of that Sibber medallion.

The note was signed by Peter Earnhardt, with a P.S. noting that he intended to travel across the state at his earliest opportunity to meet with Alderson and see the medallion. Oak Alderson had to make a decision on this one: should he tell his boss Earl Cummins about all of this? It did seem to Oak that Earl had a bit of an "ignorance is bliss" take on this whole situation.

APRIL 24TH, 1991: NEW YORK CITY

Dr. Orlow was a slight figure of a man. Nearing 70 years old, he was a professor emeritus at NYU, and still maintained a busy practice, seeing patients both at his 96th Street office, and at a home office in Riverdale. His services, as those of many celebrated psychiatrists in New York, were much in demand.

He was owl-like in both his deep wisdom and in his slightly stooped, round-shouldered appearance. He wore thin, tortoise shell glasses, and had scattered wisps of white hair. There was a little wooden figurine caricature of the stereotypical 'wise, old owl' sitting on a side table between the two brown leather chairs that faced each other in his city office. The resemblance between Dr. Orlow and the figurine was undeniable.

His first five sessions with Abigail, occurring weekly, were initially cordial, and then became like a tug of war. He got her to review basic family background: single child, father died when she was young, mother never re-married. Soon she was sharing more personal information. Dr. Orlow enabled his subject to steer the conversation – allowing her the latitude to stew in silence for uncomfortable minutes at a time when a subject came up that vexed her. Finally, during their sixth session together...

"So," Dr. Orlow asked, "you keep referring to problems you are having during intimate moments."

"Yes, and during other times, as well. Always when I'm with Eldon. There's a voice," she said.

"Tell me about it."

Suddenly, the composed young lady he had known for six weeks now experienced a physical breakdown. Her face was contorted. Her hands covered her eyes, her fingers on her forehead, pressing.

"What's wrong Abigail?"

"I can't do this...I DON"T WANT TO TALK ABOUT THIS!"

A silence ensued. She looked to her right and eyed the five shelves of books lining the wall. She looked left out of the office window and saw a woman pushing a baby carriage into Central Park in springtime New York. Above Dr. Orlow's head were the framed diplomas and awards lining the wall above his desk. A table clock ticked lightly, the second hand marching its way across the digits. It was the only sound in the room. Then Abigail began crying. She took a deep breath and tried to compose herself.

"My mother...was very difficult."

"Yes?"

Dr. Orlow watched her carefully: she was wringing her hands. He looked into her face, but she was averting his glance.

"She would say things that were upsetting to me."

"How old were you?"

"C'mon doctor, I don't know."

"Think about it Abigail; remember."

"It started when I was six or seven. If my room was messy or...God, I don't really remember what would set her off. I just remember all the yelling."

"What would she say to you?"

"She called me names. Pain in the ass, loser…I think it got worse when I was a little older. I was thirteen. She caught me kissing a boy. Then it was 'bitch'…whore'…"

"Was your mother ever charged with child abuse?"

"No. Absolutely not. I couldn't tell anyone. The shame was… it just crushed me. The shame of having her…." She was crying again now. "I tried to love her. GOD DAMNIT, THIS ISN'T RIGHT!"

She was wild-eyed now, her blue eyes bulging, seemingly enraged. Her body language displayed someone who was tense, upset, and desperately confused.

Dr. Orlow kept his neutral expression and averted her glance by looking down at his note-pad, jotting down information.

"And your father, Abigail?"

"I don't remember much about him," she said. "He died when I was young."

"I'm sorry to ask – I know this might be difficult, but how did he die?"

There was a pregnant pause. "It was…he was killed in a car accident," she lied.

"That must have been difficult for you."

"Yes," she said, swallowing snippets of the truth – pieces of which remained a mystery even to herself. "I was very young – six years old – but I remember mostly my mother being upset, and that made me upset."

She averted the doctor's eyes as she weaved the fabrication.

"Your mother was supportive of you during this time?"

"Yes," Abigail seemed upset by the question, "as I recall…"

"I'm sorry, I didn't mean to upset you, Abigail," he said. "But I'm afraid our time is up."

She took a tissue from the box on the table next to the owl figurine, and dried her eyes.

"I would like you to start taking medication, Abigail. Please get this prescription filled."

"This isn't right, Dr. Orlow," she said, looking fearfully at the piece of paper he held out to her. "You think I'm sick. You think I need to be medicated."

"Abigail, I think that if you begin taking this medication, and we continue meeting, we will make progress. The medication will help to take the edge off of these episodes you keep having. Hopefully, we can stop the episodes altogether."

Reluctantly, she reached out and took the prescription, fingering it like it was the leaf of a poisonous plant.

"God, I don't know about this."

"Please, Abigail. For the first few days, take one-half of a pill. Then, on the fourth day, begin taking a whole pill, after you've eaten. See you next week."

She nodded her head and silently headed to the door, leaving the wood-paneled office behind.

She emerged on 96th Street and approached 5th Avenue. Taxis were headed downtown, and from across the street she heard the gleeful screams and laughter of kids in a playground in Central Park.

As he jotted down notes from the session, Dr. Orlow finished his observations with a query to himself:

Not completely forthcoming about details of her past. What is she hiding?

CHAPTER FIVE

The beat of the hip-hop song was clipped silent when they shut the door. They were laughing and holding hands as they left the party, walking/falling down the front stoop and across the front yard. It was an annual tradition for Steve and Jody, now that they had been dating for three years. Soon after they had met as freshman at Simon's Rock College in Great Barrington, they had attended a party at the house at 7 Cherry Street in nearby Stockbridge, a house always rented by kids from the school. The party was held every fall, and Steve and Jody had their own way of marking the event.

"Let's go babe," he said, tugging her along into the street, heading left to the trail-head. Steve was wiry and long-faced and wore hippy garb. He had on a white hemp drawstring sweatshirt with red and green vertical lines stitched in, ratty jeans and Doc Martens. He had a scruffy, fuzzy beard and a happy, crinkly smile. His eyes were bloodshot.

"OK, OK! Stop pulling, alright?" Jody said. Her butch 'do was dyed a phosphorescent blue (oh, how her parents *hated* the blue hair), and her pretty, small-featured face was dotted by piercings and studs: one below her bottom lip, one on the right side of her nose, one through her tongue. She had on a robin's nest egg blue hoody sweatshirt and washed out multi-hued jeans, purple with pink splotches. She was barely five feet tall, wore retro pink Keds sneakers, and had trouble keeping up with her boyfriend, who stood a foot taller and whose legs made much wider strides.

There was a blazed trail that covered the swath of land in Stockbridge that lay between Cherry Street and Buck Tree Road. It contained big boulders for climbing on or around, and snaked its way through the woods. A cut-off on the path led up a fairly steep, vertical trail that ended at Laura's Tower, a fire tower that was a panoramic spot that provided views of numerous Berkshire peaks. It was 3 AM – and there was a bit of a chill in the air, but at 51 degrees it was actually unseasonably warm for mid-October.

"So, how did you like this year's version of the Pumpkin Party, sweetie?" he asked.

She skipped a few steps to keep up again. "Great. I think the magic punch did the job."

They were both still tripping on the "x"-spiked red elixir that was spooned out from a big wooden barrel on the screened-in back porch. The Pumpkin Party started at midnight every year and always included psychedelics.

"Did you see that Robin left with Joe Cunningham?" she asked.

"Really?" Steve said. "Those two hooked up?"

"You'd think she could do better than that," she commented.

"Hey, be nice," he said.

As they left the road, their feet were shuffling through the fall leaves gathered near the trail. There was a dirt component to the trail that led to a footbridge across the Housatonic River. A half moon was now low in the sky but still provided enough glow to light the way in the open part of the trail. Steve had a blanket and flashlight in the backpack he wore. After they made their way across the peaceful river – it was shallow and still here – they hit the trail and held hands looking out for their favorite spot.

It was quiet, with a light steady chirp and high hum of little creatures along the river bank, but it was too early for even the birds to begin their morning songs. Steve stopped and leaned over to kiss Jody, and she kissed him back, their tongues intertwining, and they held each other – celebrating their third year together, their third Pumpkin Party. He took the flashlight out of the backpack, zipped it back up, and they resumed walking. The starry sky was soon partially blotted out as they made their way beneath a canopy of maples and elms, some with leaves still remaining.

The flashlight beam led the way now, as there were tricky, rocky outcrops to make their way around. There was a specific spot about a quarter of a mile of the way in to the trail itself, where the land was flat and open and there were no rocky patches. It was actually at the spot of the turn-off that provided the alternate route – up the hill to the fire tower.

"Hey, here we are, babe," he said. "Our spot."

He unzipped the backpack and unfurled a small blanket.

"I have an idea," Jody said. "How about *you* go down on *me* this time?"

"Good thinking," he said. "After that, who knows?"

"Exactly," she said.

She stood and he kneeled on the blanket. When he unbuttoned her jeans, and then unzipped her pants, and worked them down her thighs, she felt the chill on her bare butt – left uncovered by her thong. He pulled the thong down, and held her hips, and his tongue was making progress in pleasuring her.

"Hmmmm," she said, and she inhaled and then moaned. "That's good."

He was experimenting, probing her with his finger and his tongue.

"How does that feel, babe?" he asked in a whisper. He resumed working his tongue around in a circle inside her.

He heard a *whoosh*, like leaves being swept off a branch, and then a crack that was really close, like the branch snapping off a tree – but louder and closer.

There was no response.

"Babe?" he asked. "Does that feel nice?"

When she still said nothing, he glanced up and there was shiny liquid on the front of her light blue sweatshirt. He backed off a little and saw a coursing stream shooting up from the top of her trunk where her head used to be.

"No, no. What the fuck?!?...JODY!" His hands fell away from her hips.

Her body toppled over like a bowling pin and there were slight kicking, reflexive movements in her legs as the last remnants of life spilled out of her headless body. His hand went to his face and he saw that blood had splashed on to him. He looked at his hands and was dumbfounded in terror. Where? What? He looked around and saw a huge creature – it had a disfigured head with stringy hair, reddish flesh that looked mutated and petrified. Its long-nailed hands were at its sides. There was one eye drooping down inches lower than the other one – the one that flashed at him. A pulsating maw lay beneath where the nose should have been – in its place was an oddly shapen lump of flesh. The maw opened and closed in an horrific display as the one eye flashed wide open.

There was blood dripping to the forest floor from one long-taloned hand – the hand that had swept clean through Jody's neck and decapitated the head.

The body was huge, broad shouldered. Steve looked to his right and all that stood out was the splash of phosphorescent blue visible on the leafy forest ground – the hair on Jody's prone head – the entire dead ball of humanity soon to be a maggot feast.

"What the fuck?" he cried out. "Why?"

The loud voice disturbed the creature – confused him. His hands came out and he approached the source of the voice.

"You shit!" Steve yelled. "You killed Jody!"

Now Steve saw the long-taloned hand coming towards him. Sweeping towards his body. After the brief disconnect in which he thought that anger and protestations might be appropriate, he snapped to and realized he better run. As he turned, the talons sliced through the hemp sweatshirt and the t-shirt beneath, deep into the flesh in the middle of his back.

"Ahhhhhhhhh!," he cried out. He tried to reach around to where his back had been gashed, but of course, he couldn't reach that far.

Now the creature was on him, punching him in the head, the force akin to being struck by a hurtling train, knocking him down. The yells had upset the creature. Now he stomped Steve to shut him up. Just shut him up for good. He crunched Steve's head in, and the cracking of the skull bone echoed in the forest – like a tree trunk felled in a storm. Steve's head was a pulpy blob of blood stained hair. He was dead, next to his decapitated girlfriend.

Driven by hunger, the creature had realized that he must leave his lair – he began to explore beyond the confines of the house on Buck Tree Road. Perhaps the forest animals had figured out to steer clear of that house. Something told him it was time to return to his lair now.

JULY 7TH, 1992: HASTINGS ON HUDSON, NY

Abigail and Eldon's wedding took place in Westchester County; it was a small ceremony – a pastoral setting by the river. A friend of the Bailey family owned the restaurant that was right on the Hudson, and they decided it would be a perfect location. There were only 25 people in attendance: old friends and distant relatives mostly. With both of her parents deceased, Abigail's closest relatives there were her two aunts – her mother's sisters – from Massachusetts. Eldon's mom was there, down from Utica, but his dad had passed away, a cancer victim.

Miles was Eldon's best man.

"How are you feeling, old man?" Miles asked him that morning – he reached him by phone prior to heading out to Hastings from the city.

"Hey," he said. "I'm fine – a little nervous, that's all."

"You're doing the right thing, man. Abigail's a great girl."

"Hell, I know that, Miles. I love her. I really do. How can a guy not have some..."

"What?"

"Sometimes I just think about our problems, that we had initially. You're the only one I've confided in about this, Miles."

"Yeah," Miles said. "You also told me she's been seeing a doctor, and things are much better."

"She's still on edge some of the time and really moody."

"Hey, c'mon, everybody has their moods."

"I talked to Dr. Orlow about it. He assures me she's fine. He thinks there are some hard knocks she's had in the past. He just tells me to be supportive of her. I guess her mother was really difficult – he thinks the mom really did a number on Abigail. I just worry, I mean, what if the apple doesn't fall far from the tree?"

"Dude, I think you're having a bit of a panic attack here. Everything will be great, OK?"

Eldon didn't know how he could trap himself into feeling such doubt on his wedding day – time to change the subject.

"So, you're still bringing your latest squeeze, right?"

"Yeah, we're still going strong," Miles said. "Hey four months and counting."

"Hmmm."

"Alright, I know," Miles said. "That's like a long term commitment for me. See, Eldon, we all have our crosses to bear. You're sitting there freaking out about entering the next stage in your life. Hell, I go sprinting for the door when a girl asks me if I'm ready to meet her parents. You're doing the right thing, buddy, OK?"

That helped. Eldon felt much better.

At the same time, in a hotel suite at the Hilton in Tarrytown, where Abigail had stayed overnight, she was sitting with her college roommate, Becky, down from Boston for the wedding. A full-figured girl with a winning personality, dark haired, and apple-cheeked, Becky was a social worker and a supportive friend.

"It'll be OK, Abby," she said, rubbing her friend's back.

"It was supposed to go away," Abby said, choking through her tears, clicking a pill out of a prescription bottle. She swallowed it and gulped down some water. "I heard it – I heard this damn voice again, Becky."

"You hear *my* voice, sweetie. I'm right next to you."

Abigail was sniffling, and using a handkerchief to dry her eyes. "It's my mother, Becky."

Becky didn't know what to say.

"Yes, yes, my dead mother. I hear her damn voice. I know, go ahead, tell me I'm crazy. It's my mother – telling me what a bastard Eldon is, telling me what a mistake I'm making."

"Honey, it's just nerves. It's understandable you'd have a little nervous episode on your wedding day. I can remember when I was ready to marry Tom. You know I asked Marie to slip me a little shot of vodka on the rocks, right before the ceremony? I was a wreck!"

Then Abigail explained to her what she hadn't shared with her before – that she had been hearing the voices in the past. She told her about seeing the doctor, and taking the prescribed medication. Becky kept rubbing her back, trying to comfort her.

"I just can't believe it came back today," Abigail said, choking back tears again. She was wearing the medallion, and now held it in her palm. She always wore the medallion.

"It's just a nervous reaction. You can do this Abigail. You're doing the right thing, I just know it. Eldon is a great guy."

She sniffled again, and felt more composed.

"There's something I didn't tell you Becky," she said. She rubbed her stomach, and looked over at Becky and nodded.

"No, you're...?"

"Yes."

"Well, yee-hah. Here's to a nice old-fashioned, shotgun wedding," she said, and she laughed.

Abby laughed too, and they hugged gleefully.

May 9th, 1993: New York City

She made it through. They made it through together. The pregnancy was relatively routine (of course, there were mood swings; freak outs; dietary adjustments); the birth was trouble-free. Abigail was continuing her treatment with Dr. Orlow, and she and Eldon were building a life together. She had to come off her medication during the pregnancy, but there was no sex during that time – and no voices in her head.

And now there was Cordus. Their golden child. That's what he was. They could sit on the blue, cushy couch in their two-bedroom upper west side apartment, hold him, and simply stare in wonderment, joy and love. He was beautiful. With his cute blonde locks and angelic face. The experience was even more joyous when he wasn't crying. The only (almost) sure-fire cure to stop him from crying was to let him be with his mommy. Abby holding him could usually help him to settle down.

His frequent crying jags were troubling for Eldon, more so than for Abby. She seemed to accept the baby's restless nature as a matter of course, while Eldon early on thought it signaled a problem. He suggested that they should consult with a second pediatrician about the situation, but Abby disagreed, feeling that the baby was healthy, and that their current doctor gave them fine guidance. Also, Eldon was far more impatient with all the crying. Abigail held Cordus now to her shoulder, lightly tapping his back for a burp.

"He looks more like you, Eldon," she said. "He really does."

She brought the child from her shoulder and held him on her lap, set across her legs, now petting his hair, stroking his head.

Eldon draped his left arm across his wife's shoulder, pulled her close, and happily gazed at Cordus. The baby was content, being with Abby. "Maybe you're right, honey," he said. "Not the eyes, though. Those baby blues are just like yours." They looked at each other, and smiled lovingly. Eldon glanced from her blue eyes, and looked back at those of his son. "Beautiful – just like yours, sweetie."

He rose from the couch, and walked over to the window, looking out on Columbus Avenue. After a pause, his thoughts had floated elsewhere.

"I don't know if it's for me, Abby."

"What are you talking about?"

"All the crap at the office," he said. "I don't if I'm cut out to be a broker at Whitestone Realty."

She was still cooing at Cordus, and happy just to be alive and a new mother. She'd heard this refrain previously from her husband.

"That guy in our office, Walter. The way he talks about the cold calling, and the tricks – recalculating measurements in office space, so you can pry a few dollars more of rent out of a new lease agreement – he seems to like it. He thinks it's a blast."

"Honey," she said, still sitting on the couch, "your vision of the job doesn't have to be like Walter's. Why can't you have your own take on what you do?"

Eldon shook his head slightly as he watched the cars speeding downtown, past the pizzeria and the gift shop and the framing gallery across the street – ten stories down.

"Because he's right, Abby," he said. "He'll get ahead. There are a thousand more offices like ours in Manhattan, with brokers looking to chop the competition off at the knees. It's so fucking Darwinian – sorry Abby," he said, looking over his shoulder, and casting a worried glance towards Cordus. "These charged up, clean-shaven, apes battling each other for every crumb." His eyes started to glaze a bit in recognition of the meaning of his work life, and what it was doing to him. Maybe he should of followed his early instincts and become a teacher. "Because, if I don't get the commission for the vacancy at 962 3rd Avenue, then it means that Brad Jacobs at Alliance Realty will get it. And our boss Stanley will be in my grill, looking at me the way he does. That disapproving scowl. What does he say, Abby? What does that so-and-so Stanley say to me? 'Bailey, that's a dinner right off your family's table. Brad Jacobs is probably taking his wife to the Four Seasons tonight. And you're dishing up pizza for your family. One measly slice for all of you to share, Bailey.'"

"Honey, that's ridiculous. It's stupid. We're hardly starving."

He barely heard her. " 'Well, Bailey? What kind of man are you? We need commissions in this office. That coffee maker in the kitchen doesn't drip for free, Bailey.' And Walter understands. He *gets* it. It doesn't bother him, at all. He mocks Stanley behind his back. He thinks it's funny. Walter is *part* of it; he enjoys it."

"Eldon, please, honey. If it's not right, you'll get out."

"I might have to, Abby." He walked back over to the couch and sat beside her. He placed his left hand across her shoulders again. "We might really have to get out, Abby. Out of New York, babe."

"And if we do," she said, looking from Cordus to her husband, looking into his eyes, "so be it. I'm with you, hon. Wherever you want to go, we're together, OK Eldon? We're a family."

"Yes, Abby," he said, exhaling a held in breath, trying to let out the stress. "Good, that's very good. I'm sorry. I guess it's just been this week."

"Eldon. I understand. I really do, honey. But it's not just this week. It's not just Brad Jacobs and Stanley Whitestone. Maybe we're not meant to be here in the long haul. That's OK. There's a big world out there. It's not just New York City or bust. Now, why don't we have that slice of pizza now?"

She looked at him and laughed, and so did he.

"I love you, Abby," he said, and he kissed her on the lips.

"And I love you," she said.

Again, they both looked down at the baby, and recognized their deep unstated love for Cordus. And it went beyond love. It was a sense of awe, that together they had created this beautiful being.

※　　※　　※

Financially, the landscape had changed for Eldon since he started dating Abby. Growing up in upstate Utica, Eldon's dad, Martin, was a successful businessman. The Baileys were big fish in a small pond. Now his dad had passed way, and his mom remained in a modest downtown apartment in Utica.

For Eldon and Abby, expenses were piling up, and Eldon's savings were diminishing. So the pressure to succeed as a broker was coming from all sides. He felt it every time he reviewed their finances, and he had to take shit from the likes of Stanley Whitestone, who wanted to see more productivity from the desk of Eldon Bailey. After all, Eldon was occupying valuable office space at Whitestone Realty; he damn well better produce.

It was Saturday now. As much as they worshipped Cordus, the constant need for attention got to both of them now and then. Infant care was hard, and it was never-ending. Eldon and Abby struck a deal that they would each get a bit of down time on the weekend. It was Abby's turn now; she was out shopping for clothes in one of the Columbus Avenue or Amsterdam Avenue boutiques. Eldon was trying to read the *New York Times* at the kitchen table, but the baby kept crying, and he found himself reading the same line over and over in a story in the business section. Flustered, he shut the paper and put it aside. He walked to the living room where the baby was.

He stood over the crib and shook the rattle.

"C'mon, Cordus," he said, trying to keep that warm, loving tone. "Stop crying, little man, c'mon."

There was simply an unsettled nature about Cordus, Eldon felt. He cried too much. Abby told him it was perfectly normal. But he had friends with different experiences – his co-worker Walter, for instance. His little girl was perfectly behaved.

The piercing tone of that cry. No, the bottle wouldn't do. Cordus didn't want the bottle now. Just more crying. It worked on two levels to get to Eldon. The crying droned on and on *and* it peaked in high-pitched crescendos that stung his psyche.

"Baby, it's time to stop now," Eldon said, a little less patience in his voice. "Stop crying Cordus. Daddy needs some quiet."

Five minutes later, it simply hadn't stopped. Eldon was feeling discomfort...pain...the crying...

He turned the TV on, cranked up the volume. He soon realized that that was pretty annoying, too, so he lowered the volume again. He was pacing now, and walked over to the crib, where the crying kept on, unabated. After a few attempts at gentle-voiced baby babble and rocking the baby in the cradle, and moving him back to his crib, Eldon was at the end of his rope. Where the hell is Abby? he thought.

He went back to the kitchen table, reading the newspaper, but could barely read a word. He walked back over to the crib, and now is voice was loud and angry: "Can't you ever shut the hell up?"

Eldon's anger was rising more, his patience ebbing. Then, there was a click in his mind, an epiphany. He heard the phrase again, even though he wasn't saying it:

"Can't you ever shut the hell up?"

What is this? What's going on, Eldon asked himself. Cordus was still crying – the screaming was stinging his ears and his brain. Eldon felt the perverse inclination to walk right over and hit the child. He heard the words again, reverberating inside his skull:

"Can't you ever shut the hell up?"

But the only voice in the apartment was the bawling wail of the baby. Eldon was feeling incredibly tense and had an uncomfortable flash of events from the past. It all seemed way too familiar. It was *déjà vu*, but more intense, more a part of him, deep inside.

He spoke out loud, to himself: "No, no, no! Don't hit the baby." He sat down on the couch, ignoring the muted show on the TV screen, and grabbed his temples. "Jesus!" he said, feeling at the end of his rope. The crying went on and on and on.

It was now unbearable. Eldon wanted to know why that phrase seemed familiar to him – "Can't you ever shut the hell up?" – but felt mixed-up because he was unsure why it resonated. He rose again and, in a dark, confused mood, walked over to the crib. Jaw clenched, he tried to hold it together. His voice was tight and strained. "C'mon Cordus, please stop it now? Stop it now!!" Eldon yelled. Then, there was that phrase again, and Eldon just said the latter half: "...shut the hell up!" and he reached down and grabbed the baby's left hand and tugged it upwards abruptly.

The crying only became louder – much louder – and all of a sudden it was a truly piercing wail. Eldon's eyes widened – he was shocked at what he had done. It was just like that time he punched Cindy in a rage when she broke up with him. He had experienced a momentary blackout; he didn't realize what he was doing.

Did he just hurt the baby? He lifted the wailing baby up gently, and inspected his tiny form. His little arm was disconnected from the rest of his body and swinging loosely behind him. Eldon had tugged way too hard on his arm when he pulled at the baby. Shit, Eldon thought. How could I have hurt my baby? What the hell am I gonna do now? Abby is gonna to want to kill me. He'd have to take the baby to the hospital, and get him examined. And tell them what? That the baby tumbled off the couch? That, ummm, his arm got caught in the side of his high chair?

Damnit, Eldon thought. I didn't even mean to do it. I didn't know what the hell I was doing. She'll *never* believe that. Abby is gonna be so pissed. Eldon's mind was racing, and he was panic-stricken. What was the right thing to do? Minutes later, Eldon was in Cordus' room, sitting with Cordus in his arms. He was preparing to leave a note for Abigail and take the screaming baby across town to Lenox Hill Hospital. Then he heard her:

"I'm home," she called out. She heard her baby crying with such ferocity that she dropped the packages down and ran to the sound. "Eldon? What's going on? What's wrong with him?"

"We're back here," he called back loudly, to be heard over Cordus' loud wailing. It was evident, upon any close inspection at all, that the baby's left arm was not in the same condition as his right. It was lifeless, disconnected, and out of place. Abby entered the room with a wide-eyed look of concern on her face.

"Hi," Eldon said, as she entered Cordus' room.

"Cordus," she called out desperately, and was reaching out to be handed the child. "What's the matter, sweetie?"

"Abigail," he said. "I think he's hurt."

"*What?*"

"I had him in his high chair, and his arm must have gotten caught between the side support bar and the base of the chair."

She was immediately frantic. "What do you mean 'must have?' What are you talking about?"

His tone of voice was even and falsely calm. "I-I tried to lift him up out of the chair; I mean, I *did* lift him out of the chair. His shoulder got tugged the wrong way."

"Jesus Christ, what are you talking about? What are you doing just sitting here?" she walked closer, and was horrified by what she saw. "Oh my God! My baby!"

"It just happened, like two minutes ago. So calm down, please." he said.

"Calm down? You're telling me to calm down, Eldon," she said, clearly about to erupt. "DON'T TELL ME TO CALM DOWN! WHAT THE HELL DID YOU DO?"

"Abby, I was looking the other way; I was watching TV while I was lifting him up. It was really stupid."

"*Stupid?*" she repeated, and then she started crying, and the volume of her voice was a bit lower. "Yes, that's one way to put it Eldon."

He was averting her eyes. He looked at Cordus. He looked down. He looked over to the side. Eldon was not a very good liar.

What kind of nightmare was this? Abigail asked herself. His explanation seemed shaky. But *that* worry would have to wait on the side for a few minutes. Get the baby to the hospital. Right away. Abigail looked at her husband with disgust, wishing he wasn't even in the apartment right now.

And now she was yelling again, wiping tears away. "LET'S GO! WE NEED TO GET HIM TAKEN CARE OF – NOW!!"

Eldon had nothing to say. He thought of continuing his explanation of the events that took place, but realized that silence was about the best he could do right now. The baby seemed to be crying even louder now. Then Eldon regained his composure a bit, and figured out that the story would have to stand. That's it.

"Yeah, Abby. Let's put a blanket over him, get our coats on and get out of here. We'll go right downstairs and get a cab. But listen to me," he said, looking at her now. She was crying, looking at Cordus and his detached arm. He couldn't catch her eyes. "I messed up, OK? But it was a mistake. I feel miserable about this."

"Yeah," she said, still crying, now nodding her head. "Yes, Eldon, you should feel miserable about this."

"I didn't do it on purpose, damnit!" he yelled. "You're acting like I did."

"Please," she said, feeling upset and confused and horrible, "let's just go. I'll get a blanket. Just carry him out now, and let's go."

"Damnit!" Eldon said. "I really don't appreciate this, Abigail."

"Shut up, Eldon," she said firmly. "I don't think Cordus appreciates it either. Let's go."

And so came the first fissure in their marriage – the solid rock of trust revealed its initial crack.

⌗   ⌗   ⌗

On Monday, two days after the incident, Eldon was in the office and made a private phone call. He was sitting in his cubicle, of course, but Walter was out on a sales call, and there was no one else within earshot if he kept his voice down. After initial salutations and inquiries over the latest updates on the baby:

"Mom," Eldon said into the phone. "There's something I need to know."

His mother, sitting in her Utica apartment, responded in a good-natured manner:

"Yes, dear. What is it?"

"Mom, I've had these strange...memories lately."

"What are you talking about, Eldon?"

His mother didn't know about Cordus' shoulder injury. It wasn't the kind of incident Eldon was about to broadcast.

"Look, Mom, I got upset with Cordus – at all his crying. I yelled at him, the poor little guy. I yelled. I said, 'Can't you ever shut the hell up?' I felt like I might lose my temper, and do something I'd really regret."

"Dear," she said, concerned, "you've got to be very patient with a baby."

"He cries too much, Mom. How many times have I told you that?"

"He's a crier," she said, matter-of-factly. "And I've told you, Eldon, you were, too."

"Yes, Mom, I realize that," Eldon said. "Anyway, I yelled at him the other day, 'Can't you ever shut the hell up'? That's what I said. And the second I said it, I realized for the first time in my life, that someone said that to me. A long time ago. Something else happened when those words were said to me. Mom, please tell me. Who did it? Was it a stranger? What the hell happened to me?"

"I don't know what you mean," she said. There was a slight shift in her tone. It was practiced now, and there was something mechanical about it.

"Mom, please, what happened to me? You've got to tell me if you know."

She was defensive.

"Eldon, honey. I really don't know what you're talking about." Her words belied her thoughts, because her mind was now racing. She felt tears welling up in her eyes, now. What should she do? What *should* she do? She couldn't ask Martin – not from beyond the grave. Her husband, Martin, had always guided her, given her advice...bossed her around.

Eldon's anger flashed. Tears were streaming down his cheeks. He peaked outside his cubicle, to make sure no one was walking nearby. "Stop it, Mom. It's deep, buried inside me. I know it's there. Don't lie to me."

She wiped a tear away, and gathered herself. She remained calm. "Eldon, I don't like your tone. I just don't understand what you're talking about."

"Mom! For God's sakes, what are you doing?"

The silence at the other end of the line spoke volumes to Eldon.

"Tell me, please. It was no stranger, was it? I know Dad drank, Mother. Of course I know that."

"Now, look, I don't know what's going on there, Eldon," she said, trying to assume a scolding tone. "Where are you?"

"I'm at work," he said, clearly annoyed that she asked. He reflexively looked around again; the coast was still clear.

"Well," she said, assuming a nurturing tone again, "please don't let yourself worry about this. I really don't see how I can help you, honey."

"Mom, I want you to stop and think. Those words, 'Can't you ever shut the hell up?' He yelled them at me. He hit me, didn't he, damnit? Didn't he hit me, when I was just a baby?"

"OK, I think I need to go now, Eldon," she said, coolly. This was more than she could handle right now. She loved Martin. He had been a very good provider. "I have an appointment at the hairdresser's."

"Mom," he said, trying one more appeal. "This thing is eating me up inside. The closer I get to the truth...I can feel it; it's so close."

"Please, Eldon," she said, looking for closure in this conversation. "Take care of Abigail and Cordus. Be there for them. Be patient. That's your job now, alright?"

"But if you could only help me out right now, Mom. Maybe I can move past this."

"I'll talk to you soon, Eldon. I really need to go now." She saw and heard flashes of Martin losing his temper. Acting out of control. That period passed though. He had been a very good man.

Now Eldon was resigned to the harsh realization that this conversation was going nowhere. There was no clarity for him here, nothing to be gained through his effort to reach out – and reach back – into his past.

"OK," he said, trying to choke back emotion. "Yeah, alright Mom. I've got to make some calls myself. Talk to you soon."

"Goodbye dear," she said. She hung up the phone and felt dizzy and light-headed. Martin deeply regretted what he had done; he *told* her that. There was no reason to betray her husband now. In any case, she felt it was disrespectful to speak ill of the dead.

⁑   ⁑   ⁑

"What did I do?" she repeated her friend's question, speaking into the phone. "Becky, I tried to stay calm. My baby was hurt. I-I tried to find out what happened."

"And?" her social worker friend Becky asked.

"I still don't know. I admit it," she said, holding back tears with her voice cracking a little bit.

Cordus was napping now, as his mother sat in the kitchen.

Becky exhaled; she didn't quite know what to say.

"Becky, how can I believe Eldon? But, on the other hand, how can I assume he's lying?" she said, composing herself.

"Can you talk to him again? Try to press him on it?"

"What good is that gonna do?" Abby asked. "If we get into another fight over what happened, what is that going to accomplish?"

Becky tried another tack: "Look, honey, maybe he's telling the truth. He said the baby's arm got caught in the rail on the side of the high chair. OK, it was a stupid mistake. But people are entitled to make mistakes. Granted, this is a big one..."

"That's right, that's a good way to look at it," Abby said. "I guess it could have been worse. After all, the doctor said that Cordus will be just fine. It was a shoulder separation. The doctor popped it back in and he stopped crying instantly. His shoulder will heal completely." But Abby started to cry lightly again. Just saying the words – actually discussing the injury of her sweet little boy – was heartbreaking to her.

"Oh God," Becky said, overcome also. "C'mon Abby, it'll be alright. I know it's awful. But like you said, Cordus will heal up fine."

"Yeah," she agreed. "He will, he really will."

"Abby, I see lots of different situations in my practice," Becky said, trying to phrase this delicately. "I have to tell you this: if there's a pattern, then you know there are some serious problems, OK? You have to call me immediately if you see any signs of domestic abuse from Eldon."

Abigail was crying, tears streaming down her cheeks.

"Abby? Just promise you'll call if anything happens. I'm here for you."

"OK, Becky. I have to believe it was a mistake, a stupid mistake. He was watching TV and not paying attention to what he was doing when he lifted him up."

That explanation certainly sounded dubious to Becky.

"Yes, Abby, that's fine. But please call me if anything happens," she said. "Or just call me anyway, alright?"

Abby stopped crying again; she was wiping away tears. "I will Becky. I'll call you in a couple of days, I promise."

"OK, Abby. I better go. My 3:00 o clock is about to head in the door. Just take care honey, and give Cordus a kiss for me."

"Bye, Becky. Thanks."

After she hung up the phone there were tears welling up in Abby's eyes again. The doubt was ever-present. Don't press the issue with Eldon, she told herself, because she needed to believe him – she simply had to. Unfortunately, that didn't assuage her gnawing suspicion that Eldon's story failed to ring true.

CHAPTER SIX

S he sat at her kitchen table crocheting a sweater for Cordus, for her lovely son, now in pre-K. He was taking a nap in his room. She had read a few books about crocheting and had completed a few smaller projects – a pot holder and a small scarf – and now she had become more ambitious. The sweater was one color – royal blue: a relatively simple project if you just followed the pattern. It would not fit Cordus now, of course. The way he was growing, it was just a miracle, she thought. So fast. The sweater would fit about six months from now. She was giving herself a lot of latitude in terms of completion time.

Pearl, stitch...pearl, stitch...

Her mother was right, that was the enormous irony of the whole damn thing. The voice was no longer there, calling to her and berating her. That's why she worked with Dr. Orlow, to eradicate the damn voice: her mother's strident tone, yelling at her, a daytime nightmare reverberating inside her head.

But after all was said and done the old girl was right: men are bastards. It must have been true of Abby's father – of course it was, why else would her mother have done what she did to him? And hell if it wasn't proving to be true about Eldon. Everything is beautiful and glossy at first – and it's all phony as a three-dollar bill. His sentimental slobbering before he bedded her down. His vows. His prolonged lust for her body during what she referred to in her mind as the honeymoon period.

Pearl, stitch…pearl, stitch…

What was it now? What had their life become?

"I'm too stressed out to talk about it, Abigail. I just want my dinner, and I'm going to watch some TV and have a few beers."

So many nights, there was nothing but silence and tension in the bedroom. Abigail reading. Eldon turned away from her, lying on his side. Where was the compassion? What had become of her dreams of a happy life together with her spouse? Hell, where was the sex? Where was the *passion* in their lives?

Pearl, stitch…pearl, stitch…

Each of them had a seemingly independent, loving relationship with Cordus. The father and mother doting over the gentle and bright child. Eldon's love for Cordus, and Abby's love for Cordus. It was no longer translating into love for each other, however. God, how she tried. She still felt it often: pangs of love. But he snubbed her. He turned her away with his surliness, his superiority. His regal role as the bread-winner, as if what she did was meaningless, worthless.

Her mother was right, after all. They want you for one thing – *your pussy*. She laughed out loud. He didn't even want her for that anymore.

"Mommy? Mommy?" Cordus called out from his room. "Come here please."

She placed down the needles and the wool on the kitchen table and went back to his room – Cordus was surrounded by a sprawl of toys and was zooming a truck along the carpet. He was a cute, sturdily-built, four year old now – his curly golden hair cut short and neat.

"Yes, sweetie," Abby responded as she walked in. "How are you doing?" she asked cheerfully.

"Good," he said. "Mommy, I don't quite understand what it means that we're moving. Will I see Michael again, and Jeremiah?"

"Cordus, sweetie," she said, and sighed. "I really think you will. We'll come back here to visit. And guess what? There will be new friends for you to meet where we're going, OK?"

"But they won't be Michael and Jeremiah, will they?"

"No Cordus."

"I don't want to go. I want to stay here."

She tried to bite her tongue, but couldn't quite do so.

"Well, Cordus," she said, "Mommy kind of feels that way, too, alright? We simply need to move. That's what's happening."

"Hmmm," he said, thoughtfully, zooming the truck around the carpet again. "Maybe I can stay with Michael and his mom and dad – here."

"Oh, honey," she laughed. "I'm sorry, but I don't think mommy and daddy want to leave you behind. We love you way too much for that." She sat down on the carpet and hugged him, pulling him close.

"I don't know why people move, mommy."

They heard the front door close. The tension increased within Abby instantly. Where had things started to go wrong? She knew that the problems started before Eldon insisted on the move to – she still could hardly comprehend it – Bangor, Maine, of all places. The argument over the move, however, only seemed to exacerbate their differences.

Business, that's what it was. The opportunity came up to buy out a realtor up there.

"Abby, hi," he called out, curtly. Then, with far more enthusiasm: "Cordus, Daddy's home."

Cordus dropped his truck and came out to greet Eldon, and Eldon lifted him up and gave him a kiss. Abby trailed behind, following Cordus out of his room and into the front foyer.

"Daddy, Mommy says she kind of feels the same way that I do," the boy said. "I don't want to move, and Mommy said she kind of feels the same way."

Eldon glared at her. This was a stark betrayal. She knew they were supposed to hold a united front over this decision in front of Cordus.

"Jesus, Abby, what have you done now?" he said, gently putting Cordus down on the floor, and then kneeling down to speak to the boy at his level.

"Cordus," he said. "Daddy and Mommy need to have some alone time, now, OK? So be a good boy and go back to your room."

Cordus turned and paced back towards his room. Eldon rose from his crouched position to see Abby glaring at him before she turned to head into the kitchen. She pulled a couple of vegetables out of the bottom tray of the refrigerator. Then, she turned to the other side of the kitchen counter, and angrily started slicing through a green pepper with a carving knife. Eldon walked away from the kitchen and into his son's room to chat with him.

Abby was knifing butter into a pan, and soon placing slices of the green pepper into the frying pan, and it started to sizzle.

Earlier that day, when she told Dr. Orlow about their growing problems as a couple, he had his concerned look – but he always seemed to have a concerned look. Could the move help them, she asked?

Dr. Orlow was like a poker player who didn't want to give up a tell. His response was non-committal:

"It's up to you, Abigail," he said. "You are half of this relationship. The way you described it to me was that Eldon feels that this move is necessary for his business. Now, is that true?"

"He could keep working here as a broker, but it's making him unhappy. He says that the stress of his job is part of what makes things more difficult at home. The business climate is decent in Maine, he says, and it's unusual that this kind of business comes on the market. It's a small operation, so Eldon was able to buy the retiring owner out. And Eldon believes there's room for growth."

"So," Dr. Orlow said, "it's not necessarily a move that *has* to be made, but your husband wants to do this, and you don't."

"Ummm, yes, I guess that's about the sum of the situation."

Dr. Orlow had this annoying habit of letting her stew in silence when there was a revelation to be made. This was his way since the first time she met him. Finally, after a minute:

"So, what are you thinking?"

"Oh, please Dr. Orlow," she said, in an exasperated tone. "I've known you long enough. I know what you want me to say."

"I don't want you to say anything in particular. I want you to say what's on your mind."

"You want me to say that I am not asserting myself enough, and that I should prolong this argument over the move."

"Not really, Abigail. *You* said that – so maybe there's truth in the fact that you are not asserting yourself enough."

She sighed. Oh God, she thought. $175 for 50 minutes of *this*?

"He always brings it back to the schools issue, you know, that Cordus is ready to begin first grade. How can we just send him to the public school and be sure that things will be OK? I guess I agree with him on that. It would be a strain on our finances to send him to a private school in New York right now. I understand that. If we move – when we move – that problem is gone. Cordus will be in a lovely little school right near our house up there."

"So that's a good thing, Abigail."

"Yes, Dr. Orlow, that's a good thing."

Again, silence hung in the air. Between the angry patches of silence that she and her husband experienced, and the extended pregnant pauses in her sessions with Dr. Orlow, sometimes she felt that the two of them were starting to drive her nuts. She laughed aloud at that, and didn't share the thought with Dr. Orlow.

"What's so funny?"

"Oh, nothing," she said. "I was just thinking about the futility of this situation, honestly. This move is happening. In two weeks. It's a done deal."

Now she flinched at the memory. She was clanking around in the kitchen, pulling a large pot out of the bottom drawer in the kitchen cabinet, continuing to work on dinner now that Eldon was home. He was with Cordus in the boy's room.

"Cordus, there will be new friends," Eldon said. "I promise."

"Not Michael and Jeremiah," he said, firmly.

"We can visit. We'll visit, OK? Daddy has to do this. For his business. Someday, you'll understand why, OK Cordus? I know it's hard now, but someday, you'll wake up in the morning, and instead of going to school, you'll go to work," he was sort of blabbering now senselessly to a four-year old boy. "Then, you'll understand better why we're moving."

Eldon understood all too well that this pat explanation didn't tell the whole story. He knew that the move was also about his own attempt to run away from the mysterious darkness that resided within him – a malevolent side that refused to leave, like one of those low-life apartment tenants who didn't pay the rent and then tried to claim squatter's rights. Eldon harbored the hope that moving away would help him to escape the events in his past that haunted him. Cordus was running his red Tonka dump trunk across the carpet. It was certainly more interesting than what Daddy was saying.

"I don't wanna go," Cordus said. "Mommy said she doesn't want to go."

Eldon's lips came together and thinned in a straight line. How the hell could she do this to me, he thought? What a low, god damn dirty trick.

"We have to move, Cordus."

Tears were next, and a temper tantrum. Eldon shut his eyes and patiently continued to try to reason with his little son. Never raise a hand, Eldon reminded himself. Never raise a hand.

"OK, Cordus. You might need a 'time out' now. C'mon, why don't you stay in here a while, and calm down, and then we'll have dinner. I'm going to close the door on you, Cordus, if you can't stop crying."

"Noooo!" Cordus bawled.

✕   ✕   ✕

As they lay in bed that night, backs turned towards one another, Eldon reflected on his feelings. Why had his sex drive for Abby waned? Why had he shut her out? There was no good reason. She was as good a woman as he could find, a wonderful mother to his son. There was no logical explanation to the coldness that had grown around his heart. In his mind, it was some immature sense of dissatisfaction with her appearance. Her distinctive face: long and thin, not beautiful. Of course, early on in the relationship everything was hinged on her sexy form, and her face complemented that in a lovely way. Now, he saw the imperfections. And, maybe her tits weren't big enough. Yes. Now, that he had Abigail as his wife, there was a burning desire to make love to a woman with huge breasts, that he would bury his face in.

But then it became more complicated, and harder to understand. That black patch when Eldon was a baby. He had that feeling again – more than a nagging suspicion – that something *bad* had happened to him in the past. It was always there, but remained beyond his reach. Whatever that flash of memory was, it contributed to the man he was now. It played itself out in the violent incidents with Cindy in Syracuse, and with Cordus when he was an infant.

Truth be told, Eldon wasn't able to clearly understand the dynamics of his own behavior. If he did, perhaps he could re-shape it – be a better man, and love and support his wife. However, he was just another emotional casualty, another damaged individual aimlessly seeking an answer, like so many others. Unwittingly, he sought out ways to undermine his relationship with Abby, thus sabotaging his own chance for happiness. Their relationship was like an hour-glass. Their love was collected at the top, only to be inexorably drawn through a hole, seeping slowly to the bottom of the glass, where it was converted into feelings of resentment, confusion, conflict and an ever-diminishing passion.

The fact of the matter was that even Eldon, if confronted with the facts in an analytical summary, would be forced to concur: Abby's mother was right after all – *men are bastards.*

A week later, Abby had her last appointment with Dr. Orlow. She told him their move was finalized. Abby resented his disapproving frown. God, she thought, do all these shrinks just want to make a mint off the patients? Does he just see me as the Fort Knox of whackos?

"We've made a lot of progress, Abigail," Dr. Orlow said, glancing at a page far back in his notes. "No more voices, right? The medication has been effective."

"Yes," she said, matter of factly. "And I am grateful for that." There were side effects from the medication. She didn't like those one bit. She had stomach pains at times, and couldn't drink alcohol, because even just a couple of glasses of wine would cause a terrible hangover the next day in concert with the medication to control depression.

"Look, here is the name of someone for you to see in Bangor," he handed her a prescription paper with a name and phone number. "You really should continue your treatment, I believe," he said.

"That's fine," she said, in a flat tone.

"Abigail, this is important. Think of what you have. You've been married for...," he paged through his notes.

"Nearly five years, Dr. Orlow."

"Almost five years now. You have a child. I'm sorry to be so blunt, but I don't know if any of this would have been possible if you hadn't been on the medication. Remember what you had been dealing with before."

"My life is different now, Dr.," she said. "I really think the past is behind me."

He looked at her with a grim expression, and stroked his chin with his hand.

"What happened when you were a child will always be a part of you, Abigail."

"Yes," she said, quietly. "I understand. My mother was very ill. What she did to me was wrong. I can't thank you enough for helping me come to terms with that situation."

Dr. Orlow's instincts, honed through nearly 45 years of seeing patients, still told him there was more to the story than what she had told him. The mother beat Abigail. He believed that was true. Something else was there. Prior to the days of modern pharmacology, and his ability to prescribe her the proper medication, he didn't know if she could have made the kind of progress she had – with some darker truth still buried inside of her. Thankfully, her moods were now controlled by the medication, and the voices had subsided.

"I wish you all the best, Abigail," he said, as the table clock indicated that their time was up. "Please feel free to contact me if you need to talk."

She stood up and held out her hand for a shake. "Thank you for everything, Dr. Orlow," she said, smiling at him.

PART II

CHAPTER SEVEN

"The last time he told me 'I love you'?" she repeated the question, looking out the window at the foot and a half of snow in the backyard. Should she laugh or cry? "I don't know... two, three years ago? God, I could tell then he didn't mean it."

Abby's blonde locks were dappled with grey patches now.

"Hmmm. That is so cold," Becky said, speaking to Abigail from her office in Needham, Massachusetts.

"That's what he is, Becky," Abigail said, sitting at her kitchen table, nervously folding a piece of paper into itself over and over: "Cold." She looked haggard and tired – circles beneath her eyes. Twelve years married, Abigail was still a young woman. It was clear there had been an emotional toll and it had weakened her. "Eldon is on a full-time power trip. He needs to stroke his own damn ego all the time. Since he started the business, it's like he's the master of his universe over there and he started bringing it home."

"So isn't it just a matter of, umm, putting him in his place?"

"Honestly, I think that requires the two of us to have a sense of humor about things – and some affection for each other still. When he started giving me shit about the way I kept the house and my cooking...You know what it is? The bastard just figured out how to push my buttons and piss me off."

79

"I don't understand why? What's his motivation for picking fights with you?"

"He's sadistic. It's that simple. Eldon has these basic insecurities and he feeds off of putting me down. It makes him feel like a real man."

"Honey, maybe the two of you aren't meant to stay together."

"The pitiful truth is that part of me still loves him. I remember the guy he used to be early on – sweet, respectful."

"But you just said so yourself: he's sadistic. It's just the simple 'honeymoon syndrome': a guy is just putting on an act for the first stage of the relationship. I hate to say it, but maybe his true colors came out, Abby."

Abby knew her friend was right. The problem was deeper than Eldon being an asshole. It was that she had lost confidence. She hadn't been working since they left New York; there wasn't the economic necessity for her to work. It was a vastly different business environment in Maine – one in which Eldon was thriving more than he had been in Manhattan. They were financially comfortable now. Unfortunately, the increasing success of Eldon's professional life did nothing to prevent the continuing disintegration of Abby and Eldon's relationship.

While the anti-depressant medication had regulated the voices, there was nothing now to prevent the onset of the malaise Abby was now feeling. She didn't have the moxie to step out of the shadows of her life. She was an easy target for Eldon, and he kept on swinging away.

Still on the phone, she floated off into a daydream about the night before. With Cordus in bed, Eldon came after her with both barrels. He still made a token effort to minimize their disagreements in front of their son.

"Jesus, Abigail, I asked you to do one chore for me. You know I needed that grey suit taken to the dry cleaners today. I mean, what were you doing that kept you so damn busy?"

"I'm sorry Eldon," she said, meekly. "I had a few things to do. I messed up, OK?" She had taken a walk in the woods behind the house during the day, and got lost in her thoughts.

"I know you messed up, Abby," he said. "That's why we're having this conversation. I work my ass off all day, supporting the family..."

"I'm sorry," she said. "I said I was sorry, damnit. Just get off my case."

"And what do I do in two days when I have to wear that suit to my meeting?"

He just couldn't let it go. That was Eldon. Like a pit bull with a bone with some remnants still left on it, he had to keep gnawing at it.

"You know," desperately trying to gather her strength for a return parry: "why don't you just fucking wear a different colored suit, you control freak!"

Then he slapped her – open handed, right on the cheek. She was crying now. Just weeping, her narrow shoulders in her night gown pulsing up and down in concert with her tears.

"Don't tell me how to run my business, Abigail! Christ, you can't even keep this house in order, god knows what you'd do if you had a business to operate."

She wanted to say something. God, she wanted to hit him back. She was so broken-hearted and depressed she just didn't have it in her. Her mind was a swirling canvass of confusion and self-deprecation. Eldon was the beast – the sadistic beast, covering up all his insecurities through utter domination of the woman who he claimed to once love.

"Abby?" Becky asked, lining up a sheaf of papers on her desk. "Are you still there, sweetie?"

"Hi," she said. "I'm sorry, you were saying?"

"Don't worry about it," Becky said, somewhat aggravated. She listened patiently to all of Abigail's woes, and then when she tried to discuss some of her own concerns, Abigail floated off to la-la land.

Abigail couldn't tell Becky the whole story. Not that Eldon hit her, even though Abby had promised, years ago, to tell Becky if he ever became abusive. It was just too humiliating.

"Oh, Becky, I'm sorry. Please, what were you saying?"

"Forget it, Abby," she said, sincerely. "It's OK. I'm worried about you. Call me anytime you need to talk, OK?"

"Bye, Becky. Thanks," she said.

Hanging up the phone, Abby felt like she was drowning and losing hold of the lifeline.

The house was empty, quiet, looming. She rose from the kitchen table and looked in the backyard – the snow-covered two acres and the woods behind. She thought about Cordus – the lovely, beautiful Cordus. He was in sixth grade now. He was a very good student, and a wonderful little athlete. There was always good in her relationship with him. But every night there was the psychological warfare with Eldon to deal with. In that battle, he had the surface to air missiles; she had the pea shooter.

There was one more variable, however, that was her rock, and helped her to forge onwards. It was a source of strength and faith, yet it remained a mystery. When Eldon verbally took the starch out of her, and she felt awful and small, she reached up to hold the medallion that always lay against her neck, attached to the thin silver chain. She felt *something* there. It was at once both unpleasant and empowering. What was it? At times, when she held the medallion and shut her eyes, she felt it and almost even saw it. What was it?

※　　※　　※

For Eldon, there was a distinct disconnect between office life and home life. He wouldn't have believed it could have happened to him, but work now represented a relatively safe haven from the problems in the marriage. His professional life was good – far away from the pressure cooker he had dealt with in Manhattan. Bangor had proven to be a wise choice. He had a solid corps of brokers at Bailey Realty now, and the agency brought in steady income through property management, as well. He was reviewing some of the information now as he compiled sales figures, actually wondering if it was time to find new space and expand the office:

- Barclay Yates – in his fifties. A very tweedy dresser, heavyset man, married, with a solid reputation in the community. Handled many of the commercial leases and the agency's residential property management.

- Barbara Simpson – also in her fifties, married to Frank, a high school history teacher. Matronly and rock solid responsible, she had meticulous attention to details. Did great with older couples looking to buy or sell homes; they loved working with her.

Then, he had his secret weapons – the two younger women in the office who helped immensely when it came to attracting – and keeping – male clientele. It was simply a matter of fact that men liked the idea of developing a business relationship with sexy women. Both of the "girls" knew the appropriate times to flirt a bit and turn on the charm and that was just fine with Eldon.

- Patti Millerton – 30 years old, dark haired and very buxom and curvy. Married to John, a blue-collar guy with a gun rack on his pick-up, Patti was excellent with office and store leasing. She had a steady list of customers and always got referrals.

- Tracy Mills – 32, and a former college track star, blonde, tall and thin with an endless well of charm for her customers. It was nothing short of a miracle that she was still single. Somehow it was an endless lure for male condo and house hunters who enjoyed the company of a beautiful broker – with the wisp of possibility that business might turn to…?

Eldon was proud of the team he had assembled. It was a well-oiled machine. Not too much tension in the office. Although, he knew that Patti and Barbara had been known to have their catty spats now and then – Barbara apparently frowned upon Patti's penchant for wearing low cut tops in the warm weather in a 'professional' setting. All Eldon knew was that those low cut tops didn't seem to hurt business.

Eldon enjoyed time with his son, Cordus, of course. As a father, he always felt like he was making up for mistakes he had made when Cordus was a baby. Eldon regretted his short temper and wished he had been more patient. That was over – they had left New York and all that pressure far behind, and Eldon was a better father now. What he especially liked were Sunday drives alone with the boy in the summer. They'd make their way across the state to the Maine coastline and sit on an outcrop off of the road, admiring in particular the sloops majestically cutting through the ocean wake.

"How would you like to have a boat like that, Cordus?"

"I hope we can," Cordus responded, with his wind blown curly blonde hair.

As far as Abby was concerned, he thought it really started to go downhill when she accused him of being selfish – always wanting to have his way. He always tried to explain that he was looking out for the best interests of the family. Eldon resented her eternal mood shifts – her darkness and negativity. She was just a downer these days. He really wondered how much longer they could stay together. Could they remain together?

The phone rang:

"What's up?" the familiar voice said.

"Hey," Eldon said. "How's it hanging, sailor?"

"Nice greeting, you freak," Miles said.

"What's going on?" Eldon asked.

"You know, just trying to finalize the Vegas trip. Are you psyched or what?"

"I can't wait," Eldon said.

He and Miles – still his closest friend even though Miles was in New York – took a Vegas trip in the spring every other year. Miles reviewed dates and times, and discussed hotel options.

"I'm definitely cutting loose out there this year, Miles," Eldon said. "I'm dying up here. I'm wound up too tight."

"Is business good?"

"Yeah, but it's not that. It's..." he was struggling for the next word.

"What? You can talk to me."

"Things at home – I don't know what's up with Abby. I swear to God, we're just at each other's throats."

"The bachelor life, my friend," Miles said, adding sarcastically, "fun, fun, fun."

"Yeah?"

"Oh, c'mon. It's not that great. Shit, I'm dating a couple of women, but nothing that's leading anywhere."

"How's the job?"

"Good," Miles said. "I'm now on the city desk; the city hall beat. Log on to the website to check out my bylines."

"I will. I definitely will," he said. "So, what do you think, maybe a trip to the Bunny Ranch this year?"

"Hey, you know I'm up for that. You really think you'll go for it?"

"Man, I don't know," Eldon said, tapping a pen against the desk. "At home, the sex is...ah forget it. You've never been married."

"Hey, Eldon, we can talk."

He tossed the pen down. "It's fucked up, Miles. We fight so much of the time. Then, we're supposed to pretend we're still into it."

"Damn, Eldon," Miles said. "Hey, I'm sorry things have gone so far downhill."

"So do I think that going to a whore house is a great idea?" Eldon asked rhetorically. "No, but I just need to do something."

"Hey, look buddy, I gotta fly," Miles said. "I'll call you next week. Let's go out there – throw some dice, play some cards. Like old times, right?"

"Yeah," he said, "Like old times."

"Talk to you soon buddy," Miles said, and hung up.

Eldon was shaking his head. The trip would be great...but what the hell were he and Abby going to do? In his heart, he had to acknowledge he was tough on her sometimes. But, damnit, she brought it on herself, brooding around. He hated her for it sometimes. Yes, it was perverse, but he hated *her* for allowing him to bully her around.

MARCH 26TH, 2005: BANGOR, MAINE

Mist was rising off of the lake surface on the quiet morning. The two women watched at rapt attention as a loon flew low over the glassy smooth surface, webbed feet just inches above the water, and then rose above the trees at the shoreline. Lake Ididginaw outside of Bangor, a quarter of a mile wide and a half mile long, was a small, idyllic body of water, surrounded by a simply carved out circular, blue-blazed trail. Stands of elm, maple and Douglas fir rose stoutly and the snow was receding now, with spring approaching. The trail was marked by large boulders sitting lakeside, providing natural rest areas by the water.

Cordus was in school and Abigail thought of her words carefully as she tried to answer her new friend, Cynthia K. ("Everybody just calls me Cynthia K.," she had said when they first met.) What was it about this older woman that drew Abigail to her? Cynthia K. dressed in dark clothes and earth tones, today wearing comfortable khaki pants and a purple and black print wool sweater. She also had on a black canvas jacket with oversized buttons; there was still a chill in the air in the early spring. Cynthia wore brown, low-ankled hiking shoes, and seemed to move effortlessly across the frosty ground, making little sound.

Her long hair was mostly gray, with some remnants of brown remaining. Her full, weathered face had a friendly glow, red cheeks, and an almost cherubic expression. She had a demeanor and appearance that made her seem at one with the lake setting. Abigail found it comforting to speak with her. And she needed a friend these days. Eldon was abusive – and then was working a lot of late nights, caught up in work. He said they were trying to attract an investor from out of town to develop a shopping mall at a site on the western edge of the city.

There were the additional hours he was spending out of the house – and the lack of passion in their lives when he was home. Their love-making was rare. Worse, when Eldon did deign to rise atop her and press into her to rapidly bring himself to completion, she knew that he was distracted, going through the motions. He never held her afterwards anymore. He would spring out of bed and she would hear the water running immediately in the bathroom. Then, he would have another chore to attend to in the bedroom before racing out of the room. Abigail would lay there uncomfortably, staring at the ceiling, or reflexively picking up a paperback from her bedside to read, feeling utterly empty. He made her feel so unloved, but what was so frustrating was that she ended up feeling guilty about it.

She was on the verge of suggesting that they go to counseling together when she met Cynthia K. at the lake. It had happened two weeks earlier, and they began sharing their lives soon after meeting. Cynthia was divorced and seemed to have few regrets about that. She was childless – fifty years old. Abigail just craved the sense of contentment in life that Cynthia K. possessed. Abigail dropped hints in their conversations that her relationship with Eldon was troubled.

As their meetings became more regular at the lake, personal details – like melting ice trickling down a mountain stream – emerged from each of them, and a greater sense of closeness developed.

No creatures of the forest ran for cover from Cynthia K. In fact, there was a cute red fox that Abigail had now seen on two occasions when she was circling the lake with Cynthia K. She had never seen the fox when she was here on her own. Cynthia would even give out a kind of 'chit, chit' sound – like one might make to attract a house cat – and the fox would look in her direction. There was no fear there when the fox saw Cynthia K. She and Cynthia would walk on and leave the fox to his explorations. They were on the far side of the circle loop, and there to the left on the downward slope of land, in between the path and the lake, someone had thrown a candy wrapper.

"How could anyone do that?" Abigail asked, repulsed by the detritus at this pristine site.

"Just selfishness and laziness," Cynthia said.

"It's so beautiful out here – such a perfect spot."

As if on cue, they heard a whistling call from a nearby bird.

"There is something I've been meaning to talk to you about, Abby" Cynthia said. Ahead of them, a sharp shard of sunlight – like a flashlight beam – cut diagonally in through a break in the trees. They crossed through it, and were back in the covered path.

Cynthia K., a fervent proponent of holistic treatments, pondered for a moment on how to present her idea to her friend. "Well, think about your life before you moved up here. Being in New York City – you were totally out of touch with this life – the feeling of being one with the natural world around you."

"I guess I never really felt comfortable in the city," Abigail said.

"Precisely," she said. "Now you're out here, but are you close enough to the earth – to the life around you?" Cynthia said, and stopped walking. She now knelt down and placed a flattened right palm against the snow and dirt trail. "I think there's something standing in the way of your happiness." She stood up straight again and placed her hand on Abigail's shoulder. She looked in Abigail's blue eyes. "I don't know if this is my business, Abigail, but I have to tell you what I think."

"What is it, Cynthia?"

"You told me about some of your 'problems' when you had been intimate – and the doctor and the medication. You're still on it, right?"

"Well," she looked down, averting Cynthia's gaze, indicating that she didn't like talking about it. How had she become comfortable enough to confide in Cynthia K? She never told anybody about the pills she took. "Yes, Dr. Orlow advised me to continue taking the pills for..."

"For the rest of your life? That's the solution?" She brushed Abigail's shoulder again, signaling to her that they would continue walking.

Abigail hadn't liked Dr. Brewster when she had met him – the psychiatrist that Dr. Orlow had referred her to in Bangor – and chose instead to consult monthly with a pharmacologist who continued writing her prescriptions.

"I'm sorry, Abby," Cynthia said. "Maybe I'm stepping over a boundary that's not mine to cross."

"No, please, don't worry. I want to know what you think."

"OK. You were in New York when you were prescribed this medication. You were in a place that is completely urban – utterly removed from..." she waved her hand upward to indicate a breathtaking sweep of tree tops to the right of the path. "...all of this. My point is: now you're back *home*. This is where you belong."

The ideas were so simple that Cynthia presented to Abigail – yet seemed to offer such an epiphany. Had she been too close to the proverbial (and now literal) forest to see the trees on her own? Abby looked upwards, spying the breaks in the trees where the sunlight shone in, and the glorious jutting branches, shooting from the tree trunks, that surrounded them. Soon the first flowers of spring would be emerging.

"Abigail, when the doctor put you on the medication, you lived in New York. I think maybe your...soul...was out of place."

Abigail had a sense of being a bit overwhelmed by her friend's words. When was the last time she had experienced a real conversation with Eldon? They had grown apart. She had no siblings to confide in – her parents were both deceased. The words swept over her like a rushing wave.

Cynthia continued: "I've read about these treatments, like Dr. Orlow's. It's all so – synthetic. Your mind is being flooded with chemicals. Maybe it's time to give Mother Nature a chance to be the balm for your troubles. Walk in the woods every day... get in touch with who you really are. Should you live your life just propped up by the work of the Pfizer company?"

"I don't know."

"Maybe Dr. Orlow didn't really understand you."

"Look, Cynthia, I've told you. I really did have some problems back then – the voices I heard – they were for real. It wasn't a function of living in New York. There was something else," she said, still holding back, unwilling to share everything because even she was mystified about pieces of the puzzle.

"Abby, it's *your* life, my dear," Cynthia reiterated. "Please, don't think that I'm trying to dictate your thinking. I just needed to give my opinion, OK?"

They were now sweeping back around the far end of the trail, circling the southern tip of the lake, headed along the trail towards the gravel car park area. Here, the trees thinned out and the sun shone brightly. To the right, set back from the lake, were camp sites for overnight visitors.

Aside from the joy of seeing her beautiful, golden-haired son move from being a toddler to growing to be a boy, and now nearly a teen, there had been little that had been going right for Abigail. Her life with Eldon was uncomfortable – filled with distrust and questions. She was ripe for a change, all too malleable and open to suggestions.

JANUARY 24TH, 2010: PITTSFIELD, MA

Oak Alderson was sitting at his desk in the sheriff's office mid-morning. He was munching on a bow-tie from Dunkin' Donuts and sipping from his green ceramic coffee mug that said **The Berkshires** in white lettering, along with a simple graphic of a few pointy mountain tops. Outside a side window in the building, Oak could see the snow falling in puffy flakes on the chilly but nearly windless day. It was winter wonderland time in the Berkshires, as a series of recent storms had left a sweet, white candyland coating in the yards, in front of the schools and on the dormant golf courses.

Oak had been conducting his own research about the medallion. He had spoken with Professor Earnhardt periodically. Earnhardt had recently been scheduled to come to town for a visit, but cancelled at the last minute. Oak thought it kind of strange that Earnhardt now had access to see a medallion that he had such great interest in, but couldn't find the time to make it across the state. Maybe he was just busy.

Oak pulled out a binder that he kept in his desk with police reports and newspaper clippings of occurrences on Buck Tree Road, along with relevant photo-copies and print-outs of downloaded web articles about the Sibber Medallion. The articles he had located were from various web sites devoted to the occult and the unknown. He kept this binder to himself.

He was also guarded about his surfing to some of the bizarre web sites he visited. He certainly didn't want colleagues at work to know about it, although if they found out, he'd just say it was case research. He didn't even talk to Claudia about the things he read. Oak found a new posting on darktruth.com, accompanied by an illustration of a medallion that looked exactly like the one he had retrieved from the house on Buck Tree Road:

The Last Words of Ann Sibber

As loyal readers of these pages know, the Sibber medallion is an artifact with provenance stretching back directly to Salem, Massachusetts, and the witch trials of the 17th century. The quarter-sized piece with its distinctive design of wheat stalks and three five-pointed stars allegedly contains power that is beyond rational explanation. This pewter amulet is said to have been worn as a necklace by Ann Sibber in 1694 when she was accused of witchcraft and executed by drowning along the shoreline of Salem. Sibber is believed to have imbued the medallion with its legacy of power.

Here at **darktruth.com** we have unearthed a document from town records in Salem that indicates the actual dying words of Ann Sibber. That infamous queen of darkness is said to have spoken this phrase to those who were about to hold her beneath the ocean surf:

"May the wrath of the innocent sufferers forever torment you."

It has been well-documented previously in these pages, dear readers, that the medallion was removed that day from Ann Sibber's neck and kept by her relatives. While it remains shrouded in mystery, this much is known:

the Sibber medallion has been passed down through the generations from one Sibber woman to another.

These women seemingly have the ability to coax mysterious forces out of that medallion. There's far too much documentation over the years to deny that the "bad luck" and tragic events that have befallen neighbors who may have run afoul of the Sibber in possession of the medallion have occurred coincidentally. Clearly, the Sibber wearing that medallion has the ability to either have her wishes fulfilled or can actually place a curse or hex on an enemy.

A further cloak of mystery envelopes this case, my ghoulish friends, since it is unknown whether the medallion is even in the Salem region. The trail of the medallion seems to have grown cold after the 1976 death of Margaret Sibber Waltham – a life-long Salem resident. Margaret was frequently seen wearing the medallion – there are reportedly existing photographs that show her wearing it. Margaret worked as a librarian in Salem. From all accounts, she was friendly and not known to have cursed any enemies – perhaps she had no enemies.

It is unknown who ended up with the medallion after Margaret. The family has numerous branches stemming off from Margaret and her husband Daniel (Margaret and Daniel had three daughters, immediately complicating matters!), and there seems to be a dearth of information about the current whereabouts of the medallion.

Certainly we at **darktruth.com** revel in the notion, friends and fiends, that this wonderfully evil pewter round piece is out there somewhere – perhaps quietly spinning a web of black magic for its beholder as you read this. The only true justice we can hope for, colleagues in darkness, is that a Sibber woman is gripping the medallion now, and that her flesh is feeling the wonders of its awesome power and vast history. Perhaps we'll find out some day...

Oak was looking forward to meeting Professor Earnhardt – if he could ever get him into town. At least the Professor could tell Oak whether the medallion he had retrieved was identical to the Sibber medallion. Surely, it couldn't be the same one. Could it? Oak closed out the file and eyed the stack of reports on his desk he had to check over. It seemed like every time he stumbled on something that further piqued his curiosity about the medallion, reality came calling. Oak had work to do and a family to support.

"Hey Oak," said Sheriff Earl Cummins as he approached Oak's desk, "come into my office for a minute, eh? Let's talk about what we're gonna do about all of those complaints we've been getting from near Pontoosuc Lake lately. Must be a bunch of damn kids raising hell out there late at night. Really, all these calls should be going to the city police, not us, you know?"

"Yeah, you're right Earl," he answered, laying his arms across his binder full of information to keep it out of plain sight. "Umm, look I'll be right in and we can talk about it."

"OK, Oak," Cummins said. Then he shook his head, as he walked towards his office, muttering, "I'm tired of these old-timers calling us about noise around Pontoosuc."

Oak closed his binder and put it away in his bottom right desk drawer. It was weird, Oak thought, Since the day after Oak retrieved that medallion, and put it away in a safe deposit box, Earl had never asked him about it again: never brought it up once. It seemed like Earl was just hoping that if he never said anything about it, then maybe Oak would forget about it, and the whole incident – and presumably the medallion – would just go away and never come back. Regardless of the cynicism Oak had previously felt towards matters of the occult and the unexplained, he was starting to accept the notion that maybe strange things *did* sometimes go bump in the night.

CHAPTER EIGHT

JULY 18TH, 2005: BANGOR, MAINE

Summer in New England. It was a glorious time. Everything about it reminded Eldon why their decision to leave New York had been so right. He could almost still feel the disgusting swelter rising off of the Manhattan pavement in July – even from hundreds of miles away.

Eldon had just hung up the phone and was ready to close up the office for the night. He told Abigail that he would be late; his dinner meeting with the investors for the shopping center would keep him out until probably around nine. He picked up his lightweight, tan L.L. Bean jacket off of the hook near his office door, walked out through the four desks in the empty outer office, shut off the main light, locked up the outside glass fronted door and stepped across the parking lot to his SUV. It had been a beautiful summer day, but had cooled off when the sun went down. The rest of the strip mall where his office was located was occupied by a nail salon, a book store, a sports/ gun shop, and was anchored by a Super K-Mart.

The space was cheap; that was its main appeal. He had his eye on a little gray stone townhouse on the edge of town that was available for conversion to commercial space. That really had much more cachet for a real estate office than his current location. Along the commercial strip of Route 14, Bangor had unfortunately taken on a rather generic appearance of big chains and fast food joints. Eldon barely paid attention to his surroundings as he pulled out of the lot onto the road, hitting the gas as he drove past an Arby's and a Gap. He had other thoughts on his mind.

Sometimes his mind wandered all the way back to discussions with Miles. Maybe he had been too rash in ignoring the signs of Abigail's illness. Well, he certainly hadn't *ignored* the signs. He had arranged for her to see Dr. Orlow in New York. But how could he have really thought that there wouldn't be problems down the line? A naïve kid, that's what he had been. Now his wife was moody and seemed to want to pick a fight with him every time he walked in the door. The sex had all but dried up between them. Who were they kidding?

The Doors were singing "Love Me Two Times" on the classic rock station – *Love me twice today. Love me two times girl* – and Eldon thought about last night's argument. So stupid…

"Look, Abby, all I said was maybe we shouldn't have the thawed-out leftovers for dinner. I didn't mean it as an insult to your cooking, for Christ sakes."

She was brooding. The silence hung in the air like a golf club perched at the top of a back swing, ready to be swooped down through the hitting zone at any second. Cordus dutifully kept eating the chicken fricassee on rice, and his fork 'clinking' the plate was now the only sound in the room. Their son just folded into himself when he sensed the tension between his parents.

Abby held her hand against her forehead, her head hanging. "You know," she said, removing her hand, and looking up at a spot on the wall near Eldon – not at him – "can't you just make an effort to say something nice once in a while? You come in through the door, I've done all I can for Cordus all day – it's like I'm a single parent, you know that?"

"Abby, it's been busy at work. How many times do I have to tell you that? I've got to keep us in house and home, and groceries, you realize that?"

"You just have a lot of nerve, Eldon, criticizing the dinner I've made."

"OK. I'm sorry…"

She knew he couldn't stop himself. He wouldn't let it die there. And she was right:

"...but is it really that hard to pack Cordus off to school and pick him up at the end of the day?"

"Damn you!" she yelled. Cordus was looking down at his plate now. He hated it when his parents fought. "You just want to slice me up, Eldon. Cut me right down to size. It's like some kind of power trip with you."

"You do tend to be a bit sensitive, Abby. I mean – it gets tiring walking on egg shells around here all the time." He got up from the dining room table, and strolled into the connected kitchen to grab a bottle of Molson Ice beer. He twisted off the lid. Before taking a sip, he held it out. "You want a beer?" It was a pretty meager effort at presenting an olive branch.

"No," she said tersely, before dragging a fork through her dinner, feeling resentment and anger. Of course, there was also the pain of knowing that her sweet Cordus was exposed to all of their nastiness.

That night they were far apart in the bed, as usual. She was so sullen, and he just wasn't up to the effort of breaking the ice. It was upsetting to just go to sleep, but ultimately less stressful.

Driving along, he shook his head and grimaced at the memory as the DJ discussed the Doors reuniting with a new lead singer.

Eldon maintained a youthful appearance, a receding hairline the main sign that he was now 37. He headed west – his destination was Hadley, five miles outside of Bangor. He pulled off route 14, onto the side road, and past the gleaming neon sign in front of the low slung building. The sign said: Snowcomber Inn. Each green letter flashed on one at a time, and then the entire name flashed on for ten seconds, and then the sign went dark for a second, before the little light show began again, the "S" lighting up first.

He didn't have to check twice where the room was. He had been here before, and gave three quick knocks on the door of #10. The door opened and Patti Millerton, the buxom broker, had on a smile and a see-through negligee. Her ample bust on her short frame stood firm and at attention, clearly visible beneath the sheer material.

"Hey, baby," she said, pressing against him as he shut the door. "What took you so long?" She had a high-pitched, little girl's voice – but she certainly had a woman's body.

He bent his knees a bit, and his lips found hers – and their mouths merged hungrily. Patti was short – 5'0" – and shapely and buxom all around. His hands stroked her ass and then pulled her close and they were already feeling each others' excitement and heat.

"You know, I had to take a couple more calls – Tracy Cox was on the phone asking me about getting a second mortgage." He was sinking to his knees, pulling the spaghetti strap off of her shoulder, pressing his lips against her breast. She pulled him back with her and they were now intertwined on the plain blue bedspread in the spartan hotel room.

He hadn't sought out the office romance. Patti had definitely made the first move, however, Eldon hardly tried to fight her off. How could he resist, really? Ms. Patricia Millerton – Trish the dish, as she was referred to by some lustful wags in the Bangor broker fraternity. Was there guilt? Yes, yes, he felt guilty. But he told himself that this was as much Abigail's fault as it was his. Hell, it was more her fault. She's the one that shut down on him – emotionally, sexually.

He stood up to begin disrobing and smiled, looking over at Patti as she lay down on the bed in the pink teddy. He sat down in the hard chair at the desk with the table lamp by the door to remove his shoes. The flash of green neon filled out the sign as the full name of the motel came on again and there was a splash of green that spilled into the room through the shades that still remained open a sliver. Eldon reached over and shut the shades all the way.

He had taken off his tan jacket and was unbuttoning his yellow dress shirt as Patti got up and pushed his hands aside so she could unbutton his pants and loosen the zipper. She helped him off with his clothes, and caressed his strong thighs – feeling his excitement, stroking him. He helped her off with the negligee, pulling it over her head, and it fell to the carpet by the bed. She walked away, and sidled across to the back of the room, into the bathroom. He was hard as he watched her round butt swish and her firm little legs strut. She turned the water valves on in the shower.

"Let's get wet tonight, sweetie," she called over her shoulder, in her sexy, innocent chirp of a voice.

Eldon had no problem with that idea, and he was naked as he followed her into the bathroom. She turned to him and caressed his strong shoulders, and ran her fingers through his dirty blonde hair. A light mist of steam was starting to rise from the shower, and Eldon grabbed her around the waist and lifted her right into the shower/bath.

"Ooh," she said, and laughed. "You animal!"

He stepped over the edge of the tub to join her, and closed the plexiglass door that served as a hard shower curtain.

In the corner of the motel parking lot, beneath the green flashing neon, a burly man with two days beard grown rough on his face, in a Chevy pick-up, fingered the handle of a 12-gauge Remington shot gun sitting on the front seat next to him. Dressed in a faded jean jacket and tan work pants, and wearing big black work boots, he looked at the gun, removed his hand from it, and pulled a digital camera out of the chest pocket in his jean jacket. He thought for a good thirty seconds – his mind whirling through a thousand images at once – wondering which implement he was going to use. Surely, if he had stopped by the bar before he hit the Snowcomber, it very well may have been the Remington. Sober, he made the ultimately wise choice of preparing to use the digital camera instead.

After getting out of the car to snap a set of photos, he got back in and dialed a local number on his cell phone. The gun still lay across the front seat.

"Hello, is this Abigail?"

"Yes, can I help you?"

"Abigail, this is John Millerton."

They had met at Eldon's office parties.

"Oh, hi John," she said guardedly, unsure why he would call. Abigail had been paging through a notebook given to her by her grandmother; one of a series of notebooks bequeathed to her. These were 'the journals,' passed down through the generations in her family. While previously never spending much time looking them over, she had recently felt a pull, almost a magnetic force, bringing her to open the musty old volumes and heed what was written there. She placed the volume down now.

"Look, I need to talk to you about something. It's messed up. I'm calling you cause I'm trying to stay under control here, Abigail – trying to act smart – "

Eldon and Patti faced each other, their hands caressing one another's body, the water soaking them, wetting them down. He soaped her bountiful breasts, and the soap was lubricating her body – his hands slid across and down her body, and she moaned lightly.

"What are you talking about, John?" Abigail asked.

"Abigail, my wife and your husband are...inside the Snowcomber Inn in Hadley, right now."

"Wh-wh-what are you saying? Eldon told me he had a meeting."

"He lied to you. He's with Patti, Abigail. I'm tempted to walk right in there and shoot the son of a bitch dead right on the spot."

Abigail was speechless. She was more angry than surprised, but certainly felt a range of emotions, finding out about Eldon's betrayal.

John continued: "As far as that slut wife of mine is concerned, hell, I could shoot her dead, too."

Eldon held her by the shoulders and turned her around – he a full head taller than her – and the flesh of her breasts was pressed against the plexiglass door. He bent his knees for better-angled leverage, and she reached behind and took hold of his hard member, and guided him in.

"Look Abigail," John said. "I'm trying to play this cool. I took a bunch of photos of their cars at the motel. I'll take pictures of them leaving the motel room. I want to get a good divorce settlement. I suggest you do the same."

"I-I-I..."

"I know Abigail. I understand you don't know what to say. Look, I just wanted to let you know what's going on between those two. He's playing you big time. She's playing me. I'll deal with Patti – you better believe that. I don't want to stay here right now. I don't want an assault rap on my record – or worse, I don't want a murder on my hands."

"Ahhhhh," Eldon cried out, as he entered her, water splattering his cheek, as he pressed her from behind against the plexiglass door, her hands and her breasts cushioning her forward and back motion.

"Oh, yeah!" she screamed, high pitched and urgent.

The rush of the water and their intermingling cries formed a storming sea of pleasure.

Abigail composed herself – feeling new resolve. "John, I promise you that Eldon will not be catting around anymore with Patti." Her fist pounded the formica kitchen counter, and then she gripped its edge, her fingers taut and pressured as she felt a surge of energy rush through her.

※   ※   ※

Eldon came home and Abby had nothing to say to him. Of course he had a desire to see the boy – a reaction to the guilt of what he had done: now it was time to play the loyal father. When he finally came into the bedroom later, and Abigail was in the bed reading, he had trouble meeting her gaze.

"Why were you so late, Eldon?" she said, in a flat tone.

"I told you Abby," he said, taking the watch off his wrist, and laying it down on the dresser. "I had a dinner meeting with the investors who are looking at the shopping mall site."

"You met at the Snowcomber?"

He was frozen for a second, and he stopped unbuttoning his shirt. She could sense the sex on him, even get a faint whiff of the cheap perfume that slut Patti wore.

"The Snowcomber – in Hadley? No, why would we do that. We had dinner at…"

"Don't lie to me," she said, viciousness in her voice.

"Shut up, Abby," he said. "Why the fuck would I lie?"

"Don't tell me to shut up, Eldon," she said, anger and strength rising in her voice. "Don't ever tell me that again. And stop playing me for a fool, you worthless…"

"What? What did you say to me?" Eldon said, louder now, turning on his stockinged feet, standing there in his boxers and his unbuttoned shirt. Then he laughed in her face. "That's a joke. *You* calling *me* worthless."

She was entirely able of ignoring his petty insults now – his endless efforts to sadistically lord his superiority over her.

"How was she – how was your whore?"

"Fucking shit Abigail. You don't know what you're talking about."

"I know plenty, shit for brains," she said. "It's Patti – figures, you go after a bimbo like that. That's what you like, huh Eldon?"

"You are so fucking out to lunch," he said. He had become a practiced liar and deceiver – he wasn't about to crack.

Abby had discovered a new found calm – within the storm of the voices and the visions of her past – there was a strength that was filling her up, certainly more pleasingly than Eldon had ever filled her up with anything: love, sex, compassion. "How did you do it with her, huh? Was she on top – or was it doggie style? Did you tell her all about what a big man you are, and how you played football and how you fight bad guys. Then you gave it to her?"

"I had a business dinner," he said, climbing into bed, turning on his side, his face away from her. "I'm trying to earn the money to send the boy to college, remember? It's more than you're doing Abigail."

She was actually going to say: "I hope you liked it tonight, you motherfucker – cause you're never riding that squat bitch again," but chose to keep that comment to herself.

※　　　※　　　※

Exactly one week later, Patti stayed late at the office. She still had a remnant of the shiner on her right eye from where John belted her when she got home from the Snowcomber Inn and her rendezvous with Eldon, and was wearing oversized dark glasses to mask it. Eldon was working late – as he often did – in his office in the back corner of the suite.

Well, fuck John, Patti figured. God knows she had had the best sex she'd experienced in years the three times she'd slept with Eldon. They both were so into it, and he turned her on – he was so handsome, and his body was firm and strong. Also, there was still the 'clandestine sex' thing happening that made it so exciting for her. John would love to play hardball and make her stop working at Bailey Realty, but what was he going to do? He'd gotten laid off from his factory job six months before and *she* was the provider. They both knew they couldn't afford to have her leave her job. Not now anyway.

John couldn't do a damn thing about that, she knew, as she sat at her desk, filing her nails. She also knew that John was whistling in the breeze talking about a divorce. He didn't have the nerve to go through with it. She put down the nail file, and started checking her e-mail, just killing time. OK, maybe no more little meetings at the Snowcomber Inn...but...

"Good night, Patti," Barbara Simpson said, with more than a hint of derisive sarcasm in her voice. She was a right-minded woman, 52 years old, and happily married for 25 years. Barbara knew what was going between those two, and had a good idea why Patti was burning the midnight oil. Barbara would never think of cheating on Frank, much less with the boss

"OK, sweetie," she called over in her little girl voice, oblivious to Barbara's sarcasm, not even looking up from her computer screen. The clock in the corner of the screen indicated 6:40 pm.

Barbara gave her head a little shake, and had a scowl on her face as she made her way out the front door. Patti was alone in the office with the boss now. She walked over and turned the bolt lock on the door, to block access from the strip mall parking lot. The office was now truly closed for the night. Today she was wearing a modest knee length plaid skirt and a cherry red blouse. She had been showing houses that afternoon. She clicked off her flats, and replaced them with the spike high heel shoes she had kept in a plastic bag beneath her desk. Then she strolled over to the back office door, which was open, and gave a cursory knock.

"Knock, knock," she said, in a sexy tone, removing her dark glasses.

"Hi," Eldon said. "How are you? Come on in. I was just reviewing some sales figures here. Did you know that we're up 4% on commercial leases for the most recent three month period, as compared to last year?"

"Fascinating," she said, with mock sincerity, as she worked her way around the perimeter of the office and methodically pulled the blinds closed on all four windows.

Eldon, in his blue blazer, khaki pants and a blue shirt with yellow power tie, still had his head buried in a ream of papers.

"Eldon," she said, now sashaying up behind him. She started massaging his shoulders, and rubbing his chest.

No reaction.

"Now don't you worry about John. He's just a big old puppy dog, and I know how to keep him right on his leash. We can still keep having our little fun."

"Hmmm?" Eldon commented. "Right, Patti. Well, I just wanted to create a new spread sheet to begin making new year-against-year comparisons on residential sales."

She walked around the side of his leather reclining office chair, and spun the chair on its axis to face her. "How about you spread these, baby?" she said, in her most seductive tone, hiking her skirt to show him her thighs. She reached out to stroke his hair.

Eldon had a quizzical look on his face.

"Are you playing hard to get, Eldon?" she said. "What's the matter?"

She came closer, her generous bosom in his face; she was massaging his chest, working her hand down, unclasping his belt. Her hand went down to feel him.

"I really would like to get some of this work done, Patti," he said.

She massaged him; she stroked him.

"What's going on, Eldon? What happened to that tiger in your tank from last week?"

He looked at her, and there was a glassy, strange look in his eye – a flat, inscrutable expression on his face. Patti couldn't figure it out. All of a sudden his personality seemed as wooden as a cigar store Indian, but unfortunately there was nothing wooden about what was between his legs.

"Well, Eldon," she said, sounding frustrated, her voice a little higher pitched than usual, "you're just as soft as a little worm down there. What the hell is going on with you?"

He pushed her hand away from his lap, turned his swivel chair back around to face the desk, and made an effort to straighten his tie. He picked up his pen to resume scribbling notes on a yellow legal pad.

"You bastard!" she yelled at him, in a squeaky wail. Then she pointed to the remnant of the black eye: "All I've gone through for you, and you just sit there like a useless bump on a log! Well, you know what? If you're gonna treat me this way, I might as well go home to John!" She turned on her high heels, and walked right out, slamming the door behind her.

Eldon gave his shoulders a little shrug, and went back to work.

✕   ✕   ✕

None of it was really Eldon's willful doing. Neither he nor Patti knew what had happened earlier that day...

After she took Cordus to school and Eldon had left for work, Abigail went upstairs into the master bedroom and took another close review of the pages in one of the journals that her grandmother had passed on to her. She thought about her time with Cynthia K., and how her new friend encouraged her to make changes. Abby had taken it all to heart, that was for sure. There were no more of those chemicals in her body from that medication. Yes, the anti-depressant pills were a thing of the past. Abigail believed she was finally being true to her family's calling, and she was beginning to truly recognize the power of Mother Earth.

Sure, she had some tough times – and it wasn't always pleasant seeing these images that flooded into her head now. There was one undeniable feeling that surged through her, however. There was a soothing sense of self-confidence. Whatever was happening to her, it was *true* – it was just right. She was finally a part of something that seemed to lend meaning to her life.

Ultimately, that belief, in and of itself, was the final piece of the puzzle that would give Abigail the power. Reading through the journals, getting a clearer image of visions of the past when she clutched the medallion – it was all adding up in her mind now. It would take her way beyond her own convictions. She would be imbued with a spirit and a destiny that had been passed down through generations of her family. Yes, for now she held the key to unlock the safe that held the dark desires expressed by Ann Sibber herself more than 300 years earlier.

Now Abigail knew that the key was her belief. All she had to do was allow herself to become unshackled from the chains of the present, and have faith in the legacy of her forebearers.

It was time. She had found her destiny. Maybe it was madness…

As she sat alone in her bedroom, clutching the journal from her grandmother, she shut her eyes. Her head began to ache and she finally clearly saw the vision: all those people screaming for Ann Sibber's death:

"Drown her!"

"Kill the witch!"

"God will reign supreme in Salem!"

"Get her! Get her!"

"Kill her!"

Even though they were closed, hers were the eyes looking up at hands and arms in the water. Abigail's eyes *were* those of Ann Sibber. She could feel the desperation of the victim, being forcefully held beneath the water. Abigail felt her own breathing strained – cut off – feeling the life being choked out by water flooding the lungs. Abby opened her eyes, and groaned aloud – she could feel the pain that Ann Sibber felt in 1694 – she was experiencing it: Ann Sibber murdered by an angry, ignorant mob.

She placed the journal down on the bedspread of stars and a crescent moon that she still possessed, and opened the book to the proper page – the page on which the incantation was written. This incantation was written completely, except for two empty spaces where the name of the person would be inserted by the speaker. She followed her grandmother's instructions to the letter.

She gripped the medallion that hung from her neck in her right hand.

"Eldon," she spoke aloud in a strong, clear voice. "You betrayed me, you shallow bastard. Like so many before you, you were ultimately weak and unworthy. Now you will pay. I need you to continue providing for me and for the boy. And you will. In fact, your life will be committed to providing for me – and protecting me."

She liked the sound of her words. When was the last time she felt so…definitive and powerful? She could feel a warmth emanating from the medallion.

"You will no longer be distracted by the sins of the flesh," she said, and the medallion started to burn in her palm. "Neither will you be dragged down by the other foibles that make men less productive. Eldon, you ungrateful piece of shit, from now on you will be both a soul-less and sex-less man. You will serve as the provider and protector – and so you will remain."

And she smiled – she looked upwards and flashed an evil, toothy grin. She looked back down at the journal sitting on the bed. She took a deep breath, and exhaled. She savored the stinging heat of the medallion. It was so hot it began searing her palm, yet there was nothing unpleasant about it. In a loud and clear voice she read the incantation:

'Blessed be the dark vision that reigns upon thee, Eldon Bailey. For this wrath is now your destiny, and you will suffer – suffer, like the hundreds of innocent who perished at the hands of the cruel, the fearful and the ignorant, those whose hatred will forever infect this earth. May the wrath of the innocent sufferers forever torment you.'

A spark of red, a light glow, transformed her blue eyes to a raging crimson for a brief flash, and Abigail could feel the burning heat of the medallion on her palm. She cried out as a wisp of smoke rose before her eyes. She had to pull the medallion off of her palm, as it stuck to the branded flesh. There before her was *not* an image of stalks of wheat and three stars on her palm. No. What was visible on the right top of her palm, beneath the forefinger, was one lone five-pointed star – branded on to her right hand.

As it fell back in place, the medallion felt warm and soothing against her neck and chest, and she felt emotionally spent. Abigail placed the journal on her nightstand and lay down on her back on the bed. For the first time in longer than she could remember, a feeling of complete calm swept over her. She knew then that her wish had come to fruition – fulfilled by the power of the Sibber medallion. Eldon was doomed with the curse of impotence. Not only that, but his focus on business and success was heightened and sharpened, as his desire and ability to seek out female flesh – and perform – was dulled and muted.

CHAPTER NINE

M iles Adamson was now associate city news editor at the paper. He had worked his way up over the course of more than a decade in journalism. Due to his skill and personable nature, he had advanced up the ladder. Hell, there were people at the Post who were serviceable reporters, but they remained reporters for 20 or 25 years.

Management liked Miles. He cut a fine figure in a pin-striped suit, tall, clean-cut and still bean-pole thin, and could bullshit about the subtle differences between Johnny Walker Black and Johnny Walker Red for ten minute stretches. His shock of red hair was flecked with touches of gray, which made him only more appealing to upper management. So he was an editor now – with his own office.

When he started his career, his bylines had been in the lifestyles section. Survey pieces about the best tacos in town, and price comparisons on music at different record stores. There were the obligatory first-person accounts from the perspective of a young, single guy in Manhattan (and he was still single now). When the bar with the computer screens opened up downtown, the place where you could send IM's back and forth to people sitting in front of different terminals at the bar, Miles was selected to write the account of his efforts to meet girls the 1990's way. He certainly provided his readers with a colorful story – of both some of the rejections he received in his overtures and the nibbles he got when he threw out the bait.

Miles was reassigned to the Brooklyn/Queens crime beat – becoming a serious reporter. In that spot, he wrote about five years worth of homicides, drug rings and violent family squabbles and then he moved on to the city political beat – which would ultimately be his entrée to the city editor job.

What was on his mind now, though, was his good friend Eldon. Their last trip to Vegas, nearly two years back now, had been great. Total debauchery: idiotic drinking and gambling, along with various and sundry dirty deeds. It was a Saturday afternoon, and the city section for Sunday's paper was put to bed – or at least dormant, pending a big story breaking, which Miles hoped wouldn't happen this week. He kept replaying in his mind the conversation he had with Eldon earlier in the week. It was mind-blowing.

Miles had left a series of messages on the voice mail at Eldon's home in Bangor. Miles was under the impression that he and Eldon were still planning this year's trip. Every other year: Vegas in April. This was their year. He hadn't heard back. He also called Eldon at his office a few times. Still no call back. Miles was truly pissed off at this point. He attempted once again, and finally Eldon picked up the phone.

"Yo, Eldon, what's up?" Miles said. He was sitting back in his chair at the office, tapping a pen on his desk. "Don't you return calls?"

"Yes, this is Eldon Bailey. How can I help you?"

"What do you mean, Eldon. It's *me*. How about our Vegas trip?"

"I'm sorry, who is this?"

"It's Miles, you crazy motherfucker."

"O.K, right. How are you?"

"Cool, I'm cool, don't worry about me. How come you haven't called back? I thought we were planning the trip this year."

"I'm sorry, Miles. Did we discuss plans to take a trip? I don't recall. I better check with Abigail because I know that..."

"What the fuck, man?" he said incredulously. "Vegas, next month – you know, we went two years ago? We went two years

109

before that? Play craps, blackjack, maybe a little trip to the Bunny Ranch?"

"Where's that?"

"Yeah, right. The fucking Bunny Ranch!"

"Again, I'm very sorry Miles…"

There was something about the way Eldon was saying his name that was…disembodied. It freaked Miles out.

"…but I don't know that I would be available. You said next month?"

"Yes, Eldon," Miles said calmly. He had now registered that something was amiss, and he had adjusted his tone accordingly.

"Next month is tight. It's a busy time for showing homes up here, and I really have to check with Abigail about this."

The whole thing was unfathomable for Miles. This was Eldon – the brother he never had. First, he doesn't return phone calls. Then, he doesn't even acknowledge the Vegas trip. The *Vegas* trip. How many times had Eldon told him how much he looked forward to cutting it loose at the craps table and getting some big-titty lap dances?

Now, he sounds like some home-spun crap-assed, Lake Wobegon motherfucker who never played a hard eight and had never even heard of the god-damned Bunny Ranch?

Many of his colleagues had left the office, and Miles stayed behind to check the Nexis-Lexis data base the paper had available. It provided an enormous collection of stories from thousands of publications around the country. There was something extremely odd about Eldon's seeming transformation. Miles never forgot that story that Eldon told him the night after he first slept with Abigail (who could forget that?). OK, they had worked out their problems, Eldon said. But what was behind it all?

Miles knew what Eldon was going through at that time – he was coming off the tough break up with Cindy. Eldon needed this relationship with Abigail to work out. The last thing Miles wanted to do at the time was convince Eldon to leave Abigail.

Then, if Eldon bemoaned the break-up, Miles would feel responsible for egging him on. Eldon was by nature more of a follower than a leader. He respected Miles' advice. Miles had to encourage him to stick with the relationship.

Now, however, he couldn't help but look back at the stories that Eldon told him about Abigail being a very troubled woman. He always remembered the name of the town that Abigail came from – it was distinctively New England: Marblehead, Massachusetts. Miles started by combing through the archives of the *Marblehead Reporter* weekly paper. He entered:

Wedding notices; Merriweather.

Sure enough, he found a six column-inch story in the *Marblehead Reporter* dated July 10, 1992 announcing the wedding of Abigail Merriweather and Eldon Bailey. He was looking for a thread that might push him along a path to more information. In the second paragraph of the story, there it was:

Abigail Merriweather is the daughter of Virginia Merriweather (nee Sibber of Salem), a resident of Marblehead.

Something struck him about the maiden name of Abigail's mother – Sibber – although he couldn't quite place it. He knew he had run across that name before. OK, Abigail Merriweather was a descendent of people named Sibber in Salem, he thought to himself.

He then dug deeper by calling up the archives of the *Salem Tribune*, a daily in Salem. Also, since Salem was a larger community and this paper was a daily as opposed to a weekly, he figured it would be a better source of detailed information. He simply entered the name:

Virginia Merriweather.

More than a dozen referenced articles appeared on the computer screen. The most sensational was the one that appeared immediately after the event that had brought Virginia Merriweather's name prominently into the papers:

Salem Tribune
October 15, 1974

Local Man Murdered In His Own Home

Author and historian John Merriweather was brutally slain in his Marblehead home last night in what police say was apparently a robbery attempt gone wrong. Merriweather was bludgeoned to death by a heavy object which was left at the scene of the crime – the base of a cast bronze statuette of a horseman that many neighbors recalled seeing displayed in the Merriweather's living room.

Police believe that Merriweather had been working in his downstairs study at the time – approximately 2:30 a.m. Police believe that the front door was opened by force. Virginia Merriweather, a native of Salem, was upstairs asleep at the time, according to police sources. She only came downstairs two hours later – at about 4:30 am – telling police she was checking on her husband.

She said he commonly wrote late at night. She claimed that she had taken sleeping medication that night and never heard anything. Neighbors indeed told police that they heard the sounds of a car driving away from the house and speeding along the street soon after 2:30 am. Unfortunately, no one called police at the time. Apparently, no information is available about the make and model of the getaway car.

Virginia Merriweather worked with police to compile a list of goods that were stolen during the apparent break-in.

"We are investigating this horrible situation. The entire community is shocked that this type of crime could occur in Marblehead," said Police Chief Dominick Scarpelli. "Anyone that may have seen or heard anything unusual last night should call us immediately."

In addition to his wife, Merriweather is survived by his six-year old daughter, Abigail.

Miles combed through follow-up stories and soon discovered that the slaying of John Merriweather – Abigail's father – remained unsolved. The car with the alleged killers drove off that night without a trace, police said.Virginia Merriweather was questioned repeatedly and was indeed considered a suspect.

Police were never able to gather evidence to convict her of a crime.

"Jesus," Miles said aloud. "Poor little girl. No wonder Abigail had the god-damned voices in her head. She must have been in the house when her father was murdered."

He wondered if Eldon ever knew about this. He specifically recalled Eldon mentioning that Abby's father had died when she was young. Eldon never explained to Miles any of these details – wouldn't he have mentioned it? But did Eldon even know?

※   ※   ※

Miles requested a day off on Friday and got the ok from his boss. He had to go out of town to visit a sick friend. That was certainly the truth.

He made the drive straight up Route 95 into Maine on Friday morning. He'd find a Motel Six to shack up at. He hadn't announced his visit. He had a feeling that it wouldn't be wise to tell Eldon he was coming at this point. In the last conversation they had, Eldon sounded as vacant as the Bates Motel on a slow Monday night.

He had their address, and had consulted MapQuest on his computer for a couple of maps to help him track down the house in Bangor. There was still snow on the ground, and it was blustery and clear, and much colder than it had been in New York.

Wearing a navy blue overcoat with a black scarf draped around his neck, he arrived at the house on Friday evening. The Bailey home was a neat, yet modest two-story Colonial in an unassuming neighborhood, painted off-white with black window shutters and a grey shingled roof. The most distinctive feature was actually the land out back – two sprawling acres – and the wooded area behind that.

When he rang the doorbell, he recognized Abigail – though clearly change had taken place. Where he had always recognized a sweetness in her demeanor when he had met her in the past, now there was a shadowy scowl. She was wearing black on black, a cape over a long skirt – her long, blond, curly hair was flecked with grey.

"Yes," she said in a flat tone, looking up at the tall, thin man.

"Ms. Bailey – Abigail – it's me, Miles Adamson. Don't you remember me?"

"Oh," she said, still in an unexpressive tone. "Hello."

"I just came up from New York."

"What brings you up our way, Miles? Are you here on business?"

He was going to say "no," but realized that was not the right answer. Don't make her think he came up specifically out of concern for his friend.

"Yes, that's right. I'm doing a feature story on New England towns for the travel section. I work for the New York Post?" It came out as a question, because he figured she remembered.

"Oh, yes I recall," she said. "Still there, hey Miles? Very good." She was glancing behind periodically, acting somewhat evasive.

"Do you mind if I come in? I mean, is Eldon here?"

"I'm sorry, he's not here. I believe he's working late."

Eldon's SUV was turning the corner and headed towards the house as she spoke. Miles noticed the even darker look on her face – he could see that something was upsetting her – and he turned around and started waving as he saw his friend in the driver's seat as the car pulled into the driveway. Miles walked towards the driveway.

"Eldon!" he called out.

Eldon was carrying a brown leather valise when he emerged from the car – always time for more work at home – and gave a noncommittal look over.

"What's up, man?" Miles said, reaching his hand out for a shake.

"Oh, hello," Eldon said with little emotion, like he was greeting a contractor who had arrived to work at his house. He had a recollection of Miles, but it was vague. His whole persona was fading away these days since Abigail put the hex on him. "How are you?" His voice sounded like he was making a tired sales pitch at a convention.

Miles was already discouraged and deflated. He could tell it was as bad as he had suspected – whatever was going on.

"I'm doing OK, Eldon," Miles said. "I hope it's alright that I'm just stopping by, unexpected and all."

"Sure, ah, Miles," Eldon said. "C'mon in, won't you?"

Abigail stood in the doorway, observing this uncomfortable exchange – her eyes squinting slightly – and she had the furrowed-brow look of a penny-pinching boss watching two employees wasting too much time at the water cooler. As Eldon led the way and Miles followed behind, Abigail moved aside and her disapproving eyes bore a hole in the back of Miles' head as he entered the house.

"Please take a seat, Miles," Eldon said, motioning to the living room to the right, which contained a large black couch fronted by a low-slung coffee table, and two high-backed easy chairs, upholstered in blood red. "Here, give me your coat. Would you like some coffee?"

After Miles sat in one of the high-backed chairs, Abigail came in and shut the front door behind her. Without even looking over at Miles, she walked rapidly straight through the entrance hallway into the kitchen – and took a seat at the kitchen table, reading the local newspaper. She wanted to remain within earshot. It would have been hard for her to make Miles feel any less welcome.

The phone rang and Miles saw Abigail rapidly move upstairs. She took the call in the bedroom:

"Abby, Oh my God! I'm so glad to hear your voice. I was worried about you. You didn't return my calls!"

"Oh, hi Becky," she said nonchalantly.

"Why didn't you call me back?"

She gave a dramatic exhale. "I've been so busy, I'm sorry."

"How's everything going? How are things with Eldon?"

"Oh, much better. I can't even begin to tell you."

"Really?" Becky asked, truly amazed.

"Honestly, things have just turned around completely. How are *you* doing?"

"I'm fine, sweetie," Becky said. "Andrew – he's 15 now – is mouthing off to his teachers, and going through a really bad teen phase, but I think he'll work through it."

"I guess they can have some rough years," Abby said. "My Cordus is fine. He's a good boy."

"Oh, he is, Abby. Cordus is *such* a sweetheart," Becky said. "But, tell me, how did things turn around with Eldon so dramatically? I'm sorry to say it, but you guys were touch and go, I mean, I really thought..."

"We're great. Eldon is the model husband."

Becky chuckled, sort of uncomfortably. Abby sounded different. So firm and assured – that was good, of course. But this wasn't quite the same Abigail she had known all these years. "Well, great! Can't you tell me what's changed? Did you use some black magic on him, or something?" she joked, with a laugh.

Abigail let out a deep, hearty laugh. It ended in a high-pitched cackle.

"Yes, dearie," Abby said, grinning broadly. "You could say I used some black magic on him!"

Becky was speechless. She didn't know whether to laugh – or ask another question. So, she did neither, and assumed it was a weird joke.

"Oh, Abby," she said. "I'm so glad to hear you have your sense of humor back!"

"Yes," Abby agreed, nodding. "Me too."

They agreed to speak again soon – though that seemed low on Abby's priority list. Abby hung up the phone and headed back downstairs, glancing over to glare at Miles as she made her way back into the kitchen.

Eldon had brought him in a cup of coffee. After a few minutes of chat, Miles remained perplexed. How could my best friend resort to small talk? he thought. The only time Eldon perked up was when he started talking about sales figures and vacancy rates. This was not Eldon – Eldon was never so fixated on business. He was a person who reveled in life – not the notion of how one earns more money to maintain a lifestyle. A boy, athletic-looking and strong – he appeared to be about twelve or thirteen– came down the staircase with quiet footfalls and glanced over to his left at the visitor.

"Hello," Miles said, in a friendly tone. "Eldon, who's this big guy? Is this Cordus?"

"Come over son, and say hello to our guest," Eldon said.

"What a good looking kid you are," Miles said. "Time really flies. How old are you?"

"I'm thirteen years old," he said, in a hushed voice. There was little expression on his angelic face. He was beyond polite – he was shy to an extreme. His eyes avoided Miles' glance.

Cordus had never liked it when his parents had fought, but now life had changed in their home. His mom was mean. She bossed the two of them around – he and his father. There weren't any more fights at home between his mom and dad. His dad did whatever she said.

"Cordus!" came a strident voice from the kitchen. "Are you finished with all of your homework? Come here right now."

The boy, with blonde, curly hair identical to his mom's (minus the flecks of grey), spun on his heels in a flash and headed in to the kitchen. There were murmured voices, and then the boy quietly made his way back up the staircase, carefully moving up one step at a time. He gave a meek wave to Miles – but didn't even look over. The boy seemed petrified of – something, and Miles had a pretty good idea that the something was his mother.

Miles attempted to broach the subject of the Vegas trip, but Eldon gave him the same pat answers. Too much work, the timing really wasn't right. During the whole conversation, Eldon seemed more machine than man. He was some kind of programmed being. Miles was disgusted. He got up – ostensibly to bring his empty coffee cup into the kitchen – and saw Abigail, her legs crossed, reading the newspaper as it sat on the white formica table.

Miles clunked the cup into the sink, and pulled a chair out to take a seat next to Abigail. She sneered at him.

"We need to talk," Miles said.

"*What*?" she said disgustedly, closing the folds of the broadsheet newspaper in a crinkled rush. "You're in my house, uninvited, and you tell me – she took on a mocking tone: " 'we need to talk,' What does that mean? I have nothing to say to you."

"Look, Abigail, I was the best man at your wedding. I've known Eldon longer than you have," he knew these points would hold no water with her, so he just got right to the point. "Who is that out there in your living room? That's *not* my best friend. It looks like him – but that seems to be where the resemblance ends."

"Yeah right. You come up here from" – here she added the mocking tone again -- "*New York*, with some kind of 'S' on your chest: Miles, the super-hero. How special. You don't know shit, Miles."

"And what about your son?" he said. "It's like he's terrified of you – what are you doing to him?"

Mentioning Cordus was crossing the line. A look of stark evil crossed her face. Her lips thinned in anger, and her eyes looked over to the right to the kitchen counter. There was a hard wood rack with narrow slits, containing four knives of varying sizes. She eyed it briefly and looked back at Miles.

"Get the hell of out of my house!" she yelled at him. "You have no right to butt in where you don't belong. Go back to your stinking city" – the mocking tone, now cutting – "*Miles*. You don't like the fact that your friend doesn't want anything to do with you. You're just a low-life, sleeping around with any slut with a pulse."

Miles was taken aback – overwhelmed by the viciousness of her rant. He remained seated at the kitchen table. He was also shocked – though not as much at this point – that Eldon didn't seem bothered by this exchange. He didn't even come in to the kitchen.

"That's right – I've heard stories about you," she said. "Mr. Bachelor – the king of the cocksmen, Miles Adamson."

"Well, if marriage was going to lead me down this road, lady, I made the right choice," he said. "Now, look, I have a right to know what's going on in this house. Also, I want to ask you some questions about this..." He pulled out a sheet of paper containing the text of the newspaper story that detailed the murder of Abigail's father. He showed it to her. There was pure rage in her eyes...and a voice calling to her.

[they're all shit; these men are all the same, Abigail, users, bastards]

Her right hand went to her forehead – the pain was there.

"What happened that night, Abigail? What really happened?"

Her voice was subdued again – the jagged pain bolting through her head was confusing her and dulling her rage. "You have no right to do this to me," she whispered. Then she raised her voice: "Get the fuck out of my house."

[he's another piece of garbage]

"Admit it Abigail," he said. "Something else happened that night."

[scum, low-life, repugnant, worthless dirty trash]

She couldn't fight the image she now saw. It was replaying in her mind, the awful reality of that night long ago. She was floating off somewhere, and it was like Miles wasn't even in the kitchen with her.

It was all too clear. Abby was a little girl. She had risen out of bed because she heard loud voices. She hid, huddled behind a corner wall at the top of the stairs, peaking out. Her daddy, seated right at his desk by the fireplace in the living room, where he liked to work, was being held down by two men. Her mother, wearing black gloves, grabbed the statue of the man on the horse, and lifted it above her head. She brought the horse statue down on her father's skull with all of the force she could muster, the black base of the statue hitting him. Abigail remembered the dull "crack" and then the louder "thud" when her father's body hit the floor. Just now she heard the "crack" and the "thud" again. Abigail remembered: there was blood everywhere – she couldn't get the sight of the blood out of her mind.

And now – like an out of body experience, because there was a release, such a cathartic release – she voiced it aloud, seemingly unaware that Miles was sitting in the kitchen.

"She did it," she said, choking the words out initially. "My mother killed him. He was a bastard – a piece of shit – a cheater, just like Eldon." Now, Abigail *was* the little girl again who had witnessed the horrors of that night.

Miles – stunned – sat in silence.

"I saw those two men in the living room. They held Daddy while she clubbed him with the statue. She held the horse in her hands and hit him with the heavy base of the statue. Then Daddy was on the floor and Mommy hit him again. And again. Then she handed the two men a pile of money. There was blood all over the place. The men left the house, and then Mommy saw me, and yelled at me to go back to bed."

Miles was unsure what to do. What could he do? Could he go to the local police? And report what?

The secrets locked in Abigail's memory were flowing like flood waters. Miles didn't even fully understand what she discussed next.

"And Nana – she wrote about Mommy. It's in the notebooks. She fought with Mommy so badly and she didn't trust her. Nana told Mommy that she shouldn't have done that to Daddy. Sibbers don't do things that way. Sibbers don't use brute force – the Sibber women use the power of the medallion.

"Nana took the medallion away from her. That's when Nana passed it to me. That's another reason my mother was so angry. She never even got to keep the medallion. It was passed on directly to me."

Miles didn't know what this was about, but he had heard enough – too much really. Maybe if he found the shrink in New York that Abigail had seen – what was his name? – and told him what he had heard. Well, at least it was a start.

"You – you – you need some help Abigail," Miles said.

His voice snapped her out of her trance. All of a sudden, her face expressed total shock. What had she done? What had she said?

"Abigail, I think you – you need to talk to someone," he said. "Look, I've got to get going now."

She looked over at the knife rack again. What should she do? Somehow, indecision took over, and she heard the front door slam shut. He was gone. What did he know? Was that bastard going to try to ruin everything she'd worked so hard to attain?

※ ※ ※

The next morning, Eldon was taking care of Cordus, as Abigail sat upstairs in the bedroom. Eldon was such a good father now that he was so – focused – on his work, at the office and at home.

Miles had stayed in the Motel Six Friday night, and packed up and hit the highway back to New York first thing Saturday. He didn't have a game plan at this point. There must be something he could do. Was the shrink in New York the answer? Maybe he could go to the cops over in Marblehead and report to them about the truth regarding the death of Abigail's father.

Great. A murder that took place more than 30 years ago. And the murderer – Abigail's mother – was long dead. What he really resented was the loss of his best friend. Who was this imposter walking around as Eldon? There must be somebody he could talk to.

He was already in New Hampshire – he had gotten an early start – buzzing past the Hanover exits. If he could touch base with a journalist at the local newspaper – ask them to at least poke around the story. What story? he reminded himself.

There was no god damn story: just a formerly personable guy who used to be his best friend, who now insisted on talking endlessly about commissions and vacancy fucking rates. And a terrorized boy who will barely take a step against his mother's will.

Meanwhile, that boy and his father were downstairs, while Abigail asked herself: why was that asshole Miles poking around here? After all she had been through – and to come out feeling so powerful on the other side. This was her fiefdom now – she never thought she'd see the day that she, Abigail Merriweather, would feel the rush of power and dominance coursing through her veins. Who know what this Miles would do, trying to stick his nose in?

He had crossed the New Hampshire line and was well into Massachusetts now, having stopped for coffee at a rest stop near Foxboro. He was sipping from the triangular space on the white plastic lid on the to-go cup; it was still too hot.

Soon, Miles was through Massachusetts and entering Providence, where the highway rose above a cloverleaf of intersecting roads below.

Abby had wandered upstairs and was quietly chanting to herself, looking upwards, reading from one of the volumes, clutching the medallion. She began speaking in a loud, clear voice...

Miles was lifting the cup, and had to swerve to avoid a cardboard box in the road that he thought might be a plank of wood. "Shit," he said, as drips of hot coffee hit his lap. The car was about to reach the bridge that rose above the cloverleaf of roads below.

Then she was intoning:

"Blessed be the dark vision that reigns upon thee, Miles Adamson. For this wrath is now your destiny, and you will suffer – suffer, like the hundreds of innocent who perished at the hands of the cruel, the fearful and the ignorant, those whose hatred will forever infect this earth. May the wrath of the innocent sufferers forever torment you."

Abigail felt the singe on her hand – and looked down to see a wisp of rising smoke and a second five-pointed star seared into the flesh of her right palm, just below the first one. Her eyes narrowed into an evil glare and emitted a red glow momentarily, as she felt a surge of warmth continue to flow through her.

Miles had been distracted by the spilled coffee, and when he glanced up there was a huge dark blot filling his center rearview mirror. He heard a deafening blast of a truck horn and looked around to see a monstrous, black truck cab bearing down on his car. He tried to head right to avoid the mad trucker, when his rear bumper was smashed with horrific force. The coffee cup flew from his hands, the car careened hard to the right and he couldn't turn the wheel to straighten it out.

He saw the guardrail and let out a desperate yell...The car surged through the guardrail, spun over in the air and smashed down, wheels skyward, on to a crossing highway 50 feet below. There was an explosion of breaking glass and twisted metal – and Miles head was crumpled and neck broken instantly by the force of the hood of the car smashing on to the highway.

Sparks leapt and metal screeched as the car rolled and then smashed through another guardrail, falling to the street and the adjoining sidewalk below the lower highway – just 20 feet from the entrance way of a defunct red brick manufacturing plant – Marinelli Screw & Nail Co.

Two onlookers strolling down the sidewalk in the direction of the crash were walking only a block away. They were shocked first by the smash of the hulking metal frame slamming against the asphalt, and then the sight of the car bursting into flame.

"Holy God," uttered a shocked Ephrain Jefferson – a retiree out for a noon walk with his wife. "Nobody's surviving that wreck, Emmy. We better call 9-1-1."

She stopped to open her purse to get out her phone.

A charred body with a broken neck lay sprawled inside the wreckage. There was no reason for Abby to worry any longer about Miles' intrusive visit.

She was flying. She was drunk with power; Lady Macbeth drunk. The only difference: her husband was not the king. No. He was the court jester – bringing in a growing sackful of quid thanks to his new-found work ethic.

The level of madness was surely more severe than the past Sibber women had reached. Not only was Abigail imbued with the spirit and power of her female forebearers; within her was also still the scarred little girl who had witnessed her mother bludgeoning her father – braining him in front of her innocent eyes.

Abigail's mother said that her father had been cheating on her; that's why she killed him. That's what started the big fight between her mother and granny. Abby's grandmother objected to her mother's choice of resorting to such brutality. Nana said that Sibber women used the medallion and used the incantations to get their way. What was this idea of bashing someone in the head with a statue?

Abby's mother and Nana had always disagreed over many issues. This made it much worse. They fought and fought. Eventually, Nana took the medallion and the notebooks away from Abby's mom – and gave them to Abigail. Nana explained to her that some day she would understand what it means to be a Sibber – and she would act upon that knowledge appropriately.

Abigail had always been much closer to her Nana than to her mother.

Finally, after so many years of living in ignorance, Abigail now understood the importance of her role. She now recognized that she was here to carry on the powerful legacy of all those Sibber women who came before her.

But in reality, Abigail's mind was like the cloverleaf of roads in Providence where Miles met his demise: messages coming from so many directions, hurtling through her brain, causing such confusion. It was best to sort it out by remaining focused on the revelation that had brought her out of her shell: Remember the incantations. Treasure the medallion and all it represents. Block everything else out, she told herself. That wasn't so easy, though.

So Abigail reveled in her raging insanity and her seemingly boundless power. Yes, her tormenter, Eldon, was now a neutered slave. And his sidekick, that man-whore Miles, was gone for good. In every fibre of her body she felt the surge of dominance and superiority where previously she had been wracked with weakness and doubt.

She reached up to her neck to grasp the medallion. It was still warm.

CHAPTER TEN

A Victorian house of once lovely grandeur sits empty at the end of a peaceful road deep in the mountainous western Massachusetts countryside. The paint has long since peeled off, and the exposed ash boards are weathered with the age brought on by numerous harsh winters. The wood is now a light grey hue. The roof shingles are tattered and lay irregularly, like stray pieces on a child's game board. Long ago, the spirit and body of "family" breathed life into the three-bedroom structure. Now the wind whistles through, since a number of the window panes have been smashed by stones thrown by neighborhood kids.

It stands two stories, with a dramatically spired turret capturing the eye of the beholder at the top right hand corner of the home. The round room within the turret contains a library of musty old volumes in a low-lying book case, an upholstered easy chair and a square oak side table. A small lamp, designed with a lacquered shade with rainbow colored ceramic chips rimming around it, hasn't contained a working bulb for a few years now. Three bedrooms are lined along the corridor down the hall from the turreted room.

Downstairs, a simple, elegant Shaker table and six chairs still sits in the middle of the dining room. A Cherry-wood cabinet with glass doors, six neat square panes in each door, still contains the fine China once used – in another home – during Thanksgiving and Christmas celebrations by this home's most recent residents, the Bailey family.

The living room features twin tall red upholstered chairs, with deep carved mahogany armrests, dramatically sloped with rounded ends, enabling the occupant of each chair to comfortably grip the ends of the armrests. Couch and loveseat, maroon-colored, sit weathered in the room. A maple coffee table is in front of the matching set. It's empty, aside from one dusty volume of The Collected Works of Percy Bysshe Shelley, unmoved for years.

Virtually everything in the house is covered by a deep coat of dust, and cob webs gratuitously spread in open spaces between the furnishings.

Emerging from the depths as the midnight hour strikes, he is buried among the cold soil, twigs and leaves beneath the front steps of the house. Experiencing a rebirth, his one still-functional right eye opens in a series of quick blinks as he tries to comprehend this once-familiar but now foreign environment. A creature of the dark, his nighttime vision is unfailing. During the day, he neither can see nor be seen. All the limbs in his immense, powerful body feel stiff. He stretches his arms and examines his eight-inch long, razor sharp nails. He sees the pinkened, lifeless flesh covering his left arm, scarred from flames long ago. The right arm – like the rest of his right side – was spared from the burning blaze. The flesh on that limb, however, is not recognizable as human. It's dried to a nearly petrified state and has a crimson-colored reptilian hardness – more shell than skin. He – or 'it' – takes the first few hours of his stay here to simply awaken and renew his senses. Following that his mind and body will function wholly. And the anguish will flood back in – human emotions affecting the form of the undead creature. This event is destined to play itself out at the exact same time each year...until the cycle ends, and he can finally experience eternal rest. The creature has got to cling to the belief that someday the cycle will end.

※　　※　　※

His place during his sentenced time among the living is spent as one connected to the mother earth. His dwelling is in a trench that lay under the front stoop of the home and is dug into the ground beneath the old stone foundation. His dirty, other-worldly form seems one with the detritus of soil, mud, twigs and wet fall leaves within which he resides. His breathing is tremulous and labored. The blonde hair is matted, long and stringy. The left side of his face is a pinkish and red tangle of scarred and scabbed flesh. There is no discerning where a cheek or jaw would actually begin or end. The left eye contains a light grey sightless ball that serves no purpose. The right side of the face isn't disfigured, but has suffered the ravages of time and space and has a wrinkled – nearly reptilian – consistency. The blue eye on the right side flashes in sensory curiosity, trying to take in enough to comprehend the strange – yet familiar – world, which the creature is periodically forced to inhabit. His maw, the left half misshapen into a downturned scowl, is never still, as it opens and closes in a constant pattern, fishlike, matching a slight bobbing of the head in a barely discernable circular motion. His body, like his mind, is in a seemingly eternal pattern of restlessness. The freakishly-long finger nails scratch through the soil as the creature seeks out what it can find for sustenance. For during these periods of earthly inhabitation, he is cursed with feeling: the desires, emotions, pains and foibles of the flesh. He experiences emotional pain, human desires, and hunger during this time. In fact, for the creature, those reminders of the horrors of human existence are the worst aspects of his punishment.

He stops moving his hands as his sensitive ears hear a light squeaking and the skitter of tiny feet across the leaves near his trench. When it is immediately upon him, he reaches out and spears the passing field mouse with his long, sharpened talons. Ravenous, he lifts the squirming creature to his maw and chomps down on it, placing the head in his mouth and biting into it mid-body. The mouse emits a final squeal as its tiny frame is crushed by the creature's mandibles. The sound of chewing is punctuated by the cracking of small bones as he bites through the frame of the mammal. The creature grunts with slight satisfaction, as his hunger is sated. Blood drips down his chin as he devours his meal. The mouse is consumed in two bites, fur, flesh, tendon, bone, blood and all.

AUGUST 23RD, 2004: BANGOR, MAINE

Cordus Bailey was a strikingly handsome, 14 year-old boy now beginning the transition towards manhood. He had an angular, square-jawed face with bright blue eyes and curly blonde hair, flowing down to his shoulders. He had filled out from his pre-teen wiry form – and was more muscular than just a year ago – and he was agile and athletic. He enjoyed running in the vast field behind the Bailey home. It was a sunny summer day in Bangor and the field was blooming with yellow daffodils and purple fleur-de-lis. Majestic oak and sycamore trees rimmed the field and marked the entrance to a trail that snaked up the surrounding hillside. Cordus was out in the middle of the field, nudging a soccer ball deftly into the air in front of him, tapping it off of first his right foot, then his left, practicing his ability to keep the ball bouncing up and down without hitting the ground. He had even taped an index card to his bedroom wall with the current record of his consecutive airborne kicks – he called it the "magic number."

Sports served as Cordus' main sanctuary – a temporary respite from the incomprehensively strange nature of his family life. He felt that he barely knew these people, the man and woman who were called his parents. His mom – he used to love her so deeply. Now, she was this awful, bossy presence, who ran the house like she was the queen, and Cordus and his dad were serfs – those servant guys he learned about in world history.

And his dad? He used to be cool. Now, he was weird and just sort of flat. It was sad but true: his dad was like some creature from another planet – Planet Zombie. Cordus either lost himself in Spider Man fantasies, or just counted down the days to his next soccer or baseball game. He tried his best not to dwell on his life at home, and what he was subjected to. It wasn't easy.

On either side of the Bailey home, also bordering the field leading to the trail, were two neighboring homes. In one lived a retired couple who enjoyed the Maine summer sunshine and fled to Florida once the cold weather moved in. In the other lived Michael and Samantha McIntyre. The McIntyre's had a daughter, a pretty girl named Jenny with straight auburn hair that ran down to her waist. She had a child's lifetime of memories compiled from her experiences in this town, and in this house – running, jumping and climbing in the spacious field she now viewed. She was sitting on a high-backed wooden rocker, sipping from a tall glass of iced tea, enjoying a lazy day on the back porch. She was watching Cordus now, and in the distance she could hear the *tap, tap* of the ball clipping his sneakers. She rocked back and forth, and entered a delightful, day-dreaming state on this warm afternoon, and her mind drifted back to another afternoon long ago, thinking about kicking the soccer ball with Cordus on a day when the weather was just as nice, but they were little kids then. They were both bursting out of that stage – she and Cordus. They were teenagers now.

Jenny's mind brought her back to the present, and she noticed that the tapping sound of the soccer ball had stopped. She looked over and saw that her friend Cordus had departed the field, probably to go back inside the Bailey home. As the years had passed, the young neighbors saw each other regularly and became good friends. Jenny and Cordus walked home from school together and often played in the field, sometimes kicking a soccer ball back and forth or playing catch with a baseball. Indeed, Cordus had called over earlier to ask her if she'd knock the soccer ball around with him today, but she waved him off, letting him know that she just felt like relaxing. Sometimes it amazed her how much like a little boy Cordus still acted, while she sensed that she would soon be leaving the carefree days of childhood behind.

Jenny was now 14, and essential changes had signaled to her that womanhood was approaching. Her first period had taken place and the nascent beginnings of breasts were beginning to take shape. She proudly informed her mother that they should go shopping for bras for her to wear. Her body was still certainly that of a young teen, but it was no longer the straight, formless figure of a skinny girl. She recognized her budding womanhood and couldn't help noticing that boys were looking at her in a different way than just a year before. In addition, she realized that the affection she had for her friend Cordus was beginning to bloom into something that stirred the feelings inside her maturing body. For even though he acted like a boy, his body was changing in shape, and she liked the appearance of the developing muscles in his arms and shoulders.

The following day, a sunny Saturday, Cordus was strolling in the field again, seeing if he could spot the fox that he occasionally saw near their house. Jenny was not on her porch, nor in the field: no, she was standing behind a big oak tree a hundred yards away, hidden from the sun and from plain sight of the eyes of residents who might be peaking out their windows into the field. She had on a white cotton blouse, cut-off jean shorts and sandals.

She peaked around the huge trunk of the tree and called out, "Hey, Cordus, come over here!"

"Oh, hi," he called out in a high-pitched voice. He walked over towards her. He was only a few yards away when he said, "What are you doing back there, Jenny? It's beautiful out and you're hiding away in the shade."

She approached him, and they were near one another now.

"I was waiting for you to come out, Cordus. I wanted to talk to you."

As he came nearer, her striking smile flashed at him and he returned it with a grin of his own. A blue jay sounded its sharp caw from a nearby tree branch.

"OK, here I am," he said. "Why don't we go play catch? I can get my glove."

"I don't want to do that right now Cordus," she said with a laugh, leaning her head back and stretching her arms behind her head, propelling her chest forward, hoping he'd notice. She lowered her glance to look into his face, placed her arms on her skinny hips, and gave him an entrancing, coquettish stare. "I want you to come here...closer to me."

He was somewhat mystified by this new look on his friend's face. As he approached he sensed the heat from her body, felt her breath on his neck, and something rapidly stirred within Cordus that was new and powerful.

"Give me your hand," she whispered. She took his right hand in her left and gently placed it on her waist. Then she moved his hand up and over, across the white blouse, to the left side of her chest.

"What should I...?" Cordus was still confused but within seconds seemed to have an instinctual understanding that he should massage her to make her feel good. While he rubbed her small breast, she leaned into him and kissed him and Cordus was literally dizzy with a flood of new sensations.

"Do you like feeling my body, Cordus?"

"Uh, uh...yes," he stammered. He kissed her again. "This is nice. Is-is it OK for us to do this, Jenny? I mean..."

"Of course it's OK, Cordus."

He felt the nub of flesh beneath her shirt rising slightly – her nipple hardening in excitement – and he was unsure what would happen next, but whatever was happening, he knew he liked it.

"CORDUS!" came the strident yell from the back porch of the Bailey home. "I want you to come in here right now!"

"I-I better go, Jenny. My mom wants me to come in."

Jenny pulled her body away from his and gave him a questioning look. "You'd rather go see your mother than stay here with me, Cordus?"

"I have to go Jenny," he said. "I'll talk to you later."

Jenny felt an odd combination of excitement from Cordus' touch, mixed with anger at him for leaving so suddenly. Cordus gave a slight wave and ran across the field towards his house.

He knew his mother would be extremely upset if he didn't respond to her call – and he didn't like it when his mother got upset. The stirrings of burgeoning lust were overwhelmed by the stark fear that his mother might be angry at him. Jenny backed away and stood alone behind the oak tree, a perplexed expression on her face, as Cordus sprinted through the field of grass and summer flowers.

He was out of breath when he reached the back door of his house. He pulled open the screen door and saw the long, mussed blonde and grey mane of hair that ran down his mother's back. She turned around and eyed him with disapproval, a squinting look she gave him that he knew so well. Her narrow face had high cheek bones, a jutting chin and a pinched nose. She had the searing blue eyes that were replicated within her son. Next to a hardcover book that she had been reading was her pair of binoculars.

"I saw what was happening out there, Cordus," Abby said, her thin lips forming a straight line indicating her disapproval with him.

"I was playing in the field, Mom. Jenny was out there, too."

"I think she wants you to perform sinful deeds, Cordus," she said.

"I don't know what you mean."

"Don't lie to me boy!" Abby yelled. "Come upstairs right now. I will cleanse you."

He said no more. He closed his eyes and dreamt that all of this would go away. His father was at work. His Dad worked longer hours now – often on weekends. Even when at home, however, his father was inept at thwarting the dominance of his wife.

She held his hand as they walked up the staircase and led him into the bathroom. He knew that she had already run the bathwater.

"Remove your clothes, Cordus." He took off his yellow Bangor Rec Center t-shirt, unbuckled his belt and slid his jeans and underwear off. After that he lowered himself into the water.

She removed her navy blue cloak, covered in a design of stars and a crescent moon. Then, she slid out of her long, black skirt. Next, she unbuttoned her paisley blouse, and removed her bra and panties. She knelt down by the rim of the tub, and her mid-sized breasts bobbed down as she leaned towards her son. Rising steam from the bath water soothed her skin.

"Touch me, Cordus," Abby whispered. "You're the only one who can make me whole."

"No, Mom...it's not right," he cried. He knew, however, that he had to appease her or suffer the beatings she would otherwise administer.

She wanted his touch. Not only on her breasts but lower, lower...She wanted him to be in the place where he had come from at birth. She murmured to herself almost silently as he massaged her. "The spirit of the flesh must return to its birthplace to be renewed. The Earth Goddess must be served..." Then in a whisper, "This is what is right, Cordus. You are returning to the flesh of the Earth Mother. Recreating the cycle of birth and life. Returning to the home in my loins where you were conceived and created."

Cordus closed his eyes and the tears flowed down his cheeks. He tried desperately to think of Jenny, to imagine that he was touching her instead of touching his own mother.

While the flirtations towards her son by Jenny could not have been a total shock to Abigail, she found the situation to be completely unacceptable. Abigail decided that she would put the lid right back on that Pandora's Box. She informed Eldon of her plans, and instructed him to act accordingly.

As summer drew to a close, Cordus was told by his mother that he would be withdrawn from school. His father was selling Bailey Realty, she said. They would be moving to a new town. Eldon sat silently in the background and nodded in agreement. Cordus looked at his father, who had always been a firmly built, strong blonde-haired man – now thinner and weaker, with sallow cheeks and a glassy stare. Over the course of the past six months he had virtually stopped communicating with his son.

While certainly Cordus had vague recollections of his father having a quick temper – particularly when Cordus had been very young – they had ultimately grown very close and had developed a strong relationship. Cordus thought of good times, when his father was a loving man who spent time with his son and they laughed together. They drove down to the coastline and his father would point out the different types of vessels that sailed past. They always discussed the various boats they saw – Eldon promising they would live on the shore one day and have their own sloop.

The changes were too much for Cordus. His mother had become completely domineering in their home. Her seeming desire for total control – and her ability to maintain that control – was frightening. This was not the same sensitive, loving mother who had raised him. What had made her a different person? Beyond that, what had changed his father? He seemed to be so bland now, so devoid of joy and without a sense of humor. There must be a connection – an explanation as to why both his parents had turned into such total weirdos.

Cordus could figure out, of course, that the excessive time his mother spent with the door closed alone in the master bedroom – where he was now never allowed to enter – and the bizarre incantations she chanted when she "cleansed" him were an essential piece of the puzzle.

"I don't want to leave, Mom. I don't want to move," Cordus said. "I can still remember the last time we moved, and now that we're here…I mean, this is our home. I like it here; my friends are here."

"You like it, Cordus…you *like* it," Abigail repeated mockingly, shaking her head in disapproval. "The world doesn't revolve around you, son, and you better learn that. Your father, who works very hard to maintain a home for us, has received a generous offer for Bailey Realty. We're going to Massachusetts. He has arranged to work as a broker, and then I'm sure he'll be able to start his own firm soon. I told you that. That's where we're going, and that's the end of it."

"Yes, Mother."

He had three days to pack everything in his room and to get ready to go. School started on Monday, and of course, he was kept at home. On Tuesday afternoon, one day prior to the family's departure, he saw Jenny walking past his house, headed home. His mother was upstairs in the bedroom and Cordus knew she wouldn't notice if he ran outside for just a few minutes. He bounded out the front door. It was a glorious sunny day with the slightest hint of fall in the air.

"Jenny!" he called out.

"Hello, Cordus," she coolly replied. She still felt the sting of rejection from a few days earlier, certain that he would have contacted her if he felt attracted to her. Perhaps her overtures had been too strong. She carried a small backpack containing a couple of notebooks. She wore a cheery lime-green short-sleeve blouse and a knee-length navy blue skirt with comfortable open toed flats. He walked along side her and touched her hand, getting her to stop walking. They faced one another.

"I'm so sorry I haven't talked to you," Cordus said. "I've been thinking of you."

"You haven't called. You haven't stopped by my house. And why haven't you been in school?"

"But I have been thinking about you...about us really. It's just that so much has been happening."

She reached up and brushed his cheek and her hand ran down to his neck, massaging him gently. He felt a tingle of pleasure course through his body. "I thought you were scared off by what happened the other day, or that you simply didn't like me," she said. "You know I think you're cute, Cordus. And I like being around you." Every time he saw her now she looked more beautiful, more womanly. There were two buttons unfastened at the top of her blouse and he craved to touch the smooth skin of her neck and upper chest. She leaned into him and shared a conspiratorial whisper. "Tomorrow night, out by the oak trees...come see me."

"But-but that's what I have to talk to you about," he stammered. "Can't I see you tonight? I need to see you tonight."

She leaned away again. A sea change instantly took place, cooling down the heat of teen lust.

"Sorry, Cordus. We're going to my cousins for dinner. I can't see you tonight."

"No, you don't understand; we're moving Jenny. That's why I've been pulled out of school." He couldn't bear to look into her eyes. Instead, he looked up into the blue sky, his eyes glassy.

"What do you mean, Cordus?" she asked. "Why are you guys moving?"

"It's all my mother's idea, I'm sure. My father is selling his company, and he's taking a new job. I just know it's my mother who's making this happen."

Jenny was very wary about insulting her friend's parents, and didn't want to say what was on her mind: Cordus' mom had become much less friendly, and had this mean look on her face when Jenny happened to see her.

"I'm sorry," she said, plaintively.

Cordus felt even worse. "If only...," he said. Cordus didn't know what circumstance could help him interpret what was happening in a positive light.

"Yes, Cordus, if only..." she agreed. She held his hand for but a moment, gave it a squeeze, and turned to walk away. He watched her move away, longed for her calves, her ankles. He wished to stroke her lovely, flowing auburn hair. He was coming to life as a sexual being, watching her teenage strut – and dying inside at the same time. Could there be a female on earth any more alluring than Jenny McIntyre? Surely not.

"I'll write you Jenny," he called out. "We'll only be in Massachusetts. It's not far. I'll write!"

A tear streamed down his cheek and he brushed it away. He watched Jenny as she glanced over her shoulder, giving him a little smile and a wave before turning off the street to head into her house. He could never have previously fathomed the depths of the pain he was feeling. He had only just discovered – days before – what the human heart could experience when it beat in such close proximity to that of another. He now realized that his body was living on a higher plane when he had been touching Jenny. Maybe it was only puppy love, but to have it snatched away as abruptly as it had been introduced into his body and soul...it was all Cordus could do not to tumble down into a heap right on the street, and crawl into a ball and weep. Here was everything he wanted and needed – a beautiful, sweet girl – and to have her tantalizingly within reach but now unattainable was sheer torture.

On top of that was the horror of the "cleansing." The combination of being torn from Jenny and his mother thrusting herself upon him...no, no, no. It was beyond what he could comprehend. There are times when life's vagaries defy rational understanding and fate takes turns venal and cruel. Cordus was feeling the pangs of anguish that would transform a strapping, clear thinking lad into a tormented boy.

The move from Maine took place uneventfully. The moving truck arrived with four men to load the boxes and wrap up the furniture for safe transport. The family was ready to go. Cordus stood in the backyard and took a last look: he eyed the porch in the back where Jenny's favorite rocking chair was sitting empty – and he pondered the emptiness of having her removed from his life.

"Cordus, did you hear your father?" his mother yelled. She stood next to the Volvo station wagon, hands on hips.

"No, what did he say?" Cordus said, shaking his head, trying to escape the daze he was in. The move came so rapidly – and he was so blindsided by his escalating heartbreak over leaving Jenny – that he had trouble accepting the reality that was now slapping him in the face.

"Do you have to go to the bathroom before we go?" his mother said. "What's wrong with you, boy? It's like you're in your own world."

"No, I'm fine. I don't have to go," Cordus said. "We can leave."

"Fine, then get over here, and get in the car."

There was a lack of communication in the car among the family members. Cordus was brooding in the back seat, his nose buried in an old Spider Man comic book he had already read. Behind the wheel, Eldon was virtually expressionless, his short dirty blonde hair neatly parted and set into place with hair gel. He wore mirrored aviator glasses; his head rigidly focused on the road. Locked within his icy demeanor, he was beyond the point at which his mind could be distracted. Cordus glanced up from his comic book to look at his mother with disdain, as she set the passenger seat slightly back in recline position, closed her eyes and assumed a Cheshire cat grin – the look of the contented matriarch. Soon she was napping.

The station wagon hurtled steadily down the seemingly featureless stretch of Route 95 south. There were infrequent patches of trees, but mostly industrial areas and outlet malls just off the highway, service areas for gasoline and food and endless streams of cars, vans, buses and eighteen-wheelers in both directions. The radio was set to a talk radio station and was barely audible.

'Oh come on John you don't really believe that, do you?' the host of the show said, incredulously.

'I wouldn't call in if I didn't think it was true, Tony,' the voice of the caller replied in a tinny tone.

'Well,' replied the host, 'I think you're a loose cannon and a disgrace to this great country of ours...'

Cordus shook his head, wondering why anyone would want to listen to these boring people spouting their opinions. He tried to disregard it and refocused his attention on Peter Parker's exploits saving his city. The world needed more heroes like Spider Man, Cordus thought, people who stood up and took action when they believed in a cause.

The route wove through eastern Massachusetts. They circumvented Boston, and that great city became only a series of green highway signs for the family. The Volvo trundled along on its route, and the Baileys made their way from Route 95 to Route 90, the Mass Turnpike. After reaching the Mass Pike, they headed west, and there spun forth another anonymous stretch of road, now featuring more roadside forests than commercial establishments, yet still a monotonous trip of exit signs marking small Massachusetts towns Cordus would never know.

Finally, the highway was behind them, and the station wagon made its way through a small western Massachusetts town, past a police station and library and a white church with a tall spire. There was a general store, a clothing boutique, two antique shops, a restaurant with a lunch counter, and a sprawling, white hotel with a huge front porch at the edge of the downtown area. It took less than two minutes to drive through this downtown section, and then the commercial district was behind them. After three miles headed south, and a number of turns on winding roads through sparsely populated neighborhoods, past a smooth-surfaced lake and a tall stand of hardwood trees on both sides, a final right turn brought them to the head of Buck Tree Road. Three-quarters of a mile down, the pavement ended, marking the beginning of a dirt tract. Cordus eyed mountains in the distance spanning his view to the right, mostly tree-covered, but with a dramatic rock face jutting out near the top. To his left there was more forest, teams of spruce, maple and pine rising gradually on a hillside, like a massive battalion of soldiers poised for battle.

The home, a two-story Victorian a quarter-mile in on the dirt tract, was painted a deep emerald green with black shutters. It was set back 50 yards off of the road. The turret in the upper right hand corner of the house was its most striking feature. An old, narrow weathered barn – once used for hatching baby chicks – lay on the property less than a hundred yards from the main house, and set much closer to the road. Apple trees, their branches spreading out and making them appear as wide as they were tall, surrounded the house on both sides. Across the street, up 100 yards back towards the main road, was a stand of forest, with a snaking trail cut through, part of a hiking path used most commonly by locals.

When the Baileys arrived, the moving men were already there. Cordus' possessions were shuttled up the stairs by the moving men into one of the bedrooms off of the corridor to the left of the top of the staircase. The men wore blue jump suits and black work boots. They made little jokes among themselves as they carried the boxes in. His mother took immediate possession of the round turreted room, to the right of the upper stairwell, identifying it as her study. The master bedroom, containing its own bathroom, was across the hall from the turreted room. A bathroom was next to Cordus' room at the end of the corridor. An extra bedroom was across the hall from Cordus' room, facing the street. Certainly, Abigail would make the decision how that room would be utilized, Cordus realized. His father no longer seemed to be making any decisions in the Bailey family.

That evening, he sat at the small desk in his room by the window overlooking the back yard, turned on his desk light with a *tick* of the delicate metal pull cord, and took out a piece of paper to compose a letter to Jenny...

Dear Jenny:

I am so sorry that I couldn't be with you again before we left. I still want to see you. I don't know how just yet, but I know we can be together. We just got here and I hate it already. I can't stop thinking about you and about being back in Bangor. Everything happened so quickly. I guess it was my father's new job and stuff like that. We had to move right away.

How is school going? I hope you don't have Miss Bolton for social studies. Everybody says she is totally weird.

When I held you the other day, it was an unbelievable feeling. I can't even describe it. I just know that it can't be the last time we're together. Oh God, Jenny, sometimes I just hate my mother. She doesn't care what I think or how I feel. I was never able to talk to you about it, but now I'm starting to figure things out. She doesn't own me. She can't tell me what to do and who to see. It's not fair, and she's not fair.

I want to come back to see you. It's not that far, Jenny. The car ride only took part of a day. Maybe I can come up there sometime soon.

I'm feeling a little tired, and I guess I'll try to go to sleep. I'm thinking about you. Please write back soon, Jenny.

Your ex-neighbor and always your friend,

Cordus

It was a difficult letter to write. As young as he was, Cordus had enough sense to know that it was too early in their relationship for Cordus to write in a 'really corny' way. He had to be realistic, and write a letter that reflected the fact that they had only held each other and kissed once. He folded the letter in half, and placed it in the top, middle drawer of the desk. He would find out the address of his new home and write it at the bottom of the letter to Jenny the next day, so she could write him back. It wasn't enough to put it on the outside of the envelope; he wanted the address to be on the letter as well.

He felt a tiny bit better about the situation, knowing he could at least write to Jenny, and that he could wait for her reply. Cordus switched the light off and laid down under the covers in his bed – the same bed he had in Maine, but it felt so different now.

An hour later, Abby quietly opened the door. How she knew to search Cordus' desk was the result of a mystical connection between son and mother: a twinge from within that had signaled to Abigail that it was so. With bare feet, her footfalls were light on the floor, but the old floorboards still emitted a couple of tell-tale *squeaks* and *creaks* as she made her way towards Cordus' desk.

He stirred lightly; she froze momentarily in the light from a full moon. He rolled over from laying on his right shoulder to laying on his left – so he was now looking away from her direction, towards the wall – and Abigail took another step in the direction of the desk.

She reached for the middle drawer, delicately lifted the top piece of paper out between her forefinger and thumb, and quietly unfolded it. In the moonlight gleaming in the window, she saw the initial salutation: Dear Jenny. A nearly flat, half grimace/half smile spread across the middle of her narrow face. As her eyes squinted in an evil glare, she looked over to see that Cordus had rolled over again, so that he was now facing her. His eyes were shut, however, and he slept on. She turned and moved out of the room, stepping as quietly as possible.

Cordus had awakened, however, and knew exactly what was happening. While she was exiting the room, he shut his eyes and feigned sleep. Now – after his mother had departed – he let out an angry, anguished, quiet mutter; "*ahhhh,*" and slammed his fist down on to the bed. After that initial flash of ire, the tears came. They streamed onto his pillow and he felt confused, helpless, and so, so alone.

Cordus' puppy love letter had soon been crumpled and burned to ash in the turreted room that Abigail had claimed as her study. The remains lay in an ashtray on her window sill. She whispered aloud to herself:

"So, he'll try to contact that little whore," Abby spit out with bile, as she reviewed a letter she herself had typed earlier. "He's filthy, in his thoughts and in his actions. Cordus needs my guidance, so he will not be led astray by the 'Jennys' of the world. Such lustful, vile inclinations; I will not have my Cordus bespoiled by the likes of little Miss Jenny McIntyre."

As this soliloquy continued, the mother carefully placed an envelope into the 1960s-era Underwood typewriter she used for correspondence. She typed out the young girl's name and address on the envelope, and her son's name and only "Stockbridge, MA" in the upper left hand corner, omitting the actual address.

"A dirty, dirty girl," she muttered, rolling the envelope out of the typewriter. "Disgusting."

She picked up the letter to look it over one last time:

To Jenny:

I am moving on to a new life, in a new place. I know that things will be good for me and my mom and dad here. It is clear to me that there is no reason to stay in touch with you in the future. I have nothing against you, Jenny. I just have no feelings for you.

You should move on and be happy in the things that you do. I know that I will find happiness here in my new house, in a new town. Please do not contact me. There really is no reason for you to try.

Goodbye,

Cordus

Abby's sharp features broke into a smile, and a gleam shone in her blue eyes, as she folded the letter twice and inserted it into the typed envelope. She placed a postage stamp on it and placed it on her desk, next to the typewriter. Surely, her first errand the next day would be to take a trip to the post office.

When he awoke, Cordus decided to 'play dumb' about the stolen letter. It would do him no good to confront his mother now, and certainly, he told himself, he could re-write the letter and mail it out to Jenny. Little did he know that his mother was already planning a full-on barricade in every manner possible to prevent that from happening. Not only would she squelch any efforts he made to send out a letter; in addition, Abigail decided the Baileys would have no phone and no computer. Eldon had a cell that he used for business, but Abby would make sure that Cordus never laid his paws on that.

Cordus approached his mother in the kitchen, where she was picking items out of moving boxes and putting them away. Eldon had already found a job at O'Neil Realty in Great Barrington, and had left for work. "Mom, where is the school where I'll be going?"

"You will be home-schooled, Cordus," she told him in a flat tone. She didn't look at him, continuing her task of transferring canned goods from a box into the kitchen cabinets. "I'll teach what you need to know."

Cordus was silent. He grimaced and looked down at his shoes, swallowing words he knew he would regret saying – because they would enrage his mother. He tried to gather himself, as he heard the *clack* of cans being stacked on a shelf. He stepped closer towards her.

"But I've always been in school, Mom. Why would you want to do this now?"

She placed one more can on the shelf, and stopped. She turned to face him. "It's best for you, Cordus. Your father and I have decided this," she said, reaching up with both hands to brush her blonde and grey curly hair back. He saw – and not for the first time – the strange markings on her right palm.

"What is that, Mom?" he asked, pointing at her hand. "You have a tattoo now? What's going on with you exactly?"

She quickly pulled her hands down from her hair, and let them drop to her sides, palms hidden. The two stars branded on to her palm were a constant reminder for Abby about how her life had changed for the better – and how great her own power had become. Her eyes crinkled in a distasteful glare.

"That's none of your business, boy."

"What do you mean? You pry into my business all the time."

She stayed focused on him with a withering dirty look, but decided to let that remark go.

"Now about your education," she said, turning back to resume her work storing cans. "This is what's best. And that's that." She paused and looked out the window, at the bare rock face of the mountain in the distance. "To be perfectly honest, I didn't like what was starting to happen to you back in Bangor.

You are our boy, Cordus; you are *my* boy. I felt that you might be changing; your mind wandering."

"Because of what happened with Jenny?" he said, asserting himself. "There was nothing wrong with that. You took me away. I think you were jealous!"

She turned, and her open right hand swept through the air and pounded his cheek with full force. She looked at him in rage, eyes practically bulging out of her head. He rubbed his cheek and felt its sting and narrowed his eyes at her, feeling nothing but hatred for his own mother. Tears welled up and his view of her was slightly distorted.

"*Me* – jealous of that little slut-in-training? Don't be a fool, Cordus!" she yelled. "She's nothing," she pointed a forefinger in his face. "You can't associate with trash like your sweet *Jenny*," she spit out the name with bitterness. "You don't even understand what you are and what you can be. That's part of the problem. I must educate you here, boy."

He wiped the tears from his cheek, and moved backwards out of the kitchen. The desire to shrink into a ball and weep was again there within him – but so too was the pride of a boy aching to attain the early vestiges of manhood. He would cry no more. Rather, he would swallow the rage that was building within him. And it *was* building. Like surging river water pounding against a dam near the bursting point, the rage was gathering and expanding within Cordus.

He took three steps up the staircase, heading to his room, when Abby called out to him, a tinge of false sweetness back in her voice:

"Cordus, I'll be upstairs in a few minutes. I wish to cleanse you..."

OCTOBER 15TH, 2010: PITTSFIELD, MASS

"Hey, pleasure to meet you, Doc," Oak said cheerfully, extending his hand for a shake, as Professor Peter Earnhardt rose from the bench in the sheriff's department entrance/ waiting area.

"Hello Burt," Earnhardt said. "Nice to meet you. Again, please call me Peter." Earnhardt was nearly as tall as Alderson, but his thin frame was in stark contrast to Oak's thick girth.

"Sounds good, thanks. I'm really glad you finally made it over. Let's head outside, alright?"

Earnhardt was carrying a black leather valise under one arm. He remained skeptical, convinced this trip was a waste of time. This guy, Burt Alderson, really had been persistent, though, calling him every few months.

"Maybe we should take my car," Earnhardt suggested.

"Why, you don't want to be seen driving around in the squad car?" Oak said with a smile.

"I suppose that's true. I'm not ready for my perp walk yet, Burt." Oak laughed.

"Hey, by the way, most people call me Oak, so feel free."

"Oak, eh?" Earnhardt nodded.

Oak punched in a number on his cell phone.

"Hey T.K.," he said. "It's Oak. Look, I'm not gonna be in the car for the next hour and a half or so. We're going to Patrick's for lunch, and then I'll be in Lee briefly, and then I'll be back at HQ. Yeah, just call me on the cell if anything comes up. We're driving around in my visitor's car, so I can get to wherever you need me. Thanks."

Earnhardt led them in the direction of his Subaru, and Oak got in the passenger side.

"Drive out and take a left," Oak directed, "and we'll go to Patrick's Pub downtown for lunch, OK? They do a great burger."

The two men were finishing up lunch, and chatting about Oak's find, and some issues related to the medallion and Earnhardt's research.

"There's something I want to show you, Oak."

Earnhardt reached down towards the floor to the leather valise. He pulled out a small sheath of documents and photos, and shuffled through them.

"Here," he said, unfolding and handing him a glossy sheet of paper. "Take a look at this."

Oak grabbed the sheet, and saw a blown-up, glossy copy of an old color snapshot. An old woman with a neutral expression on her face was looking at books at an outdoor sale – perhaps a yard sale. She wasn't looking at the camera – her eyes were on the book in her hands – and it was a fairly close shot of her head and upper body, with a couple of people milling around at another table behind her.

"Kind of looks like my grandma Gertie," Oak said, with a shrug.

"Her name was Margaret Waltham: maiden name, Sibber. You see, I make it a point to comb through estate sales and such up in Salem, Marblehead and Beverly. I find some interesting stuff – you know, related to my Early American history research."

"I know about this woman," Oak said.

Earnhardt looked surprised.

"It's been a while since I first contacted you, Doc. I've done some digging on my own, and I've read about Margaret – she was the last person definitively identified as having the medallion."

"That's right. Here," Earnhardt said, pulling a magnifying glass from his valise, "take a closer look at this photo. Look at her neck."

Oak took the glass, and studied the woman in the photo.

"That's it," he said. "She's wearing it!"

Around her neck, the woman was clearly wearing the pewter medallion with the wheat stalks and stars, hanging from a thread-thin silver chain.

"She was. She was indeed. This photo is from the early 1970s."

"What do you know about Margaret Sibber Waltham? Did she put the voodoo hex on people, have them killed or something?"

"I don't know," Earnhardt said. "I tried to find out, believe me. But according to what I learned, she lived a rather benign existence. She was a librarian in Salem. Married for more than 50 years, ended up outliving her husband – who died peacefully in his sleep – by just two years. They had three daughters, who all remained in the region. One of them, Virginia, stayed right in Salem and was involved in a strange incident. Her husband, John Merriweather, met a nasty fate. Bludgeoned in his own house at 2:30 in the morning, back in 1971."

"Really? Bludgeoned with what?"

"The base of a bronze horse statuette. It was in their living room. He was killed with his own object d'art."

"Who did it?"

"They never found out. Two guys were heard driving away in the middle of the night. Some valuables were stolen from the living room. Virginia said she only came down later, and found her husband – dead. The couple had a young daughter, Abigail, who was in the house at the time."

Oak flinched at the mention of the name Abigail, but didn't say anything about it.

"The wife said she heard nothing?"

"The husband was an academic. Spent a lot of late nights writing downstairs, according to the wife."

"But, uh, come on," Oak said. "That's a lot of stirring around downstairs for this woman to sleep through. And the little girl, too?"

"The police suspected Virginia from the start, from what I've read. They just couldn't prove anything."

"What about the medallion? Any connection? Were these killers – alleged killers – trying to steal the medallion?"

"No," he said, definitively. "John Merriweather wouldn't have had the medallion. If anyone in the house did, I figure Virginia would have had it. There's no evidence that the killers went upstairs. And even if they had, there are just too many unknown details about the situation."

"What do you mean?"

"Well, I can't seem to get confirmation that Virginia had the Sibber medallion. You can see Margaret with it on – right there in the photo. The situation just gets murkier from there. For one thing, Virginia had two sisters, and one of *them* may have been given the medallion."

"Right. Margaret Waltham had three daughters – I read about that, too. So that's where the trail got lost."

"Yes. It's all just part of the mystique, I suppose. Stories trickle out. People speculate, they surmise. But nobody knows for sure what happened to the medallion, and what it all means."

"I'm sure you'll be interested to see what I've got stored away."

Earnhardt again swallowed his words, and nodded politely.

"Well," Oak continued, "let me pick up the check, and we'll head over to Lee to take a look."

"Why are we going to Lee?" Earnhardt asked.

"That's where the medallion is," Oak said, waving to get the attention of the waitress. "We have it there in a safe deposit box at the Lee Savings Bank."

"Huh," Earnhardt said. "Remember that material I faxed to you back when you initially contacted me? What did you think about that?"

"Fascinating stuff. It made for interesting reading. Sounded like the makings of a Poe story," Oak said. "What the hell was going on with those people?"

"Who knows exactly what was happening? But that story is just one of many," Earnhardt said. "I've got write-ups of other accounts that are similar. The stories revolve around one of the Sibber women, in possession of the medallion, wreaking havoc."

"*Allegedly* wreaking havoc," Oak added.

Earnhardt looked over at him with a thoughtful glance, propped his elbows on the table, and placed his chin on his hands.

"Oak, we *are* talking about the occult here. There's no way to get around that. After the drowning of Ann Sibber in 1694, there are no records of indictments or apprehensions of any sort in connection with...," Earnhardt was at a loss for a few seconds, "crimes that may or may not have been committed. No one has had any hard evidence that a Sibber woman committed a criminal act of any sort."

"Unless you consider the case of Virginia Merriweather," Oak said.

"That's right," Earnhardt agreed. "But, again, they couldn't find any proof."

Oak left the tip on the table and signaled to Earnhardt that they could get going.

"Well," Oak said, "I'm interested to have you take a look at *my* medallion. You can tell me once and for all if it's the Real McCoy!"

Earnhardt gave a knowing nod. Here comes another let down, he told himself.

⁂   ⁂   ⁂

The bank official who led them in had left the safe deposit box room and closed the door. The box was unlocked, and pulled out – like a tray in the coroner's morgue – and was now jutting out from the wall of boxes. Oak slid the metal lid open, and removed the medallion attached to the thin silver chain from the box. He placed it on a table nearby. Earnhardt looked at it closely, using the magnifying glass.

"What do you think?" Oak asked.

Earnhardt kept examining it – he was shocked by what he saw. He picked it up to feel the weight.

"I can't believe it. It's the first time I've ever seen it – other than in photos," Earnhardt said with wonderment. "God. It's beautiful. All that history."

"So this is it?" Oak asked.

"Definitely." He pulled his digital camera out of his valise and snapped a few photos. After Earnhardt stopped clicking his camera, they both stood in awe for a few seconds. "I think I'll bring over a colleague of mine to test it for age, if that's OK."

"Sure," Oak said. "That's fine."

"But I can tell you right now: this is it," Earnhardt said, feeling stunned…and stupid that he hadn't previously taken the time to check it out. "I'm sorry I didn't come sooner, Oak, it's just that…"

"You don't have to apologize."

"No, I want to explain the situation to you," Earnhardt said. "I've received numerous calls in the past like yours. I've traveled around to look at pieces – and ended up seeing a bunch of reproductions. And then other things kept coming up that made me postpone my visit. I really am sorry."

"It's OK, Doc, don't worry about it," Oak said. "I'm grateful to finally learn that this is the real deal."

"It's incredible," Earnhardt said, snapping more photos.

"Let me ask you," Oak said. "What do you think this thing is worth?"

Earnhardt gave him a sideways glance with a raised eyebrow.

"I mean," Oak added. "I'm just curious."

"Oak," Earnhardt intoned, "I don't want to see this medallion listed for sale on e-bay."

Oak let out a chuckle.

"I'm just kidding, Doc. Figured I'd get a rise out of you."

Earnhardt failed to see the humor in it.

"It's amazing that it's here," Earnhardt said. "It must be the first time in more than 300 years that it hasn't been in the possession of one of the Sibbers. I can hardly believe it."

Oak had a decision to make here, and realized there was no turning back now. He still remained uncomfortable about how he had initially retrieved the medallion – stealthily intruding on a crime scene. But he had to now share some information with Earnhardt, to broaden the conversation. He started with a question.

"That little girl in the Merriweather house – you said her name was Abigail?"

"Yes, that was Abigail Merriweather."

"Look, I have something to tell you. She was here...she lived here – down in Stockbridge."

Oak proceeded to tell Earnhardt about an event that had made a big stir in the Berkshires, but had amounted to nothing more than a slight ripple elsewhere. He told Earnhardt what he knew about the events of October 14th, 2007.

CHAPTER ELEVEN

Abby awoke just after 6:00 a.m. to pore over the incantations in the notebooks left to her by her grandmother. There was still much more to read, so much to learn.

Later that morning, she was sitting in a kitchen chair across from Cordus, and beginning a math lesson. She displayed patience as she discussed beginning geometry with the boy. They moved on to a discussion of early American history. After this came a discussion of literature. They read through the first half of Poe's *The Raven* together. For much of the time, Cordus clenched his teeth and put on a front of acceptance towards this arrangement. He made a façade of conversing pleasantly with his mother. How long could this really go on, he wondered? Surely, she would get sick of having him around all the time, and playing the school-marm.

Having his mother as his teacher was far less than ideal. Having her as his lover was utterly intolerable.

Late that afternoon, with dusk settling in, Cordus sat in his room upstairs and watched his father wander out to the backyard. A stack of logs was piled up and his father, dressed in a red and black-checkered flannel shirt, jeans and work boots, had toted out an ax to split the wood. Cordus heard the hum of the grinder when his father switched it on. It was set up right next to the house, so Cordus couldn't see his father sharpening the ax, but he heard it. There was that high-pitched stone on steel sound as his father honed the blade.

Eldon took the logs one at a time, placed them upright on a wide tree stump and gave them a *thwack*. It was breezy out – it had been a cloudy day – and there were strong gusts kicking up as his father continued his work. The work proceeded in a mechanical fashion, as the split logs fell aside. After chopping through three logs, he placed the ax down and stacked the newly halved logs along the back of the house. Then he resumed his chore. He would later bring the logs into the cellar for storage.

Cordus now lay on his bed, reading an old Spider Man comic again. His mother was in her study. The family knew not to disturb her when the study door was closed. She had purchased navy blue curtains for the windows that curved around the turreted room, and she pulled them closed when she hunkered down in that room. Cordus put the comic down, left his room, and went to the head of the stairs and sat there, waiting for his father to return. A few minutes later, the door opened and Eldon placed the ax to the side of the front door, next to an umbrella stand along the half-wall in the entrance corridor. Cordus paced down the stairs to approach his father. They rarely spoke anymore. Eldon didn't seem to talk at all at home. He merely rose early in the morning, ate a light breakfast, went to work, returned in the late afternoon, ate his dinner silently, and then read in the living room, sitting in one of the twin tall red upholstered chairs.

Cordus walked into the living room and swallowed nervously prior to speaking up. The chair in which his father sat was across the living room on the far side of the love seat and coffee table. The chair faced the stairwell, its back to the front door and foyer of the home.

"Dad."

"Yes, Cordus," Eldon replied. He put his book down, and gave Cordus an emotionless glance. Cordus got the feeling his father was looking right through him.

"I need to talk to you about something…something important."

"Is everything alright, Cordus?"

"No, it's not. Everything is not alright. As a matter of fact, everything seems to have changed recently."

"Well, we did move, son. That's a big change to be sure," Eldon said, folding his arms across his chest and giving an agreeable nod.

"There's more to it than that," Cordus said. He shifted his feet, struggling for words. He decided to sit in the other tall-backed red chair, next to his father. "Mother is acting in a very strange way. I don't know how to explain."

"I see, Cordus," he nodded his head, knowingly. "Maybe it's the move. It can be very stressful. I'm in a new job, and your mother is adjusting. Perhaps we've been so distracted we're not paying enough attention to you, heh? Maybe that's the problem. It's understandable that you're upset."

"I don't think that's really the problem, Dad."

"Certainly it is, Cordus. You can't see it as clearly as I can. We've moved to a new state, a new town. It can all be quite upsetting."

"Jesus, dad. She...makes me touch her."

"What? Who? What do you mean, boy."

He was battling back the tears now.

"Mom...in the bathtub. She makes me touch her...sexually. She gets...excited when I feel her..."

"Cordus," Eldon said, looking right through his boy again. "Don't imagine things. I understand you're upset. My gosh, the ramifications of being in a new town, being home-schooled. Maybe you need some help: someone to talk to about all these changes?"

"Mom doesn't let me leave the house. I can't stand what's going on here much longer," he said, at this point more to himself than to his father. Cordus firmly believed the man didn't actually comprehend what he was saying. His inability to connect with his dad was only adding to his anger and confusion.

Eldon maintained his vapid expression with a dopey, mock-supportive grin. His eyes were vacant. Cordus wondered if those eyes saw anything at all. "We understand what you're going through, son. The teen years can be rough; all the changes that a young man experiences in his body. I promise that your mother and I will make an effort to be more sensitive to your needs," he paused, and flashed a toothy smile. "We'll do a better job of listening to your concerns in the future."

Cordus was silent. He shook his head and looked down at his feet. He rose from the chair and started to walk towards the staircase. Who was this creepy guy he was talking to? It clearly wasn't his Dad. Eldon lifted his hardcover book from the coffee table, up into his lap, and looked at Cordus' back as the boy walked away.

"I'm really glad we took the time to have this talk, Cordus," he said, as his empty-eyed look returned back to the book in his hands. "There's nothing like a heartfelt father-son chat."

Nighttime had fallen, and the wind continued to howl. It was a chilly fall night, and getting colder. Upstairs, in the turreted room, Abigail stood in a crouched position in front of a tall, cylindrical silver cistern that sat atop an electrical heating coil, steam rising from the gurgling mixture within. Adjacent to the cistern with its bubbling brew, were four candles burning in their silver holders atop two small, circular side tables. A throw rug was rolled-up and propped against the wall. On the wooden floor, where the rug often lay, was a pentagram painted in deep red. She stood outside the pentagram, feeding a handful of crushed poppy flowers into the cistern. Small brown glass vials with black caps were on a shelf to her left. From these vials she poured in a tincture of henbane and two pinches of belladonna. She added crushed hemp flowers and a betel nut.

Abigail was dressed in a black skirt that fell to her ankles. A black blouse fit tightly across her neckline. The navy blue cape she wore with silver stars and a crescent moon was around her shoulders. She stood back, behind the mark on the floor of the pentagram and went down to her knees, her eyes fixed on the cistern and the surrounding candles. She pulled open one of the blue window curtains enough to enable her to drink in the black darkness of the cloud-filled night. And she chanted in an even, steady tone:

> Thee I invoke the bornless one
> Thee that didst create the Earth and the Heavens
> Thee that didst create the Night and the Day
> Thee that didst create the darkness and the Light
> Hear me, and make all spirits subject unto me
> So that every Spirit of the firmament and of the ether
> Upon the Earth and under the Earth
> On dry land and in the water
> Of whirling air and of rushing fire
> And every spell and scourge of God may be obedient unto me...

She stepped around the pentagram, and from a plastic bag on the shelf to her left, she removed locks of hair, one from her husband and one from Cordus. She dropped these locks into the steaming cistern. She stepped back around to the far side of the pentagram to bow again, to the cistern, to the candles and to the spirit of the night.

Cordus had gone up the stairs, away from his father – whom he felt was no longer really his father – and had made his way quietly down the hallway, just outside the door of his mother's study. Perhaps at another time he would cower in fear at the idea of eavesdropping on her. But the mounting anger in Cordus' mind made fear a secondary consideration. Boldness joined rage; now partners hand in hand in Cordus' mind. His ear was to the door and he heard her chant:

> Enjoin me Hecate and provide me the strength to become one with destiny;
> For I am she! The truth!
> I am she, that lighteneth and thundereth
> I am she, from whom is the shower of the life of Earth:
> I am she, whose mouth ever flameth
> I am she, the Begetter and Manifester unto the Light:
> I am she, the grace of the world...

Cordus felt both awestruck and disgusted by the strange ramblings his mother proclaimed. The acrid odor of the herbal mixture seeped under the door frame and filled his nostrils. There was some undeniable power harnessed within that room. He could sense it; he could feel it. His head throbbed with waves of...something awful, he couldn't quite comprehend. It was dark and evil and suddenly Cordus understood that it was his responsibility to ward it off. He was like Peter Parker and he could imagine that his mother was one of the villains that Spider Man vanquished.

Her chants were reaching an apex and her voice rose:

The man is nothing. He will do my bidding. He will provide for us and consume sustenance, but his desires for fornication will remain in check. He will do my bidding without question and without quarter. He will not touch me, O Hecate.

But there is no girl right now to take my place. Who can carry the Sibber mantle forward? Who will ensure that the legacy of the Begetter and the Manifester lives on into coming generations?

The boy will continue to serve my needs. For, above all else, I am weak, Hecate, and I beg for your mercy. I continue to succumb to the desires of the flesh. And he is the one who must fulfill that need. I see it in his eyes. They glow with brightness like my own. They are not dull with a canine ignorance like those of the father. We are one – myself and the boy – and when we join as one I feel whole. The boy will learn to embrace his role – and perhaps he can grow to understand this calling. Can you provide an answer, a portal to help me find my way amidst the darkness, Hecate?

Abigail rose, stepped around the pentagram, licked her forefinger and thumb and extinguished each of the candles with a light *hiss*. She kneeled in the room, in the darkness on this moonless night, and muttered to herself. The electric coil heating the cistern emitted a faint orange glow. Steam rose from the frothy, pungent concoction before her. Her voice was lower now; too low for Cordus to hear. All of a sudden, Abigail paused in her quiet chanting, as a new idea came to her. It hit her like an electric charge, a gift from beyond. She whispered to herself: "Maybe there is an answer. O, Hecate, o great one. Have you given me a sign? Have you now helped me to see a beacon in the darkness? For just because the boy is in his current mortal form – it does not mean he must remain so. Changes can take place, yes," she whispered. "Oh, thank you great Hecate. You are all powerful and all wise." A gleam in her eye brightened. Yes surely this was the perfect plan. All could be made right. Even her evil, sinful desires could be squelched...

Cordus stepped away as quietly as he could. She was talking to herself and did not hear his light footfalls. He had an experiment he wanted to try. He went back downstairs and into the living room. Eldon acknowledged him with a smile. Cordus didn't even look at the man. He walked right by and reached the front foyer. He father rose from his chair and had an alarmed look on his face.

"I'd like to go out for just a minute, Dad," Cordus said. "I'm going to take a walk down the street."

"You can't go, boy," he said in a stern tone.

"Why not? I just want to go to the trail-head and back."

Eldon approached the boy and had a strained look in his glassy-eyes. "It can't be done. Your mother and I have decided that's not right."

"Mom's upstairs. What's *your* opinion? Why can't I walk out for a breath of fresh air?"

"Your mother understands what's best for you. What's best for all of us. Stop it now, Cordus. Don't leave this house!"

Cordus defiantly took another step towards the door and reached for the door handle. His father rushed over and pulled the boy's hand off of the door. "Stay inside boy. Don't make this harder than it has to be."

Without a word, Cordus walked past his father back into the living room and sat down on the couch.

"I know what Mom thinks. But what do you think? Do you have any opinion at all?"

"Your mother knows what's right," he said, as he calmly sat back in his chair, picking up his book and opening it again.

Cordus realized that the father had become nothing more than a pawn in this chess game in which his mother had cast herself as queen. That's why Eldon always sat in the chair reading when he was at home. He was a sentry, a jail guard, preventing Cordus from venturing outside. When she couldn't watch over Cordus herself, this neutered husband of hers, over whom she'd cast some kind of spell, did the dirty work for her. Anger, frustration, desperation and confusion were flooding Cordus' mind.

Abigail knew her spell was cast and drawn over Eldon. She could feel the utter domination she held over him. Gaining complete sway over Cordus would not be quite so simple, she realized. For Cordus was her equal. She saw it in his eyes. And it was in his very being, through and through. He was not a dullard, like the father, one who had fallen easily into the callings of the incantations. This new idea, however, could be the answer – the final solution. She nodded her head. So many thoughts were battling for attention. This could truly kill two birds with one stone. Yes, what she needed to do now was have a quick chat with Eldon in order to put the plan in motion. There was no time to waste. She didn't want to "cleanse" Cordus again. Not ever again.

CHAPTER TWELVE

With deep nightfall, the wind picked up, and the old house became drafty from stiff jabs of autumn wind. Outside, neighborhood trees were losing their red, orange and yellow seasonal leaves, which were now blowing across the yards, and the apple trees on the Bailey property slightly danced to the rhythm of the strengthening gusts. A storm was approaching. Abby went downstairs now. She looked over at her husband, who was in his usual chair. Her son must be upstairs in his room. She stood at the bottom of the staircase.

"Cordus!" She called out. She waited. She called again, louder: "CORDUS! We need to see you!"

She heard the doorknob turn, and Cordus emerged from his room. He headed downstairs silently.

"Sit down here, on the couch, Cordus," she ordered, and he did so.

"Eldon," she said.

"Yes?"

"Get up. Walk over behind Cordus."

"Alright," Eldon said, making his way behind the couch.

"Now, grab him! Hold him!"

Cordus tried to get up, but Eldon still had enough of the strength he possessed from before the time he became a fraction of a man to hold him down, writhing in his arms.

"Get the hell off me, Dad. Let go of me!" Cordus cried out.

Eldon held his arms firmly, remaining behind him. Cordus kicked out. He knocked the coffee table over.

161

"Wait for one minute," Abby said. "I'll be ready." She went into the kitchen.

Cordus tried to thrust his head backwards to hurt his father. Eldon repositioned himself slightly to the side, and was able to keep Cordus down in a sitting position on the couch. Abby came back with a serrated-edged paring knife in one hand and a huge carving knife in the other. She walked over to upright the coffee table, and then put the knives down. If only he could break free and grab a knife, Cordus thought.

"Take him to the barn, Eldon," she said. "Here, take this and tie his hands together," she added, giving him a short stretch of rope. She held up the big carving knife, and shoved it beneath Cordus' chin. "Don't move, boy. Don't budge while he ties that knot, or I'll slit your throat right here, right now."

"Goddamn you," Cordus muttered. She moved the knife upwards, making contact with his chin.

"Button it, Cordus," she said. "Are you done back there, Eldon?"

He tied Cordus' wrists up using a half-hitch, a sailor's knot.

"Yeah," Eldon said, completing the tie. "All done."

She drew back the knife and held it at her side.

"Good," she said. "Now, take this," she handed Eldon a black sock and a roll of electrical tape, which he grabbed with one hand, keeping a firm grip on Cordus' wrists with the other. "Put it in his mouth and tape it if he won't shut up. TAKE HIM TO THE BARN NOW!"

Eldon guided him up from the couch, and started pushing and directing him towards the front door.

"No...what the hell is going on here?" Cordus said, struggling as best he could, kicking out backwards at Eldon, jerking his head around.

"Let's go, boy," Eldon said, guiding him around the half wall that separated the living room from the front foyer.

"Aggghhh, that hurts. What are you doing? You're both so fucked up!"

After the door opened, Cordus, started to yell:

"HELP, HELP!"

Eldon turned Cordus to the right, in the direction of the barn.

The owners of the closest house down past the barn were a New York couple who used the house seasonally, and then only on weekends. They weren't even in town. With the wind blowing steadily from west to east, those were the only neighbors with much of a chance to hear him. And beyond that house in the same direction, there wasn't another house for a good 500 yards. To the left out of the circular gravel driveway, there was nearly a quarter of a mile to the nearest house: old man Walker's place. Across the street was solid woods, and then 100 yards in the direction of old man Walker's lay the head of the Buck Tree Road hiking path. Nobody heard Cordus, though he continued calling out. A rumble of thunder sounded in the distance, and provided further cover for his futile screams.

"HELP, HELP, SOMEBODY PLEASE HELP ME!"

A light sheet of rain was now sweeping across Buck Tree Road, and the eastward wind was gusting harder. They felt the rain, virtually blowing sideways, hitting them from the left. While the boy was yelling "HELP!" again, Eldon shoved the sock right into his mouth, knocked him down to the ground on his back, and then stepped on Cordus' chest to keep him down. He tore off pieces of the black electrical tape, and then reached down and taped the boy's mouth shut.

"Well, that should do it," Eldon said, pulling him up off the leaf-matted, cold grass. "Now let's go."

Their feet swept across the ever-dampening ground, each of them with work boots on, swishing through layers of autumn leaves. The front wooden barn door slid open, along bottom and top metal guides. The two were then in the dark barn; it was narrow, and claustrophobic. It had warped old boards on the sidewalls, laying vertically, a small bell tower at the top, and hay and dirt strewn around the grimy wood floor. An old broken down wheelbarrow sat in a corner.

Abigail, in her black skirt, black blouse and navy blue shawl, was on her way to the barn now. The rain was picking up in intensity and the sideways showers hit her and she felt the cold sting. She had a black canvas bag of goods. Inside were the two knives, more cuts of rope, a flashlight, disinfectant and bandages, and one of the notebooks of incantations from her grandmother. She came in with the flashlight, shining the beam at Eldon and Cordus.

"Lay him down, Eldon, on his back," she said. "That's right... right in the center of the barn."

She handed him additional pieces of rope. Cordus was squirming, and emitting faint grunting noises.

"Eldon," she said. "Tie the ankles. Extend each tie to a hook on the wall. See those hooks?"

Eldon rapidly tied knots around Cordus ankles, using half-hitches again, and stretched the pieces of rope taut, tying them off on metal hooks that were in the warped boards on each side of the narrow barn. A flash of lightning from the growing storm lit up the interior for a second, the white bright visible through the high windows in the barn.

"Yes, Cordus, oh yes," she said. "There's only one solution to the problems that are going on here."

"ahhh....mmmm...!" Cordus grunted.

A boom of thunder blasted outside seven seconds later and a hard rain was pelting the roof of the barn, now leaking through, lightly dripping on to the barn floor in a few spots. Wind was seeping through the old boards in the barn, and the entire structure was creaking.

After the knots were secured – Cordus hands tied behind him, and his legs prone by the additional ropes – Eldon moved to the side wall nearest the house, and stood, watched and listened.

"You, boy, have evil, lustful desires. I, on the other hand, have certain...needs that you fulfill – but I recognize that it is forbidden. My mother would not approve of it. My grandmother would not approve. The mighty and great Hecate is surely frowning on the...things that we do in the bathtub."

Cordus tried to move his head and swung from side to side as he lay prone on the floor. He grunted.

"And you might as well know, boy," she said. "I can tell you now. I am part of a great legacy, Cordus, a long line of powerful – incredibly powerful – women. This line stretches back hundreds of years. I can't let that end. I need a…girl in this family. I don't need a boy anymore." It was now clear to Cordus – if he had any doubts before – that she was completely insane.

"I will make you that girl, Cordus. Yes," she added, dreamily, removing the smaller, serrated-edged knife from the bag. "We can do this. And everything will be fine, then."

Cordus grunted louder. He struggled mightily, but couldn't escape.

"Alright, Eldon, hold his head in place, now."

He stepped to the center of the barn and did as he was told.

"Cordus," she said. "This is what must be done. Eldon, let go of his head for a second, and then undo his pants and pull them down. Then pull his underwear down."

Lightning flashed again. The rain was steady and hard. The boom of thunder followed just three seconds afterwards.

Cordus was wide-eyed, trying to yell – the sounds were more grunts and indecipherable exhortations, louder now. She held the knife by Cordus' neck as Eldon had to struggle to get the pants down, since the boy's legs were angled outward, not lying straight. He had to pull one leg down a little, and then couldn't seem to work the other pants' leg down.

"These pants don't want to…come down," Eldon said, straining.

"You know, I don't give a shit. Rip them off him." She got up and reached in her bag for the big knife. "Or here, take this knife and cut them off."

Eldon took it and made a cut down the middle of the blue jeans, below the zipper. Cordus' eyes bulged. The pants ripped open, and soon, they were down to his knees.

"Yes, that's good," she said. "Then, pull down his underwear."

Eldon was able to rip the crotch while pulling, then he sliced through the elastic waist band with the large carving knife, and then tore the boxers in half. The torn halves fell to the sides of the boy.

"Give me back the knife, Eldon."

He did so.

"You, Cordus, will no longer *be*. I will perform quick surgery here, and you will be well on your way to being…hmmm… Cordelia. Yes, that's it. That will be your name. I will remove that evil member from between your legs. Then we can start you on hormone treatments. I've read about that." She placed the bigger knife – the carving knife – back in the bag.

Cordus eyes were again bulging out of his head. He continued to grunt and struggle.

"I think the paring knife will work for the first cut. Keep a tight hold on him Eldon."

Abby propped the flashlight on the side of the old wheelbarrow, the beacon spreading light across the 'operating' area. She grinned, her eyes widened, and she raised the paring knife, getting ready to cut through his penis at the base of his pelvic area. Slice the whole damn thing right off.

"I'll make a woman of you yet, boy!" she called out in a firm pronouncement.

One more lightning flash, and then a gut-busting boom of thunder. The storm was upon them now at full force. The barn seemed like it might splinter in a raging wind gust, but clearly, like a tough, wiry welterweight, this thin barn had held its ground against many of these storms before.

The adrenaline was cranked up now. This was a matter of survival for Cordus. That was obvious. He *was* Spider Man. With a tremendous burst of strength from his right leg, and a *crack*, the hook on the right wall came flying out of the weathered board. Cordus had one leg free, and he was now kicking wildly.

"Get him tied up again, Eldon, goddamn it!"

As Eldon moved to grab him, Cordus sent his leg straight up and kicked his father right in the balls with his heavy work boot.

"Owwwww," Eldon cried out, just before dropping to the ground in a fetal position.

She had the knife in her right hand, but couldn't move in to do her work. Cordus was kicking out and pulling with his leg strength every way he could, and with great agility and speed, he was repositioning his body for more leverage. Soon the other hook, on the left wall, broke off with a *crack* of weathered wood. He was up, his hands still behind his back, and his mouth socked and taped shut. She ran at him with the knife, but he was able to dodge her. In an absurd dysfunctional family tableau, Eldon was balled up on the ground, Abigail held her knife, not knowing what to do next, and Cordus was up and running, trailing along cords tied to his ankles with hooks dragging along the ends of each tie of rope. He slid the door open, and sprinted out of the barn and back towards the house.

Abigail looked down at Eldon. He moaned. She moved to the front of the barn, peaked out of the door and saw, amid the bright flash from a lightning bolt, that Cordus was going back into the house. The thunder boomed mightily seconds later.

"Get up, damn you," she said. "Stop whining. Get over it. Get the boy!"

"Ohhhhh," Eldon uttered.

"GET THE BOY!"

He tried to rise to his knees, and began to get some mobility back. He started to breathe again, deeply in and out.

"Get up or I'll stick you with this knife," she said, and then put down the paring knife in her canvas bag, and pulled out the carving knife. "Or maybe I'll use this one! Get up now!"

After a few more seconds, Eldon was on his knees, breathing heavily. She showed him the big knife again. He rose to his feet, and pretty much staggered to the front of the barn and out the door.

"Bring him right back here, damnit," she called, as he exited the barn.

Eldon walked out, took a left outside of the barn and walked back towards the house. He was gradually regaining his strength, trying to ignore the crippling pain in his groin. It took him a few minutes, and he had to stop in his tracks a couple of times, kneel down again and wait out the recovery time from a swift kick in the gonads. Rain poured down on him. He then stood up straight again and was moving towards the house. His breathing slowly became steadier as he was about to enter the front door. He walked in, his clothing sopping wet, and took a left turn around the half-wall separating the foyer from the living room. He stopped and stood behind the two, high red-upholstered chairs.

"Cordus," he called out. He waited. He heard nothing. "Come to me, boy. Your mother wants you back in that barn – now!"

Cordus, cold and wet with only a white t-shirt and work boots on, tried to squelch the sound of his breath while he lay crouched, nearly naked, behind the couch that was near the staircase, out of sight. When he had initially sprinted into the house, he went directly for the formica kitchen counter, and with all the strength he could muster, worked the tie of rope that bound his hands together against the sharp edge of the counter, pulling the tie taut, and racing his hands back and forth against the counter side, as fast as he possibly could. With friction from the sharp edge, he was quickly able to start cutting bits of the rope. Once the rope became weaker through little cuts, it was soon easier to continue the process and slice through the rope entirely. Adroitly, he untied the other ropes that had been knotted around his ankles, and left them on the kitchen floor, each with a hook attached at the end. He then ran out of the kitchen, freed of the ropes that had bound him down, went straight for the front foyer, where there sat something he desperately needed; he grabbed it, and went back into the living room.

Eldon walked through the living room, soaking wet, approaching where Cordus was hiding.

"Boy," he said, his voice sounding a bit wary, his face gleaming from the rain. "This is no game. It's time to come out. I'm your father. You do what I say. We've had enough of your insubordination. After all we've done for you, this is what we get in return?"

He was about to step past the couch now. Cordus heard him getting closer, and then sprung up from behind the couch. Gripped tautly in his hands was the big ax his father had used for chopping wood; Cordus had snatched it from where Eldon had left it sitting against the wall in the foyer.

Without as much as a word, Cordus swung it sideways like a baseball bat.

"Nooooooo!" Eldon called out.

The freshly sharpened ax sliced into his left ribcage with a muffled 'crack,' as middle ribs were shattered. Eldon went down in a heap, grabbing his side as a hot surge of pain flooded through him and blood spurted out.

"Aaaaaaaaaaahhhhh," he cried.

A blast of thunder kaboomed, and the rain continued to pound down. Immediately, now that Eldon was down and prone, Cordus worked his way behind his father, positioning for proper leverage. He swung the ax overhand this time, and brought it down square on the right side of Eldon's head. This produced a loud crack, as the ax split the skull. Eldon fell backwards, from a position where he was grabbing his side, to going flat on his back, and his shattered head hit the floor with a "thud."

Blood geysered from the head wound, and splashed onto Cordus. Dappled red drops stained the sidewall of the staircase, and spattered the wood floor and room furniture. More blood was seeping across the floor from the wound in Eldon's side. A free flow of blood spilled out of the mortal head wound, and it was spreading across the floor where Eldon lay. His right foot spasmed and shook in a last reflexive moment before death.

Cordus pulled the ax back and emitted a growl – an animal response to this enormous release of stress he had held back for so long, All the frustration, anger, confusion, unrequited teen lust...and disgust at the sexual abuse he had been subjected to from his own mother. He fully understood now that Eldon wasn't responsible for what had happened to him. It was all mommy's doing. But Eldon couldn't have been spared: no, not now.

He held the ax tight and headed upstairs, slowly climbing each step. After he caught his breath, Cordus entered his room. While his hands were shaking, an inner resolve helped him stay focused. He put the ax down, removed his boots, and then opened an upper drawer in his bureau and took out a pair of white underwear. He opened the lowest drawer and removed another pair of blue jeans. He put them on, and then stood in his room with the lights off, keeping the door open, hiding in the shadows. His breathing was heavy, and a bizarre, incongruous silence – that Cordus knew couldn't last for long – filled the house. The ax head dripped blood, and it was splashed all over his arms, his t-shirt and his face. He didn't care. A strange feeling of power, and a surge of adrenaline, were mixing around within his mind and stomach, co-hosting a ghoulish gala inside of Cordus, along with party guests: nausea and, yes, even guilt. He methodically pulled his boots back on and laced them up.

Abigail waited in the barn. Soon, she sensed that something was amiss. It was that psychic connection with Cordus that she always had. She felt slight sensations, signaling hints about his thoughts. Yes, something had gone wrong. She pulled the disinfectant and the bandages out of the canvas bag, and lay them on the barn floor next to the paring knife. She edged out of the barn, sliding open the door, shut it again, and slowly approached the house. Rain pelted down on her, sometimes from above, then sweeping horizontally, right into her face. Abby carried the large carving knife in her canvas bag along with the book of incantations. Her black skirt, her shawl, and her long grey and blonde curly locks became storm-soaked. She winced, and her craggy, sharp features formed a grimace in the pelting wind and rain.

She entered the house, turned left around the half-wall from the foyer into the living room, and saw a spreading puddle of blood at her feet before her eyes took in the source of the blood: her bludgeoned husband. There was no need to check for a pulse, that was for damn sure.

"YOU LITTLE SHIT!" she yelled out. "YOU UNGRATEFUL SPAWN!"

Cordus stood upstairs, silently, out of sight.

She pulled the carving knife out, with its sleek brown, treated wooden handle. It was in her right hand, and the canvas bag was draped over her left shoulder. She needed the contents of that bag. Holding the knife in front of her, she walked past the staircase and made the blind right turn into the kitchen: no one there.

"I'm coming," she said in a firm tone. "I've got you now, you little piece of shit. You're gonna learn – the hard way, boy." Her voice dropped to just above a whisper. Yet she believed he could still hear her. "No matter what happens, you'll regret this night forever…forever and a day."

The rain was still pounding down outside, falling straighter now, as the wind subsided a bit. Lightning flashed, and then a far-off, fainter thunder boom sounded a full ten seconds later. The storm was moving east.

She started up the stairs. She felt no fear. After all that had happened, what was there to fear now? She rose up the staircase, slowly and steadily. At the top of the staircase, she didn't take the left turn to take a peak in Cordus' room, even though she suspected he might be there. This had gone beyond that stage. That was not where she wanted him now. She turned right, and headed to the turreted room. She walked to the end of the corridor, reached to her right, opened the door, and took out the book of incantations from the canvas bag. She left the bag in the room, left the door open, walked back out into the upstairs hall, and placed the knife at her feet. She held the book now, open in her left hand. And she reached up below her neck, and closed her right palm around the Sibber medallion. Three dark wishes fulfilled for the holder of the medallion. One for each five-pointed star. She had one left. Then it would be over.

He emerged from the room, carrying the blood-stained ax.

"I hate you, Mom," he said, his once-angelic face blood-stained, and looking mean – its innocence lost. "Look what you've done. Just think about…"

"What *I've* done?" she interrupted him, and then laughed an evil cackle. "You're the one who just committed…I guess that's what they call patricide, eh bright boy?"

"He wasn't my father, anymore," Cordus said. "I loved my father, and you turned him into a fucking zombie."

"Yeah, right, Cordus," she said, mockingly. "You know it all, don't you?"

"I wish I did, you bitch. I wish I had known *more* much earlier, that's for sure. Why I ever let you touch me, you filthy slut…"

"How dare you say that to your mother!"

"I'll show you, *Mom*," he said, mocking her with his tone, now. He held the ax up, over his shoulder, and walked towards her. "I'll show you how your little boy has made good, mommy. I'll make you eat this ax!"

He looked up and she caught his gaze. She had *the power*. It wasn't just madness surging through Abigail Merriweather Bailey. No, she was a direct descendant in the Sibber line of women. She had a dark power, as real as the storm that was now blowing by. And she had the Sibber medallion. When she caught his gaze, and their identical blue eyes met, she froze him in his tracks. Slowly, the ax was lowered from above his shoulder, and gradually came down, until the bloody ax head settled on the floor, facing away from Abigail. Gripping the ax handle in both hands, Cordus swallowed, but couldn't move.

"This has gone far enough, boy," she intoned. "It's over. For all of your sins, you will now pay the ultimate price."

He heard it, but it was murky, like he was listening to a muffled speech from far away. With the book in her left hand, she began to feel warmth emanating from the medallion that was gripped in her right. She started her pronouncement:

"Upon your death, Cordus, you will find no rest. For you will return to this cursed soil, every year. You will suffer the sharpest pangs of human misery imaginable – even after your death. For a certain period of time, each year, on this firmament – 100 hours to be exact – you shall return each and every year. Yes, after your death, you are hereby punished to renew your awful existence on this earth every year – and your punishment will continue for eternity."

The medallion was getting much hotter now, as she grasped it in her palm. Her chanting was dark, even and smooth – a monotone somehow both soothing and satanic.

"And, upon my guide, the great earth mother Hecate, I promise that each year your ceaseless pain will grow progressively more unbearable and you will recognize how much you crave the final peace of true death. You will search for that peace, for it will be all you can hope to attain. And you will never find it. Seek as you may in your cursed soul, you will never discover the halcyon calm of final rest."

The medallion was starting to lightly sizzle in her palm now. She looked to the book, to begin the actual incantation.

'Blessed be the dark vision that reigns upon thee, Cordus Bailey. For this wrath is now your destiny, and you will suffer – suffer, like the hundreds of innocent who perished at the hands of the cruel, the fearful and the ignorant, those whose hatred will forever infect this earth. May the wrath of the innocent sufferers forever torment you.'

She once again, for the final time, felt a flash of light rush before her eyes, and those blue eyes gleamed a bright red in a climactic moment. Abigail moaned with pleasure this time, as she could feel the burning heat of the medallion on her palm. She cried out lightly – it was like an evil orgasm – as a wisp of smoke rose before her eyes. Once again, she had to work the seared medallion off of her palm, as it stuck to the branded flesh. The medallion felt hot and pleasurable as it settled against the base of her neck.

Now there were three five-pointed stars branded on to her right hand. She lovingly lifted the Sibber medallion over her neck, and let her eyes float away from his. Slowly, he started regaining some of his senses, as her eyes were no longer locked upon his. Abigail went into the turreted room, and placed the book of incantations in its spot on the shelf. She put the medallion in the jewelry box her grandmother had given her. Then she went back into the hallway.

Cordus was nearly fully charged up again, averting her eyes, now free of her powerful psychological hold over him. She reached down, and picked up the carving knife. She walked towards him.

"It's not going to go according to plan, eh, Cordus?" she said, trying to catch his eye, but to no avail. He looked to the side, he looked at the top of her head, anywhere but in her eyes.

The ax was now rising. Abigail ran towards him with the knife, trying to stab at his shoulder.

She cried out: "I'LL KILL YOU!"

He timed his first swing perfectly to intercept her onrushing body; it was at a three-quarters angle, a chop that swung half-vertical/half sideways. He connected flush into her left arm, and she cried out, "Aaaaaahhhhhh!" She was now helpless to finish her stabbing motion, as the knife fell from her right hand when her right arm grabbed for the gash in her now-crippled left arm. Cordus had no second thoughts, and had enough adrenaline surging through him that he was a killing machine. She fell to her knees, her head was down. It would be easy; like pounding a stake into the ground with a sledgehammer.

"Remember boy," she said in a strained voice, and then she groaned: "Ohhhhh...," she looked up at him, her voice weakening. "It's not over for you. No. You will wish to eternity that it could end, but Hecate will see to it that..."

"Shut up, you crazy bitch!," he yelled, as he brought the ax down into her forehead.

It "thwacked" into her cranium. He pulled the ax back. She fell and she was just lifeless meat when she thudded. The blood spurted out of the head wound, and from the arm gash. It was soon trick, trick, trickling down from the upper corridor, dripping down to the first floor – only a few feet away from where Eldon lay.

Cordus left the ax next to her corpse and, in a dazed state, walked to the bathroom to wash himself off. His hands shook from both adrenaline and nervousness, and his face and clothes were splattered by blood. He turned the faucets on in the sink to start scrubbing his hands and washing his face. He eyed himself in the mirror, instantly realizing that he was a killer – never to be just a simple boy with a real future to look forward to. He continued to splash warm water onto his face to remove the blood. The white sink was dappled with red, and he kept wiping at spots on the sink to send the blood down the drain.

Cordus felt drained and utterly confused about what he would do next. He had to leave the house. He slowly descended the stairs, drinking in the still scene of death around him. At the base of the stairs he took a left into the living room to head out the door. On his way out, he glanced to his left and saw blood drops hitting the floorboards. He looked up and saw blood dripping over the edge of the floor from the upstairs corridor, flowing from his mother's lifeless form. He had to step over Eldon's corpse.

He left the carnage behind, and pulled open the front door. The rain had finally stopped, yet there were still gusts of wind blowing. He proceeded out into the chilly night, and was awakened from the daze he was in by the stiff, cold breeze. He staggered down the front landing steps, still wearing his blood-stained jeans and t-shirt. Something drew him to the barn, and he made a turn to his right to approach it.

He slid open the door of the old barn, tried to catch his breath, and just sat in the darkness, right in the center of the barn, among hay strands and wood shavings and dirt. On the floor, like a twisted still-life from hell, sat a bottle of disinfectant, a package of bandages, and the paring knife. Cordus was cold. The wind was howling through the openings in the slats of the weathered barn's façade, and he could swear there was a voice in it calling to him in whispers:

"Cordus..." it said. The voice was strained and raspy, and unmistakably female. "Cordus...Cordus..."

Cordus put his fingers on both temples, and pressed and massaged his head. Maybe he could make the voice go away.

"...Cordus..."

His whole body was shaking and he felt cold and so very alone. There had been nothing that he wanted more in that moment of madness in the house than just...getting rid of his mother and his damn zombie father. He had that now – but somehow he felt no better than he did before. He only felt pain. The pain of being unloved; the pain of despising those around him, and now the horrible, pressing pangs of guilt for the awful events that he had wrought.

"....Cordus!..." the voice became louder, "CORDUS!"

He grabbed the golden hair on the sides of his heads and actually pulled it as he let out an anguished cry of fear and confusion: "Aaaagghhhh!"

Just at that moment a plume of fire, like a lightning strike from the depths of the netherworld, jutted up through the wooden floor of the barn. The flame burned hot and true, just to the left of where Cordus sat. The old floor planks fueled the blaze and a searing heat enveloped the left side of Cordus' face. "Noooooooo!" he screamed in pain. The flesh on his left arm began to singe and bubble as the heat intensified. He reached up and felt the melting epidermis of his cheek. The blaze initially seemed to remain in a small area of the barn, just within a slight radius of where Cordus sat. The left side of his torso, arm and face were sizzling as the seemingly mindful flames directed their destructive plumes.

The fire intensified and acrid smoke filled Cordus' nostrils and lungs. He let out painful coughs and gags, and clung to his throat with desperate hands. He was soon unable to scream – his very life burning away – and he now suffered in silence. His mouth was open but no sound emerged. The poison of the deadly smoke soon mercifully choked the life out of the boy.

Back up Buck Tree Road to the west, a few hundred yards away, old man Walker, a skinny retired railroad engineer, wearing a navy pea coat over jean overalls, and a weathered grey cloth billed cap with ear flaps, was taking his black Labrador for a stroll. He heard a blood-curdling scream in the distance, smashing through the peace of the windy, but now rainless evening. Walker had waited for the rain to subside before taking Rudy the black lab out. After the one scream, there was silence again. He walked beyond the paved section of the street, onto the dirt road, over a rise in the road, and saw the flames lapping at the barn as he approached the Bailey house. A barn burning after that rain storm? It seemed strange. But, there it was.

The wind gusts that continued that night helped the intensifying flames inside the barn to ultimately bake out the wetness of the exterior of the barn, and even after the storm, the barn became engulfed in flames. Walker knew this home as that of the Caulfields, who had lived there for 16 years, prior to moving out to California. He knew nothing about the new residents who had moved in just a couple of months before. He witnessed the hungry flames intensifying as they devoured the exterior of the barn. Within seconds, he heard burning boards falling and crashing, succumbing to the destructive force of the fire. He watched the dramatic night-time blaze for another minute, and then shuffled back to his house as quickly as his old, spindly legs could take him, so he could put in a call to the fire department.

While the blaze would soon overtake the wooden barn structure and bring it crashing down in an ashen heap, the corpse of Cordus Bailey was not to be found within. His form, only partially burnt, had been whisked away to a place of darkness and unrest, deep down in the netherworld. The power of the medallion would ring true and the incantation would prove to be fact. The hex that Abigail placed on the son who betrayed her would come to fruition.

With great fanfare, the red fire truck came speeding down the road, but it was soon obvious to the five men who rode inside that while they could hose down what remained of the blaze, there was little that could be salvaged in this: what was once a barn would ultimately be nothing more than a smoldering ashen heap. Flames rose in the chilly night, and small side blazes continued to burn, as three of the firemen unwrapped the hoses, preparing to douse the fire.

One of the other firemen approached the main house, knocked twice, then opened the unlocked door. As he entered the foyer and peaked around the corner into the living room, he was greeted with the sight of the face up, gashed open head of Eldon Bailey, and a vast pool of blood covering the floor. He failed to notice the dripping of additional blood from the upstairs landing, continuing in a steady metronome of crimson drops hitting the floor below.

"Heyyyy!" he called out, spilling back out of the front door and waving his fellow firemen over. "Come in here. We got a crime scene...a dead guy!"

The assistant chief of the department, the highest-ranking fireman on site, immediately put a call in to have police back-up sent over to investigate the scene. When the Stockbridge police made a more thorough examination of the residence, they found the bloodied corpse of Abigail. The wound slicing through her arm, in addition to the one that crushed her skull, indicated that two separate strikes were made to ring the death knell, just as two hacks chopped Eldon's body downstairs.

Meanwhile, a tremendous plume of smoke had risen from the fire scene when it was first doused by the hoses by the firemen. Soon the flames died down and there was only smoke and charred cinders that remained of the barn. The firemen had nothing more to do here, but kept running the hoses to make themselves feel useful. When some of the smoke subsided, and all of the flames had died, two of the firemen donned heavy white, cloth gloves, and walked through the remains of the barn. They found only ashes; there was nothing they saw that resembled man nor beast. All that turned up was the blade of a paring knife – not old, not rusted out – set on the floor of the former barn, and nearby that, a melted plastic trace of the bottle that contained the disinfectant.

The following day, two detectives from Great Barrington were dispatched to help the Stockbridge police comb through the house and glean what they could from the gruesome scene. The detectives found an ax, discarded near the woman's body upstairs. There were plenty of bloody fingerprints on the ax handle.

The police soon discovered, through a phone call to O'Neil Realty, where Eldon had worked as a broker, that the Bailey family consisted of three members. Having apparently disappeared from the scene of the crime, the boy, Cordus, was the most viable suspect at this point. He was nowhere to be found, and there had been no traces of his body in the house nor the barn. Once the detectives could finally trace down

Cordus Bailey's fingerprints, a match would be made with those bloody prints on the ax handle and in Cordus' bedroom.

Over at the barn, fire investigators found no indication of incendiary liquids (gasoline, turpentine) being used to start the blaze, nor any other common device used by an arsonist. It seemed possible – though not definite – that the fire was started by someone holding a match or lighter to hay that had perhaps had been strewn about the floor of the barn. The old boards inside the barn were quite flammable and the fire would surely intensify rapidly. Upon further inspection, the police detectives still found no trace of a body in the barn fire. They looked for two days, but could find no trace of a human form; there were neither bones nor teeth to be found in that heap of ashes.

The end result: an all-points-bulletin was send out for a young man by the name of Cordus Bailey, now wanted as the prime suspect in two murder cases. Even the normally staid *Berkshire Eagle* couldn't resist running a sensational, front-page headline in its October 16, 2007 edition (two days after the murders; the October 15 paper was long-closed and sent to the printers when the killings took place):

Couple in Stockbridge Ax Murdered; Suspected Son is On the Loose

STOCKBRIDGE – In a horrific double slaying, Eldon and Abigail Bailey of Buck Tree Road were both slaughtered by the same ax in their home Tuesday night. Police know that the new village residents had a 14 year-old son, Cordus, who is now missing. All signs in this early stage of the investigation are pointing to Cordus Bailey as the possible killer – or at least the most viable suspect.

"It's too early to know exactly who committed this terrible crime," said Stockbridge Police Chief Thomas Eisler, in a prepared statement. "The Baileys had only moved into town a few months ago. Not many people knew them. The boy's father, Eldon Bailey, worked at O'Neil Realty in Great Barrington. No one in town that we've talked to ever reported even seeing the wife or the son. We are continuing our investigation, and are classifying these killings as unsolved at the current time. We are now searching for Cordus Bailey."

One area resident claims to have witnessed the fire that same night that burned down a barn on the property, adjacent to the Bailey house.

"I heard a loud scream while I was out walking my dog," said Jed Walker, 74, of Buck Tree Road. "We went on down the road, and I saw the barn burning away. It was a strange sight after the heavy rain storm we had gotten earlier that night. I just turned around and scurried back home to call in the fire."

A member of the local fire department, investigating the nearby blaze, first found the bodies in the Bailey home, sources say.

There was no record of Cordus Bailey being registered at Monument Mountain High School. This much is known: the family moved to Stockbridge from Bangor, Maine, in August of this year. At that time, Eldon Bailey began working as a real estate broker in Great Barrington.

"Eldon was a hard-worker, from the day he started here," said Mary O'Neil, president of O'Neil Realty. "He had just sold his own firm in Bangor, and when he started here, it was clear he was a true professional. His nose was to the grindstone right from day one. It's a tragic loss, and our hearts go out to the surviving family members – wherever they may be."

From sources in Bangor, the police were able to receive a preliminary description of Cordus Bailey. The police are warning area residents to look out for a 14 year-old, Caucasian boy, strongly built, with shoulder-length, curly blonde hair. If any sightings are made of a stranger in the area fitting this description, police ask that you call your local department immediately.

※ ※ ※

The Berkshire County coroner's report contained little out of the ordinary – considering the brutal manner in which the lives of Abigail and Eldon were brought to an end. The coroner did make note, however, of the three five-pointed stars that appeared to have been branded onto Abigail Bailey's right palm.

No trace of Cordus Bailey, either dead or alive, was ever found, and the crimes remained unsolved.

CHAPTER THIRTEEN

OCTOBER 17TH, 2010, 11:14 P.M.

N ow well into the anointed period of time he must spend on this cursed earth that had once been his home, Cordus, a creature most comfortable in the slice of netherworld where he most often resides, was being subjected to stinging bolts coursing through his powerful form. These painful strikes were the direct result of the curse his mother had placed on him. During these periods on Earth, he was punished by a stream of raw, unadulterated human emotions: feelings that took on tangible form. The entire process was a coldly, sadistic exercise that brought about horrible suffering in the creature. Bolts of actual human anguish would pierce his brain. The most extreme forms of human loneliness and unrequited love took form and stabbed at his heart repeatedly. Feelings of complete rejection and utter isolation took the form of small, sharp, stinging blades, jabbing him repeatedly across his legs and arms.

The creature's misshapen mouth opened and closed continuously and he quietly emitted groans of pain and anguish. He flexed his long-nailed fingers, desperately trying to escape from the stabbing punishment that wouldn't cease. His entire body pulsed in a dance of the most emotionally and physically crippling sensations imaginable.

He continued to consume – whatever and whenever he could – since a searing, unending hunger was one of the human foibles to which he was subjected. Whatever crawled by his lair, be it mouse, squirrel, beetle or worm, he would spear it with sharpened talons and place it in his pulsing maw, ravenously crunching and swallowing.

Since he was now in the third year of his sentence, he had gained a bit of familiarity with the cycle of pain he must experience. This was now the third time his cursed form had been destined to 'revisit' the earth, according to the hex his mother had placed on him. During each journey to the land of the living he would suffer for precisely 100 hours. At the end of that period, his form would return to its natural home, a space within the netherworld reserved for certain cursed, heinous beings, a location that formed a neat wedge halfway between the living and the dead. While there, the creature was devoid of feeling and there existed an absence of any sort of experience at all. That 'nothingness,' however, was what felt most comfortable for the reptilian, charred form that was once Cordus Bailey. And the creature knew enough to recognize that anything was better than what he was now experiencing. He was now in the 71st hour of his suffering.

And then he heard it. It sounded very close. First, there was a door being shut, and then there were footsteps. Someone was in the house, the house that he knew was where he had last resided while among the living. He tried to ignore the painful emotional attacks he was subjected to, the jabs that shot throughout his body and mind, and suddenly – amazingly -- he was able. For curiosity was another human emotion, and he could immerse himself in that feeling, and he realized it didn't bring about pain. It soothed his brain in a strange way. It was a healthy expression of emotion, and it was being fed by the sounds that came to him from inside the house.

He heard voices, low and laughing. Then he heard one voice that had a higher pitch to it. He heard that voice again, speaking in an extended dialogue. Then he heard chair legs scraping against the floor. There it was again...that higher-pitched voice, and his mind conjured new thoughts; different than anything he could previously recall. For this voice reminded him of Jenny, an image that his mind had not comprehended since his initial departure from this world, *and all of a sudden he couldn't stop thinking about her. Pangs of desire and the pure lustful feelings of a teenage boy filled his mind and body with a soothing balm of pleasure. He heard that voice again and wanted to be there, wanted to be in the house, to be close to the dulcet tone of that voice...*

OCTOBER 17TH, 2010, 9:58 P.M.: LENOX, MASS.

"I don't believe you, Dennis," Charlie Merrill said, his unkempt, brown hair running down below his neck in a mullet, topped off by a yellow and black John Deere baseball cap. He was a tad under six feet, lanky and athletic. He had a thick, but neatly cut mustache that turned down past his lips – Fu-Manchu style – and a seemingly ever-present grin. "You're gonna call up Elliot tomorrow morning and just say, 'Hey Elliot, I quit.' You're not gonna do it. I think it's the booze talking."

"No, Charlie, you got me wrong, man," Dennis Riley said, shaking his crewcut head back and forth. He had a wide, angled face, broad shoulders and was short and squat. "I'm telling you, Elliot is an asshole. He was a different guy when we knew him back in school. He's just a prick...so uptight about every little detail."

"The guy's got a business to run," Charlie said, finishing the last of his drink, and clunking the glass down on the table. "I guess that can make a guy a lot more serious. Anyway, what the hell are you gonna do after you quit?"

"No big deal man," Dennis said, waving his hand, dismissively. "Lots of jobs out there, Charlie."

They were sitting at a small round table at the rustic Five Chairs bar and restaurant on Route 7 in Lenox, ten miles up the road from Stockbridge.

Charlie looked over at an approaching woman with two filled glasses in her hands, each containing a leaning thin red straw. Charlie gestured over at her, nodding his head her way, smiled at Dennis, and balled his right hand into a fist to give a 'yeah, alright' pumping gesture. "Now is this a great girlfriend or what, Dennis?" he asked rhetorically. "She even buys a round when it's her turn."

"I agree I'm one hell of a catch, Charlie," Terry said as she clunked the cocktail glasses down on the table. " But the least you could do is go grab the third drink off of the bar." Terry was a firmly built woman, with a Teutonic fullness that covered her frame from her thick thighs and behind to her full, jutting breasts and even a slight muscular tautness in her shoulders. She had been a competitive swimmer in high school and still had an athlete's build – plus about ten pounds. She had pretty, yet weather-hardened, features. Her long, straight auburn hair flowed down to the small of her back.

"I can do that," he said, pushing his seat back and walking over to the bar to get the other glass.

"Thanks, Terry," Dennis said, as he took hold of one of the scotch and sodas she had brought over to the table. Charlie came back with Terry's vodka and cranberry.

They were all in their mid-thirties, had gone to school together at Lenox High School, and had remained close ever since. Charlie and Dennis were best friends who tended to feud now and then, both being a bit hot-headed. Generally speaking, however, Charlie had assumed the role of 'leader' and Dennis more the 'follower' in their friendship. Terry and Charlie had been dating for just over two years now, each of them having broken off long relationships at around the same time – no, perhaps it hadn't been coincidental – and began seeing each other.

Dennis fit into the picture quite comfortably. He was like a brother to Charlie, and he felt like he and Terry had a brother/sister closeness. Dennis and Terry had, in fact, dated briefly, nearly five years earlier. Both of them moved on from that seamlessly, and remained friends. Now, the three of them spent a lot of time together and truly seemed to defy the old "three's a crowd" adage.

"Now our man Dennis here says he's gonna quit working for Elliot. Whaddya think of that, babe?"

"Dennis is an adult," she answered. "He can figure out the right thing to do for himself."

"Yeah," Charlie said, "but he better not come over grubbing dinner off of us after he's out of work for a couple of weeks."

"Oh, I get it," Dennis said, nodding his head with a knowing look on his face. "So, now I gotta be self-conscious about dropping by your house? Some buddy you are."

"Don't listen to Charlie," Terry said, giving her boyfriend a punch in the arm. "You're being a jerk, Charlie. Come over anytime you like, Dennis."

"You're gonna regret you said *that*," Charlie said, the tone of his voice lifting higher and the last syllable hanging in the air.

"Hey man," Dennis said, "don't be such a dick."

"C'mon buddy, you know I'm just kiddin' around."

Dennis rolled his eyes, gave his head a derisive shake, and drained a deep sip off of the scotch and soda. He wasn't sure if Charlie was totally kidding. Maybe Charlie was actually worried that Dennis might take advantage of him and Terry, and scam too many dinners. Dennis was actually a bit offended. Charlie knew it was time to change the subject.

"O.K., how about what we were talking about earlier," he said. "You know, like, let's head down South County."

"You're back on *that* again, Charlie?" Terry asked.

"You really want to do it, huh Charlie?" Dennis said. "You want to go over to the Bailey house. Shit, man, everyone says that place is haunted."

"You know what happened there, Charlie," Terry said. "Someone went nuts-o and took an ax to the husband and wife."

"Yeah, everyone says it was the crazy son." Dennis added.

"Yes," Charlie nodded in a conspiratorial voice, his mischievous grin widening, "and the son was never found. So everyone is sure the place is haunted. By who, though? The mother and father? The son still living there? Ha! How scary could that be? C'mon, finish those up, I'll go get us another round."

Charlie walked to the bar to buy three more drinks. Everyone was feeling pretty tight at this point. Particularly Terry whose head was bobbing to the right...and then to the left just a bit.

"You know," Dennis said, "my little brother and two of his friends went into the Bailey house this past summer, in August."

"They did?" Terry asked, sounding surprised.

"They said it was just full of old furniture and books, with cob webs growing over everything. Hell, nothing happened to them. They sure didn't see any ghosts."

Charlie made a path to and from the bar three times. He brought over two scotch and sodas, and then he grabbed the vodka and cranberry. On his third trip he brought over three shot glasses of Mezcal tequila, along with three slices of lime.

"Alright," he said, rubbing his hands together enthusiastically. "Let's have a party and get the hell out of here. We're going to see that house, once and for all."

"You want to mix, Charlie?" Terry asked, already slightly woozy. "I don't want a shot of *that* to chase down vodka."

"Alright...alright," Charlie acquiesced. "Me and Dennis will split the third shot. Don't sweat it."

After five more minutes of sipping and slugging, and now emboldened by a sturdy alcohol glaze, the three friends piled into Charlie's forest green Subaru, pulled out of the Five Chairs parking lot, and chugged south down Route 7.

❊　　❊　　❊

Oak Alderson was tapping keys on his computer at his Pittsfield home, and then closed a file and again started looking at the papers spread out on his desk. Tonight he had brought home the binder he kept at work containing information related to the Sibber medallion, and he was reviewing all the material carefully. It wasn't the first time he connected the dots in this case – and he wasn't alone. He shared his concerns with friends and some county officials, but nobody knew exactly what to do.

The slaughter at the Bailey house on Buck Tree Road occurred October 14, 2007. Cordus Bailey, the #1 suspect, never turned up. Following those murders, major law enforcement agencies across the country, including the F.B.I. – and even

Interpol – had been notified to look out for the suspected teen killer.

Alex Corrigan and Jeremy Stiles were killed in front of the house on Buck Tree Road on October 16, 2008. No killer was ever found. It was attributed to a crazed black bear. While he thought it was possible that a bear had been responsible, Oak had an inkling that it seemed unlikely right from the start. Following those deaths, Oak was asked by his boss – on the down low – to retrieve the Sibber medallion. It was now stored away in a safe deposit box in the Lee Savings Bank. Oak thought back, realizing how brazen it was, and downright wrong, that he circumvented proper procedure by walking in after nightfall to pilfer the medallion. Now he realized that Cordus' mother, the murder victim Abigail Bailey, was a Sibber descendent and must have had that medallion.

Steve Halberstram and Jody Greenberg, those two kids who had been at a party on Cherry Hill Road in Stockbridge, were the next victims. Mauled to death by another phantom, ill-tempered black bear that was never spotted. Those killings took place on the Buck Tree Road hiking trail on October 15, 2009. That was about a half-mile away from the house on Buck Tree Road.

October 14th, October 15th, October 16th...

What the hell? Oak thought. Was this the work of some kind of serial killer obsessed with the Sibber medallion, motivated to kill on – or around – a certain date? How could that be possible? Should he again contact the FBI? If he had just one solid lead to hang his hat on, maybe he'd start making more phone calls. But he had nothing. No survivors. No witnesses. No suspects (aside from Cordus, who had seemingly disappeared). No solid clues.

In the past few nights, Oak had even made trips south to Stockbridge, on to Buck Tree Road, and parked his Ford near the house on the nights of October 14th, 15th *and* 16th. Even earlier tonight – right after work – he again went out of his way and drove by the house to take a look. Each night he sat in his car for at least an hour, watching and waiting, hoping he might get a lead or see someone or something suspicious. He hadn't seen or heard a thing. Just a slight old man walking his black Lab one night – they chatted briefly. What the hell else could he do?

He had to cut it off somewhere. He couldn't get obsessive about this, when there were absolutely no solid leads, and no apparent suspects in the picture. The only links were the dates, the medallion and Buck Tree Road. He couldn't leave the house tonight again anyway. It was Claudia's night out "with the girls" and they were taking in a movie and catching a drink afterwards. Oak was taking care of the kids, who were now in bed. Oak tapped his pen against the desk, shook his head and looked back at his computer screen. He e-mailed Peter Earnhardt and let him know that he had toured the area again tonight, and had neither seen nor heard anything of note. Then he called Stockbridge P.D. and spoke with the officer on duty, asking him to patrol the road.

"I would if I could Oak," Officer Alan Gaines told him. "You know how it is. I'm the only one on here tonight and I'm holding down the fort."

"All right, Alan," Oak said, with resignation. "Have a good night, OK?"

"Yup," Gaines said. "Same to you."

Oak hung up the phone, and reviewed his binder of clippings and copies with a feeling of frustration – he couldn't seem to make a dent in cracking the deeper, darker secrets behind the strange events on Buck Tree Road.

※　　　※　　　※

The radio was playing a bimbo "rock" song – damn, who was it, Britney, Paris, Lindsay, Ashley, Jessica? Hard to tell.

Charlie guided the Subaru through the quiet downtown of Stockbridge, lights gleaming in the lobby of the town's main attraction, the sprawling Red Lion Inn. He took a left turn at the corner, around the old hotel, and continued south on Route 7. Three miles south of town, he took a right turn and headed off onto smaller roads, finally arriving at the entrance to Buck

Tree Road, just east of the town of Housatonic. The radio was now playing some gangsta rap lite, and Charlie turned it off.

"I don't like this, Charlie," Terry said from the passenger seat. "Let's go back north; let's go back to the bar."

Dennis sat quietly in the back seat, torn between trepidation and curiosity. He had been following his friend Charlie's lead for years, and doing that made him more comfortable than anything else. About a quarter of a mile past a small, cheery A-frame with one light on in front and scattered lights on within the house, the circular driveway in front of the Bailey house came into view on the right. Terry looked out the front passenger side window and her eye was drawn to the dark, striking turreted room, rising up, silhouetted against the starry sky.

"That place is kind of scary looking at night, Charlie," Dennis said, peaking out the back seat window. "Why don't we go in during the day some time?"

"And take all the fun out of it?" Charlie said, turning the steering wheel to the right to pull into the gravel driveway. "Hell, you got to go into a haunted house at night."

"We don't *have* to do anything, baby," Terry said, rubbing her hand along his thigh, now feeling truly frightened. "Let's go home now. We've seen the house, let's just turn around. You know, 'been there, done that,' " she said with a slight laugh that got caught in her throat.

Charlie turned the ignition to the off position, grabbed a steel-handled flashlight out of the glove compartment, and pulled open the driver side door. "C'mon you wimps," he said, ignoring any effort at debate. He flashed his trademark grin, and made it particularly toothy, as he said, in a mock Boris Karloff inflection: "Let's go meet the Bailey family."

When Charlie sprayed the flashlight beacon across the house's facade, they could see that window panes were smashed, and paint was peeling. The whole place looked so run down and ill-maintained. Local kids had popped the lock off the front door. Charlie pulled the door open slowly, it squeaked on its hinges, and the three of them strolled in. They moved around the half-wall, into the corridor and skulked into the living room. Terry, last of the three, was now standing in the exact spot where Cordus had split open his father's skull.

"See," Charlie said, "there's nothing here. It's just this ratty old furniture, that's all." He shined the flashlight beam, and ran his hands through cob webs and brushed off a thick layer of dust from an armrest on one of the tall, red upholstered chairs.

"God," Terry said. "I think it's awful."

Dennis clicked on light switches along the entrance wall in the living room, and one bulb in an overhead light, covered by a smoked glass, half egg shell light fixture, actually came on. Dennis strolled through the living room, past the base of the staircase, and into the kitchen and dining nook where Cordus' mother had home-schooled him. The kitchen counters were covered in dust. As he approached the refrigerator and peaked around it, a thick web brushed his face and he brought his hands up, frantically pushing the web away. It simply ended up wrapped around his fingers.

"C'mon, let's look upstairs," Charlie said.

"Why, Charlie?" Terry asked. "What's wrong with you? I mean, we've come in here with you; we did what you wanted. Now we can go home, right?"

From his subterranean perch, beneath the floor boards, Cordus heard that voice that spoke in a higher pitch. That was what conjured up recollections of Jenny, and created positive vibes, good feelings of pleasant emotions soothing his weary body and soul. His pain was buffeted by healthy human curiosity; recollections of pleasant times – the carnal lust of a teenage boy.

"I'm going upstairs," Charlie said, ignoring her, perched on the landing. "What about you, Dennis?"

"This just makes no sense, Charlie," Terry said. She reached out for him and held his arm, and tried to give him a seductive look, and she whispered: "C'mon, baby, we have better things we could be doing at home."

He shook off her arm.

"That's for later, Terry. I heard there's weird shit up here." He made his way slowly up the steps. Dennis was confused and curious, and stood in the middle of the living room.

Terry stood back a few steps from the landing. "Be careful, Charlie..."

Cordus was moving, and getting excited by that voice. He was out of his lair and approaching the front stoop of the house.

"...you don't know what's up there."

Cordus long-nailed hand reached for the front door and pulled it open. He took two steps inside and heard that lovely voice again.

"Don't open those closed doors up there, Charlie," she called, looking up at Charlie walking along the corridor, headed towards the turreted room.

Cordus stepped around the landing, looked to his left, and saw a long-flowing head of silky auburn hair. He was right. It *was* Jenny; it had to be. Dennis had made his way towards the kitchen, and then looked back towards the front door.

"Holy shit!" he yelled. "What the fuck is that?"

That first yell created confusion and fear within Cordus, and the spears of pain began shooting through him. Dennis beheld the massive creature that was as big and wide as an NFL offensive lineman – but a hell of a lot uglier. The flesh on one side of its form was crimson, reptilian, and scaly. On the other side, there was awful pinkish-white scarring and malformed features. The mouth went in different directions: straight on one side, horrendously downturned on the other; it opened and closed in a horrific display, the jaw shifting from side to side as much as it did up and down. One lifeless eye was covered in scarred flesh, while the other flashed at him and opened extremely wide to take in the scene. Its clothes were rags, strips of clothing: the remains of a pair of blue jeans that gave scant covering to his legs, one scaled, one burnt. The mottled and dirty strips of what was once a white t-shirt fell about his form in strung together pieces.

"AAAHHHH!" Terry screamed at ear-piercing volume when she turned to see the beast.

Cordus felt shooting arrows of pain searing through his chest cavity, as confusion and fear racked his brain. He had to hold Jenny; he needed her to comfort him. He crossed the room and his eight-inch nails, caked with dried blood and dirt, reached out to stroke her hair. Charlie sprinted down the upper foyer and took the stairs down three at a time. He took a flying leap on top of the beast, and anger surged within Cordus. Charlie punched the thing with all his might, landing a powerful right on the side of its head. It had little effect. Cordus reached back and scratched at Charlie, who screamed in anguish, "Yaaaahhh!" as Cordus' nails dug inch deep gashes into Charlie's back and shoulder.

Terry was screaming wildly and Dennis – in a state of shock – was backing away into the kitchen. Cordus shoved Charlie's body against the bannister along the staircase, sending surges of pain into Charlie's lower back upon impact. The body fell with a thud and Cordus picked up Charlie – his nails digging in – and flung him headfirst against the far wall at the rear of the house. There was a loud *clunk* and an audible *crack* as Charlie's neck snapped upon crashing into the hardwall. His body – now limp and flimsy like a scarecrow – fell in a heap and lay still, bloodied and broken.

Cordus turned to Terry – who he knew to be Jenny, she *had* to be Jenny – and held his arms out to hug her. She cowered in fear, emitting wordless whimpers of terror. As he felt her soft hair, she let out a shriek, and it caused such pain within Cordus that his right hand slipped down and scratched a gash across her left eye and her upper cheek and disgorged part of her nose, leaving it hanging off of her face. Blood spurted out and she was screaming again.

Dennis came out of the kitchen and made an effort to grab the beast, but Cordus simply kicked backwards and sent Dennis sprawling across the living room, knocking over the red upholstered chair, the one upon which Eldon used to sit night after night. Dennis' head slammed against the floor. He reached back to feel the wound, and when he looked at his hand, saw that it was smeared with his own blood.

In a wild rage of lust, confusion, pain and madness, Cordus scratched at Terry's chest. His nails shredded her clothes, cut deep gashes into her shoulder, and actually sliced through her left breast. The breast was now hanging off of her body, attached by shreds of flesh. She was losing blood rapidly, passed out and close to death. In a state of horror and confusion, Cordus picked up Terry's bleeding body – part of the nose hanging off of the face, half a severed breast swinging from the upper torso. He held 'Jenny,' trying to stroke her face, but all he did was create more scratches and gashes.

Dennis was bleeding from the back of his head. He saw that Terry's body was being torn apart and slashed and gashed to a bloody pulp. He backed away, towards the front door. He was feeling woozy, and he saw that there was nothing for him to do now. He ran out of the house. Staggering out, he felt dizzy. He wandered to the car, and saw that Charlie had left the keys in the ignition. He didn't trust himself to drive, though. He felt that he might black out. Dennis walked as rapidly as he could up Buck Tree Road, crying and breathing in fits and starts.

Cordus lay the tattered body of Jenny on the couch. The pulse was gone. Terry's one eye that wasn't gashed and bloodied was opened wide in a final stare of horrific fear. Cordus stroked the brown hair again, beginning to feel pleasant surges within him, feelings of desire and what was as close as the creature would recognize as love.

Dennis regained strength and started to run as fast as he could until he reached the A-frame house. He knocked but got no answer. He kept frantically knocking, with an old iron knocker that sounded off a *clunk, clunk, clunk*. After another minute and another three *clunks*, old man Walker said angrily, "Who's there? Damnit, it's nearly midnight."

"Please," Dennis yelled. "Open up. I need help. There's been a terrible attack."

"What?" Walker said. "What's going on out there? You trying to trick me, so's you can rob my place?"

"Please," Dennis moaned. "Just open up the door and look at me. I'm bleeding from a gash on my head."

Walker peaked out and saw that Dennis looked pale as a sheet, and he saw his hand red with blood.

"Christ," Walker said. "What the hell happened to you?"

"Call the police," Dennis said.

"Let me get you a wet towel, so we can try to clean you up a bit. Come on in."

"Call the police, please. It's at the Bailey place."

"*The Bailey place?*" he asked incredulously. "You didn't go there on purpose, now, did you?"

"My friend wanted to go. He's in there. Charlie's in there. So is Terry."

Walker hung his head low and shook it back and forth. "You're messing with *evil* there. There's some things that man has to know well enough to leave alone. That Bailey place," he shook his head again, and now fear was evident in his leathery, thin face, "that's a house the devil himself would steer clear of."

"Please," Dennis pleaded. "The police. Now."

Walker grabbed a cotton towel from a closet, and ran water on it and handed it to Dennis, who placed it over the gash on his head. "You sit down here," he told Dennis, directing him to a hard-backed chair. Then Walker called the Stockbridge Police Department.

"Yeah, this is Jed Walker, over on Buck Tree Road."

He listened to the reply.

"Yeah, that's right. That's me. I got a young man here in my house says there's trouble at the Bailey house. Big trouble down there."

He listened again.

"I *know*," Walker said. "I told this guy he and his friends made a big mistake going down that way."

He listened, and nodded his head.

"I hear ya. I'm not going near the place. But someone's got to take a look-see down there, and I think it's your job, being as you fellas are paid to police this town."

He listened once more.

"Yeah, will do," Walker said. Before hanging up, he added: "Whatever you do...just be careful down there."

CHAPTER FIFTEEN

Police Chief Morris Tewksbury had just finished up the lunch that he had purchased at Shanahan's, the only deli in Stockbridge: a chicken salad sandwich on whole wheat and a bag of cholesterol-free potato chips. He had been advised by Dr. Singh during his most recent check-up to lay off the cheeseburgers. The chief was 52 years old, six feet two inches tall and tipped the scales at 270, and Dr. Singh warned him that he needed a seriously revised lifestyle if he wanted to make retirement as a reasonably healthy man. An empty unfolded sheet of waxed paper sat on his desk containing a few strings of lettuce that had fallen from the sandwich.

Tewksbury was relatively new to the job: he had assumed the chief's position in Stockbridge only eight months prior, after the fatal heart attack that had felled poor Tom Eisler (struck down while buck hunting in Vermont; at least he had been indulging in his favorite hobby when he was called to the great beyond, the locals mused.). Having worked clear across the state in Worcester for the past 15 years, Tewksbury didn't place much credence in these rumblings he had heard about the Bailey house since he had arrived in town.

The chief, ruddy faced with muscular arms and nearly bald, with a rim of white hair encircling his head, was diligently clearing out sandwich remains from his front teeth with a wooden pick when his first deputy – Officer Alan Gaines, eight years on the force – walked in accompanying Dennis Riley. Riley was unshaven and his eyes were bloodshot. A bandage was wrapped around the top of his crew-cut head, as a result of the wound he had received during the battle with the monster that had taken down his friends.

Riley had spent the night in the Stockbridge lock-up. Now he'd get his chance to clear everything up with the police chief, he figured, and get the heck out of here. The chief cleared his throat dramatically before he spoke. Officer Gaines, tall and wiry with a bushy brown mustache, stood dutifully by the door, across the room from the chief's desk.

"Mr. Riley," Chief Tewksbury said. "You told an officer last night – and Officer Gaines today – quite a story." The chief followed this statement up with another pick at his teeth, before he tossed the toothpick onto the waxed paper on his desk.

Riley sat down in front of the chief in an uncomfortable straight-backed wooden chair (brought in to the office to specifically create discomfort in certain circumstances), and now assumed a slumped over posture. His head was drooping a bit, and leaning to the left. Dennis Riley had been in a state of shock from what he had witnessed the night before, and all he'd gone through. When he was brought into the police department and placed in a holding cell, he soon passed out from exhaustion. Now he was having trouble firmly coming to terms with reality. He had been informed that both Terry and Charlie were dead.

Tewksbury rose from his chair, hooked his thumbs in between his khaki pants and his substantial gut, and ponderously walked over to the window to his right that looked out on Main Street. The storm from the previous night had moved on, and it was a beautiful autumn day in the Berkshires. He saw the steady line of cars – autumn leaf-peepers cruising through Stockbridge. He turned on his heels and glared at Riley. "Let's hear it, Riley."

"I-I-I told your men, sir," Dennis stammered. "We were out drinking…"

"Who," Tewksbury asked. "Who exactly?"

"It was me and Terry and Charlie."

"Anybody else?"

"No," Dennis said. "It was just the three of us. We were at the Five Chairs. We all got pretty tight, and Charlie insisted that we go down to the Bailey house. He's been talking about it for a while."

"OK," the chief said. "So, you and your ex-girlfriend..."

"What are you talking about?" Dennis blurted out.

"Oh, I've been doing some research, Mr. Riley," Tewksbury said, as he slowly sauntered back from the window to behind his desk chair. When he sat down, he thrust a forefinger towards Dennis' face. "People talk, Dennis. In a small town like Lenox, people talk."

"OK," Dennis said, genuinely unsure of where this was headed. "So what?"

"You used to date that girl...that Terry."

"What's this about?" Dennis replied incredulously, shaking his head. "This is ridiculous. I dated Terry for a few months. That must have been...like five years ago. We're...we were friends, really good friends."

"As I was saying," Tewksbury resumed, "You and your ex-girlfriend, and your alleged friend Charlie – who happened to be dating your ex-girlfriend..."

"Charlie is..." Dennis stammered, "was...my closest friend. Charlie wanted to drive down there. We went into the house together. Charlie went upstairs. Terry and I stayed downstairs. The place is just creepy looking, all cob-webs and stuff."

"OK," Tewksbury said.

"I don't know where he came from, or...it, or whatever that thing was," Dennis said. "He was huge. Must have been close to seven feet tall. His face was just completely messed up. I mean, his flesh was all pink and red and scarred. He had one eye. Where the other should have been there was just drooped over, scarred flesh. He had long nails – really long nails. He wore ripped up pants and a tattered t-shirt. His hair was stringy and long."

"That's some boogey man you saw there, Dennis," the chief said, letting out a contemptuous snort and a laugh. "What do you say, Officer Gaines? That the boogey man over there in the Bailey house?"

"Didn't find him there, Chief," Gaines said, matter-of-factly. "Didn't find the boogey man. We were searching the area all night. Haven't found a monster."

Gaines opened the door of the Chief's office, slipped out, shut the door again behind him, and saw a familiar face and large form entering the police department.

"Oh, hey Oak," he said. "How ya been?"

"I'm OK." Oak Alderson said, shaking hands with Gaines. "How ya doin' Alan?"

"Not bad. No complaints."

"What's goin' on in there?" Oak asked, gesturing with his head towards the Chief's office.

"We got the guy who murdered two people at the Bailey house last night."

"Yeah, we heard something about that on the two-way up in Pittsfield. But what are you talking about? You have Cordus Bailey in there?"

Alan cocked his head to the side, and gave Oak a half-smile. This must be his idea of a joke. "Huh? Yeah, right," he laughed. "We found Cordus Bailey, sure."

"Well, who do you have in there?"

"His name is Dennis Riley, from Lenox. He claims he went to the Bailey house with his two friends – apparently Dennis' ex-girlfriend *and* her new boyfriend – and he says a monster killed the two friends. Well, the Chief is sure, and it sounds likely to me, that this was a crime of passion. Dennis lured these two to the house, and sliced 'em up good, cause he felt rejected, you know?"

"Crime of passion, huh?" Oak repeated. He wasn't buying it one bit. Oak had learned more than enough about the Bailey legacy – and the Sibber medallion – and all that went along with it. He had gone from 'total skeptic' to 'believer,' now. What it *was* precisely that he believed in precisely, he wasn't sure. But, he had a strong suspicion (close to 100% suspicion) that this guy was being set up for a patsy by the new Chief trying to make a name for himself in Stockbridge. "Just how passionate is this Dennis Riley?"

"Well, he's denying everything, of course," Gaines said. "Claims there was some big monster down there, a creature. And the creature killed the other two."

"Alan, you know I was worried about that house last night. That's why I called."

"Look, Oak. These people went down there on their own, and got into some kind of altercation. It's a free country. This all could have just as easily occurred up in Lenox."

"But it didn't! It happened in the Bailey house, right? Just coincidence?"

"I don't know what you're driving at here. Are you telling me this guy is innocent – and the ghost of Cordus Bailey killed these people? That's crazy talk."

"Fine," he said. "You say it's crazy. Just keep saying it. Look at the facts, Alan. There's been a series of murders on that street. It started with the Bailey killings."

"Right," Alan said. "Their kid went nuts. A year later, there was a black bear lurking near Buck Tree Road. He mauled those two guys in front of the Bailey house. The year after that, a bear got those kids on the Buck Tree Road trail. It was probably the same bear."

"And you believe that?"

"Yes," he said emphatically. "Yes I do. I personally combed all of those crime scenes. I didn't find evidence pointing to any other possibility."

"Look Gaines, there was no forensic evidence linking a bear to any of those kiliings!"

"Well, what the hell else could make those kinds of marks on a body?"

Again, Oak felt stalled. "I don't know, but I'd like to find out," he said. "So what about last night?"

Gaines shrugged. "It's just like the chief says. This guy Dennis did it."

Oak exhaled through pursed lips and held his tongue. He could keep talking for hours here. He wouldn't get anywhere. If he couldn't be sure himself what the hell was happening, how could he get someone else to see things his way?

"All right," Oak said. "I admit I don't know exactly what happened down there. But damnit, Alan, we all better accept the possibility that something *else* is down there on Buck Tree Road. I don't think it's a bear. And I don't think this guy Dennis killed anybody. Also, I think there are going to be more victims if we don't come up with a plan. I wish I knew the answer..."

"Oak, I'm sorry, but I don't know what the hell you're talking about. We investigate crimes one at a time – and we solve 'em one at a time. Sometimes they're not solved. That's the way of the world."

Oak was done talking to Alan Gaines. He was frustrated and feeling helpless – and upset he hadn't done more to prevent the latest tragedy. Alan shook his head and then removed a small wire-bound notebook from his pants pocket and was paging through it.

Oak had some big decisions to make. The Chief had the authority to override Oak's ideas on this case. Stockbridge was the Chief's jurisdiction; Oak was a county man from the Sheriff's department. He would certainly try to intervene, but how exactly? Would Oak stake his own reputation falling to the mat for some poor schmoe from Lenox? How could Oak tell the Stockbridge Police Chief, with conviction, that he *believed* that a monster may have committed these murders, and maybe they should just turn their suspect loose? This was truly a dilemma. And he had to work it out in his mind.

"Does this guy Riley have an attorney?" Oak asked Gaines.

"I don't see one."

"Well, you better just tell him, Alan, right now, that he's entitled to get one, pronto."

"What are you talking about?" Gaines asked. "This piece of scum murdered two people last night. Let him figure out when it's time to find a lawyer."

"No," Oak said. "Do it now. I believe it's simply known as due process, Alan. Stockbridge is still part of the United States, isn't it?"

Gaines gave Oak a downturned look of disapproval, and made a move to re-enter the Chief's office to let him know that the Sheriff's department was sniffing around – and insisting that they let Dennis Riley get an attorney. Chief Tewksbury wouldn't be happy about this development.

"I'll go in to see the Chief in just a minute to let him know, OK?" Gaines said.

"Fine, Alan," Oak replied. "I'll wait right here. And, in a little while, I'd like a chance to talk to your suspect."

"OK," Gaines answered in a flat tone.

Dennis' eyes were glazing over now as he tried to accurately recount what he had seen – and experienced.

"This thing," Dennis said, "Charlie tried to get him; he was protecting Terry. This creature just mauled Charlie, and then he threw him against the wall. Then he went after Terry. I-I-I couldn't help them. There was nothing I could do."

The chief cradled his hands behind his head, and his black leather office chair emitted a squeak as he leaned back. After a pregnant pause, the chief shot back forward in his chair, and then nearly doubled the volume of his voice: "OH, YOU DID PLENTY, BOY!" He then spoke a quieter voice again. "Yes, you did quite a job in that house."

Dennis was shaking his head back and forth, and let out a meek reply.

"What...what are you talking about?"

The chief smiled at Dennis. It was a broad smile, and it spoke volumes.

"I'm talking about revenge, Riley. I'm talking about an old-school love triangle."

"You don't really believe...?" Dennis said.

"Oh, yes I do," Tewksbury said. "You're the one who suggested going down to the Bailey house."

"No, I didn't!" Dennis said, desperately.

"You lured those two out to the Bailey house. You had a couple of weapons stashed nearby there. Yup. I believe you had a nice heavy slice and dice device or two that you hid out there. I think you had a knife – and a bat or a sledge hammer. When the three of you went into the house…Slash! Bang! Bam! You killed both of 'em. Then you crushed their heads against the wall to help make this 'monster' story of yours stand up."

Dennis was holding his drooped-over head in his hands. He looked up, his eyes now glassy with tears.

"Then where are the weapons?" Dennis asked, his voice breaking. "If I killed them, what happened to the weapons?"

"That's no big mystery, Dennis," the chief countered. "Hell, you could have driven Charlie's car away from the scene – we found the keys in the ignition – and you probably found a nice secluded spot to drop those weapons into the Housatonic River, for instance. Wash yourself up a bit along the riverbank, then you drive back, and play all scared when you walk over to old man Walker's place."

"God damnit!" he cried out. "This is ridiculous! This fuckin' monster killed my friends! It kicked me clear across the room. How do you think I ended up with my head gashed open?"

"I think Charlie got one in on you during the struggle," the chief said matter-of-factly.

" 'One' what? What do you mean he got one in? I witnessed two murders. What…what do you want me to say?"

"Just confess, Dennis," the chief said, leaning back in the chair again. "It's easy. C'mon. You were jealous of Charlie. He had your girl." The chief paused, and then asked, "Who's *your* girlfriend, Dennis?"

Gaines re-entered the office and stood quietly. He certainly wasn't about to interrupt his boss right now – to tell him they better let the suspect call a lawyer.

"Well, I'm in between relationships right now…"

"OK, well isn't that just neat and tidy," the chief said. "Face it, you never got over losing that girl. You were jealous of Charlie so you killed him. Then, you figured, if I can't have Terry, nobody can."

"No-ooooooo!," Dennis yelled, desperate to sound more credible. "It was the monster! It was this – thing. His flesh was all scarred and messed up and he was strong as a bull. *He* did it!"

"Dennis," the chief said, exhaling dramatically, "you better hope you can find a damn good lawyer, and a jury that believes in the boogey man."

Gaines shrugged. There it was. The chief just told him he better get a lawyer.

"This is crazy!" Dennis said, starting to weep again. "What are you talking about? I didn't hurt anyone. They were my friends."

Tewksbury pulled back away from his desk, rose up, and slowly sauntered over by Dennis, glaring down at him. He moved on towards the door, Gaines stood aside, and Tewksbury pulled the office door open.

"Officer Gaines, lock this man back up," the chief said, glancing into the corridor and upwards to drink in the large form of Oak Alderson. He nodded acknowledgement – they were casual acquaintances with one another. Alderson asked Gaines: "When did that county DA say he'd be here?"

"About an hour, sir," Gaines said. "He should be finishing up with the back nine real soon."

"Well," the chief laughed, and then nodded in Dennis' direction, lifting his eyebrows for emphasis, "looks like we got a regular hole-in-one over here."

Oak held his tongue, and tried to figure out exactly what he was going to do. Officer Gaines ushered Dennis out of the room.

"I didn't do it!" Dennis wailed. "Why won't you listen to me?"

"Officer Gaines?" the chief said, ignoring Dennis' plea.

"Yes, sir?"

"You and the boys keep combing the woods around the south end of town and in Housatonic," the chief said, leisurely taking a big stretch, his arms out wide, and his gut expanding. "Maybe you'll find a boogey man..."

Gaines gave the chief an expressionless nod and then took the accused back to his cell.

"...but I doubt it," Chief Tewksbury added, turning to re-enter his office.

"Chief, I think we should talk," Oak Alderson said.

"Come on in, Mr. Alderson," Tewksbury said, not even looking at him. The chief took a seat at his desk and reached over to take a sip from the cup of coffee on his desk that had long grown cold. "What do we have to talk about?"

It was pulsing through him now. Anxiety and fear: stark human emotions that produced punishing shards of pain throughout his body. For he could sense that it was close. There were brutal, searing bolts shooting up one leg, through his torso and down an arm, caused by the anticipation of what he would soon experience – paradoxically accompanied by the awareness that relief would arrive shortly after. Cordus Bailey was nearing the end of his 100-hour sentence on the Earth...for this year. He scratched at the soil around him in his lair beneath the front steps of the house. The scratching was the only release he could find.

The reactivation of lust – something he had not known for the three years since his family's demise – had only served to bring about new levels of torture and suffering. For now he had seen Jenny, but she had rejected him...screaming, her eyes bulging wide – looking at him as if he were...some kind of monster. How could he forget her screams and her terrified visage as he tried to hug her and hold her close?

He could sense a stirring in the ground nearby. A grey-green garter snake slithered along the matted fall leaves atop the soil. Cordus reached up and stabbed at it with his long, sharp talons. His nail punctured clear through the skinny, foot-long snake's body, and the creature writhed desperately, contorting its body into a last gasp "s" as Cordus brought it close. Cordus' misshapen maw opened wide and he bit through the reptile's cylindrical form, splitting the snake in two. Blood trickled down his chin as he took sizeable bites of the freshly killed flesh of the snake. The reptile's skin was crunchy and the innards chewy. Cordus would eat it whole in four pieces.

This was the period of the most dread. Cordus had developed a sixth sense of sorts: he knew when the end of his 100-hour stay on Earth was approaching. Most horrifying were the actual moments of transformation. A bolt would shoot through his body – up his spine, stinging his brain – for the few minutes it took for the time travel he would experience. He would return to the netherworld, a place of nothingness and relief. He would reside there for 361 days, until it was time to return to Earth again, to experience suffering that would be ratcheted up to a new, more excruciating level (such was the curse his mother had placed upon him).

This anticipation was a particularly difficult time. It was coming any second, but he couldn't tell exactly when. The precise moment that his 100-hour term ended, the transformation would hit him full force. When it hit he would see his mother. He would envision himself in the bathtub, and her craggy hand reaching down to touch him. Then he would experience the deaths again – the ax, all that blood. Most crushing was the reenactment in his mind of all the confusion, anger and raging madness of a once-innocent teenager driven over the edge – beyond the boundary of rational thought.

And now all he could do was wait. He finished chewing the last segment of the snake, gulping it down. Seconds ticked away as the time approached. Cordus held his one working eye shut as tight as he could, bracing for what he knew would soon hit. And in that moment, awaiting the transformation, he was the young boy again. A trail of tears streamed from the lone eye and dripped down his scar-ravaged face. His body shuddered lightly as he quietly wept. It would come any second now: a period of crushingly painful recollections and suffering as his body hurtled through the time and space continuum. Then he would reach the calm of the netherworld. All the pain would cease and his mind would be blissfully blank. He knew it was fast approaching as he...

THE END?

Breinigsville, PA USA
02 August 2010
242857BV00001B/1/P